Danger in the Night

Danger In The Night

Nothing is ever as it seems…

Wyatt Stone tries to talk his extremely attractive ex-sister-in-law out of buying a rundown haunted hotel but it doesn't go at all as planned. Despite his misgivings, she turns the tables and he finds himself agreeing to help restore the money trap.

Antonia Ross always thought Wyatt got a raw deal in his marriage to her sister, but she never thought about him in a romantic way. He might be handsome, sexy, and fun but she's all about her career. Spending her days and evenings in close proximity isn't going to change that.

Except that it does. She's never been afraid of ghosts and monsters but how she's beginning to feel about Wyatt is truly terrifying.

Hidden treasures are supposed to be valuable – not a dead body that has been stashed away for years. Shaken by what she's seen, Antonia desperately wants the killer brought to justice. What will happen to their growing passion when she finds out Wyatt has a connection to the victim?

Danger in the Night

Danger Incorporated

Book Five

BY

OLIVIA JAYMES

www.OliviaJaymes.com

DANGER IN THE NIGHT
Copyright © 2016 by Olivia Jaymes
Print Edition

Chapter One

❦

ANTONIA ROSS SMILED with satisfaction as she surveyed the expansive property she was planning to purchase. The old, rundown mansion and grounds were absolutely perfect, and she was getting them for a bargain price. The house had stood empty for years basically rotting until Toni had come along. No one wanted to buy a home that was reputed to be haunted.

Except for her. As far as Toni was concerned, the stories of ghosts were a major plus. It wouldn't be hard to lure amateur ghost hunters and other paranormal lovers to this place. Even the guests that just liked a good scare were going to love this estate when Toni was done with it.

"Are you sure you really want to buy this place?" the real estate agent queried, her forehead wrinkled with concern. Bea Wilson was an older woman but well-maintained with her short blonde hair, blue skirt and blazer, sensible heels, and meticulously applied makeup. Clearly, the woman was successful which was why Toni was surprised by the question. The woman – and the bank – should have been thrilled to sell this home after all this time.

"I do," Toni replied firmly, her gaze sweeping the dusty foyer of the home. The floors were still in good shape but the carpets and furniture had seen better days, although some rooms were better than others. "It's everything I've been looking for and then some."

Bea twisted the leather strap of her handbag, a conflicted expression on her face. Toni could tell the woman was fighting an internal battle with herself and she really didn't need to. Toni had done her homework thoroughly before asking to look at the house.

"The house is haunted," the agent blurted out, red flags of emotion high on her cheeks. "At least that's what people say. Strange things happen around here and I've seen it for myself. The last two owners didn't last six months between them. It's been empty for over twenty years. The only time anyone visits this place is when kids come on a dare from their friends."

Toni smiled as her fingers ran along the beautiful woodwork on the bannister. Who cared about a so-called ghost when there was a hand-carved staircase in the entryway? Her guests were going to love it.

"I'm counting on this place being haunted. Well, that's not true, actually. I'm going to make it haunted and people will come from all over the country to stay here. Scaring people is big business."

Toni ought to know. She owned her own monster and Halloween novelty business. Her designs were used all over the world in haunted attractions and this estate was the first step in opening her own ghostly destination. Because of its reputation, she didn't even have to create a mystique about the house. Everyone already believed. Except Toni, of course. In all her years of hanging around dark, spooky locations she had yet to see a ghost and honestly didn't expect to. Everything could be explained logically if people would simply look beyond the surface.

"You…want it to be haunted?" Bea shook her head in disbelief. "I'm not sure that I follow."

Toni could barely keep up with her own thoughts so she didn't expect the people around her to understand them most of the time. She wasn't always effusive with words, preferring her designs to speak for her instead.

"I'm going to fix up the property and turn it into a hotel. A haunted hotel. With the stories that have circulated about this place I won't have to do much. People will see ghosts if they really want to. I'll also put in a haunted pathway attraction on the property for those that just want to pay to be scared but don't want to stay at the hotel. People love spirits and I'm going to give them what they want."

Toni didn't mention that was what she already did. She was sure Bea Wilson had done her homework on Toni's creditworthiness before this appointment.

"You think people will pay their hard-earned money to be scared to death? I find that hard to believe. People in town avoid this place like the plague."

Toni chuckled at the woman's tone of disbelief. "It's true— otherwise I wouldn't be able to pay my bills. And I bet some of those people would come here if there were others just as brave. Guides to walk them through the grounds or simply someone by their side. This is why people ride roller coasters and watch horror movies. They want to be scared but feel safe at the same time. This hotel will tap into that need."

"I'm sure you know what you're doing," the real estate agent sniffed, clearly not meaning a word of her statement. She was looking at Toni like she was slightly insane and needed intensive therapy.

"I do."

Toni didn't bother going into the details of the business she'd built, slaved over, and sacrificed for these last ten years. But if she hadn't known what she was doing, she wouldn't be the successful person that she was now. She'd shown all the naysayers that Antonia Ross wasn't a businesswoman to be trifled with. She was in charge, in control, and loving every minute of it.

"I can have the paperwork ready for you this afternoon in my office," the older woman finally said, apparently giving up on talking Toni out of this purchase. "Have you contacted the bank about financing? How much were planning for a down payment?"

Before Toni could answer, the overhead lights and the wall sconces flickered for several seconds and Bea's face went quite pale, a hand fluttering nervously to her throat. Her gaze flitted around the foyer and up the stairs before coming back to rest on Toni. It appeared that the real estate agent might believe in ghosts. It would be the best luck in the world if the semi or completely undead were puttering around this old mansion but there was no way Toni could be that fortunate.

I'll need an electrician to check for a short in the wiring, first thing. I don't want the place to burn down.

Toni's smile grew wider and the toe of her shoe tapped impatiently on the scarred hardwood floors. Her mind was already whirling a thousand miles an hour with ideas for the house and grounds. The sooner she was able to get in here and start the work, the better.

"No financing. I'm paying cash. How soon can I get the keys?"

✦ ✦ ✦

BUSTED AND BROKEN down.

Those words described just about everything on Wyatt Stone's little farm, from the fences to the ancient barn. In the past year, he'd been working for Jason Anderson's consulting company and he'd barely had time to maintain the property. Not that it was in the greatest of shape before he'd taken the job. This land had been in his family's possession for three generations and everything about it was old.

Sick and tired of the traveling, Wyatt was happy to have some time off. He needed more alone time these days than he was getting and frankly, people were starting to piss him off. The littlest things were beginning to grate on his nerves like people on their cell phones driving too slow in the left lane or standing in line for hours at the DMV only to be told he didn't have the right identification. Everything felt like a conspiracy to ruin his day and since Wyatt preferred to be happy, he needed some rest and relaxation away from the job.

The thought of stretching out on the sofa and reading a good book or rolling up his sleeves in the kitchen and cooking a meal sounded like heaven. No calls on his cell in the middle of the night. No being tied to his laptop doing research. And definitely no boring paperwork.

For the next four weeks he was as free as a bird, and he intended to enjoy himself to the fullest.

Just as soon as he finished the list of repairs that simply could not wait any longer.

That's what brought him to the hardware store this morning, looking for supplies to fix the latch on the barn door, which was rusted and falling apart. He was contemplating purchasing a new rubber mallet as well when a brightly colored movement out of the corner of his eye caught his attention. He turned to examine what it was and his entire body tensed, his teeth gritted together.

The woman who had created that blur of color was trying to hide behind a circular rack of sandpaper but it hadn't been so long that Wyatt didn't recognize her.

"Antonia, I didn't expect to see you here today."

That was an understatement of epic proportions. As far as he knew, Antonia Ross lived in Denver these days and the only reason she was familiar with this area was because her older sister had lived in town for a short while.

As Wyatt's wife.

Antonia was his ex-sister-in-law and someone he'd never thought or hoped to see again. It wasn't that he didn't like her. He did. She was a nice girl, unlike her sister, but she brought up a whole host of unpleasant and downright awful memories. It wasn't her fault, but seeing her today sucked.

Toni stared down at her pink Chuck Taylor tennis shoes, unable to meet his eyes. Even she knew that she brought unwelcome thoughts of the past. He wanted to tell her that it was okay but he'd be a liar. "I just…um…came to get a key made for the construction crew. I…um…bought the old McMahon place."

He couldn't have heard what he thought he did. She wasn't going to be around town all the time. That could not happen.

"I'm not sure I understand."

She lifted her gaze, her little chin stubborn. Toni had always been one tough cookie so it had been a surprise to see her unsure of herself even for a moment.

"I bought the old McMahon place. I'm turning it into a haunted hotel and scare attraction."

Wyatt struggled to make sense of what Toni was saying but the last part was giving him problem. "Considering the state of the property last time I saw it, I would think it wouldn't take much to frighten the hell out of any sane person. Are you serious that you bought that huge money pit? Have you lost your mind, Toni?"

He and Toni hadn't been close but he'd always liked her and he sure as hell didn't want to see her make a huge mistake. Buying the McMahon property had to rank right up there on the "going to be a massive regret" scale. They'd once been family and he didn't let family do stupid shit.

A smile spread across her face, showing off two dimples and even white teeth. She was quite pretty, although in a completely different way than Carla had been. His ex-wife had been blonde and blue-eyed, model slim and always perfectly made up even when they'd lived on the farm. It had felt like her entire wardrobe had been made up of floaty, pastel dresses and she'd played the fairy princess role to the hilt.

Toni, on the other hand, favored bright colors to go along with her long and curly sable-colored hair. Today she had on ordinary blue jeans but the bright fuchsia blouse that matched her lip gloss would have stood out wherever she went. She wasn't a woman that looked to hide in the shadows nor did she try to be sweet or quiet. Toni could be brash, outspoken…and a real pain in the ass.

"I have not lost my mind but thank you for asking. I acquired the property in a shrewd business deal that's going to pay off big, if you must know. I have my own company now, or have had actually for the last several years. Don't worry, I know what I'm doing."

Well, that made one of them.

If Wyatt had a lick of sense he'd high tail it out of this hardware store and not look back. Getting involved with the Ross family, even in this tiny way by showing interest in her life, was going to come back and bite him in the ass.

"I didn't know about your company but it sounds like it's quite successful. Congratulations."

It didn't surprise Wyatt that Carla had never told him much about Toni. The sisters had an uneasy relationship at best and Carla had often said that Toni had a screw loose.

The younger sister really wasn't crazy but she hadn't given any fucks about other people's opinions. She'd always been a little different than most folks, spending all her time drawing strange-looking pictures and reading instead of going out to football games and pizza parties. Carla used to tease Toni that she'd die a virgin. The good Lord knew Carla wouldn't.

"What? Carla didn't tell you all about it?" teased Toni, her bright amber eyes sparkling with mirth. "It's so unlike her. She loves to extoll the virtues of those orbiting around her."

Wyatt had wanted to avoid the touchy topic of his ex-wife

completely but he found himself laughing along with Toni. Even when they'd argued about politics or climate change, she'd been good at making him laugh. "Orbiting is a good word and I haven't spoken to your sister since the papers were signed. I guess it's been about five years now."

Toni rolled her eyes and sighed. "You lucky dog. I had to see her two Christmases ago."

He didn't really want to talk about his ex any longer and this meeting hadn't been nearly as traumatic as he'd expected it to be. Maybe it wouldn't be so bad having Toni in town. He traveled quite a bit for his job so it wasn't like he'd see her on a daily basis. Just now and then. He could handle that, he was sure.

"I know I'm going to regret this but just what is a scare attraction?" Wyatt heard himself ask, cursing inwardly that he wasn't bringing their encounter to an end. Just because it wasn't painful didn't mean that he had to prolong it. "What makes you think anyone in their right mind would want to spend the night in a haunted hotel?"

If he'd shocked her with the baldness of his question, she didn't show it. Lifting her wrist, she checked the time as if she had an appointment. "I can explain it all. How about I buy breakfast?"

Chapter Two

THE TOWN CAFE was decorated in a mixture of subtle and not-so-subtle shades of green, with painted ivy vines on one wall. The kitchen was in the back with two large swinging doors that Toni was sure were going to smack some poor, unsuspecting waitstaff right in the face. There didn't seem to be any system such as right door in and left door out, yet somehow it seemed to work. So far.

"I think I'll have the French toast."

Toni placed her menu on the table and studied the man sitting across from her in the booth, perusing the menu. His brows were pulled down in concentration as if selecting his breakfast foods was the most important thing he'd do all day. But then that was Wyatt Stone. He did everything that way – all out – the best he possibly could. Failing at marriage must have driven him insane, although the downfall of that relationship was hardly his fault. Carla was a woman who never should have married in the first place.

He'd aged in the seven years since Toni had last seen him, a few silver strands in his short, dark hair. His face was tanned with lines fanning around the eyes but his body was still trim and muscular. All in all, time had been good to Wyatt. He still had that manly vibe that had attracted her sister to begin with.

The waitress came and took their order, barely even making eye contact or acknowledging Wyatt's request for more coffee, instead disappearing into the kitchen leaving them with two half-empty coffee cups.

"Do you think we'll ever see her again?" Toni asked, watching the swinging door for their server. She was something of a caffeine addict and this one cup wasn't going to cut it. She'd need at least two more. "Do you think it's some sort of parallel universe back there and on the other side of that door is me and you but we're not the same? You know what I mean?"

He was looking at her like she'd lost her mind, which honestly she was used to since she'd been seeing that look on various faces all her life. She was different and always had been. She'd made peace with that years ago and now she enjoyed it, reveled in it really.

"No, I can't say as I do. I think she will return and I'm almost positive there's no wormhole on the other side of the door. I've been in the kitchen but it's been years. A buddy of mine in high school worked here."

Toni sighed and sipped her coffee slowly, wanting to make it last just in case he was wrong. He'd always been a rather literal kind of guy and apparently, that hadn't changed. He wasn't taken at odd moments with flights of fancy.

"I'll take your word for it but isn't it more fun to imagine different scenarios? What if she was a spy for MI-6 with a license to kill?"

His lips quirked up at the corners and he shook his head.

"Kathy? A license to kill? That might be dangerous. Last I heard she was mad as hell at her ex-boyfriend and was threatening to string him up in the nearest barn if he so much as looked at another girl. And as for MI-6, I don't think she's even been out of the state. I doubt England is recruiting agents out of Wyoming."

"It would be interesting though, wouldn't it?" Toni challenged. "Everything isn't always what it seems."

Her entire livelihood depended on it.

He sat back in the booth and seemed to contemplate her words. "That is true, Toni. I'll give you that. So tell me more about this business scheme you have going and then I'll try and talk you out of it."

He certainly tried.

In between bites of his bacon and eggs, he tried valiantly to pick apart any and all of her arguments even when she had data to back up her facts. By the time he'd cleaned his plate and his second cup of coffee, it was clear he was frustrated and over the entire subject.

"I guess we're going to have to agree to disagree," he finally capitulated, at least as much as he was capable. "I don't understand the lure of haunted houses, ghosts, goblins, and things that go bump in the night. I don't like witches, pumpkins, the occult, or dressing up in costumes. I'm not against those that do but I just don't get it. I'm probably a lost cause."

Wyatt Stone was more stuffy and uptight than Toni remembered.

"When was the last time you did something out of character, something fun?"

He regarded her steadily over the rim of his cup. "You say that as if both of those things are inextricably entwined. I don't necessarily consider doing something out of character as fun. Knocking over a bank is not something I would do. Does that sound like fun?"

He was too used to being around women like her sister. Toni was too intelligent to rise to the bait.

"I'm not engaging with you. I think it's sweet that you're so worried about me and all, but I've got this. I know what I'm doing. You can either huff and puff and generally be a jerk or you can be happy for me and smile when appropriate. It's your choice."

"It doesn't feel like my choice," Wyatt grumbled although with a good natured tone. "I have the feeling that this was always going to be the outcome. You always were stubborn."

Slapping her cup down in indignation, Toni took a sharp breath to hold onto her temper. This was why she didn't date often. If men didn't get their way, they started throwing around words like *stubborn* or *short-sighted*.

"I am not stubborn. I've simply made a well-researched and calculated business decision and I'm asking you to respect it. Frankly, your patronizing tone pisses me off."

His brows went up but to his credit, he held onto his own temper; that is if she'd succeeded in making him angry. It took a great deal to get Wyatt to drop his calm facade and Carla had excelled at it. Toni remembered one particular weekend about ten years ago like it was yesterday.

He and Carla had been visiting her parents and Toni had been home from her senior year in college where she was studying art and design. It was Carla's high school reunion and she'd spent the weekend dangling old boyfriends in front of Wyatt's face while reliving her glory years as prom queen and all around party girl.

Toni had a sneaking suspicion that the reason her sister had been popular didn't have a thing to do with her sparkling personality.

The couple had spent Saturday and Sunday – when they weren't out socializing with Carla's old friends – tensely arguing behind the closed door of her childhood bedroom. Toni's parents had turned Carla's bedroom into some sort of pink and purple shrine so poor Wyatt was forced to sleep in a canopy bed with his wife and about two dozen stuffed animals, mostly teddy bears and unicorns. It was no wonder he'd been growling at everyone he came across by Sunday afternoon. Toni had simply did what she always did when her sister was around.

Stay away as much as possible.

"I didn't mean to impugn your ability to take care of yourself and your business and I'm sorry," Wyatt said, making Toni's jaw drop almost to the Formica of the table. In her experience, he wasn't a man that admitted when he was wrong all that often. "I just think of you as a young girl and I worry."

There were worse things in the world than having a nice man concerned about her well-being. Perhaps she should cut him some slack. He didn't have a clue about her life since she was in college.

"I'm over thirty now but I do appreciate your interest. I'm all grown up and I can handle things on my own. I've been doing it for awhile and I like it that way."

Hopefully he'd get the hint that while it was nice that he was worried, he didn't need to keep it up. He could move on to other things such as his own life. Last she'd heard, he was holed up on his farm playing the part of a hermit.

He was squinting at her now. "There's something different about you and it's not just that you're older. I thought at first that had to be it but it's not. You don't look the same."

"I am the same except now I have to worry about laugh lines." She dabbed a napkin over her lips. "You've changed too."

Rubbing his chin, Wyatt chuckled and grinned. "I'll bet I have. Older and not a bit wiser. I'll be forty next year and my hair is turning gray and my knees protest when I get out of bed in the morning. Getting old isn't for wimps."

"You're not old." He really wasn't. Ten years ago she would have thought forty was ancient but now it didn't seem all that bad. He looked in great shape, far better than most men his age. "I bet you are wiser though. You got away from my sister."

He choked as he drank his coffee, coughing and trying not to laugh out loud. "That I did. Your sister did teach me a valuable lesson though."

Toni couldn't imagine Carla teaching anyone anything.

"How to pick out the perfect shade of lipstick?"

Wyatt placed his cup on the table and leaned forward, a smile playing on his well-shaped mouth. If anyone around them was watching, it looked like he was going to tell her a funny secret that only they would share.

"Everything isn't always what it seems."

Chapter Three

WYATT SETTLED BACK in the leather recliner, his legs stretched out as he pressed his cell phone to his right ear while throwing handfuls of popcorn in his mouth with his left hand. The television was turned down low but he didn't need to hear the dialogue. He'd seen *The Godfather* at least twenty times. He knew it by heart.

After a long day outside fixing the barn and a few spots on the fence, he'd been looking forward to a quiet evening with just a beer and Michael Corleone for company. His boss Jason Anderson, however, had other ideas apparently.

"I hate to ask but we really need to have this company meeting next week. There is a long list of potential new recruits and you know that I don't like hiring people unless everyone agrees they're a good fit for the team. Is there any way you could conference in for just the interviews?"

Jason's law enforcement consulting firm was growing by leaps and bounds and if more employees meant Wyatt managed a good night's sleep once in awhile, he'd be available. "It's just two days, right? I can fit that in. How many are you planning to hire?"

"Two, but I need to put these guys through their paces. The last thing I want is what happened with Millner."

Christ, that had been a mess. In the interview Andy Millner had seemed like a solid, dependable guy but in the field he'd folded like a cheap tent. Any stress sent the man into a full-blown panic attack. It had taken both Zach and Wyatt to calm him down after pulling him off a night stakeout that should have gone easily and smoothly. Jason had let the man go, leaving them short of resources when business was ramping up steadily.

"No one wants that," Wyatt agreed heartily, already making a mental list of things he wanted to ask the recruits. "I have a few ideas of how to vet them but I'm not sure that I'm that great a judge of character, to be honest."

He'd been blind to all of Carla's faults, although in his own defense she had tried to hide them in the beginning. It was only later she hadn't bothered.

When she had another richer man on the line and didn't need Wyatt any longer.

"I think you underestimate yourself. You know a good person when you meet them."

"My track record would say otherwise."

Jason knew whom Wyatt was referring to. It wasn't a state secret about Wyatt's acrimonious divorce although he didn't make a habit of chatting about it. But he'd taken a bunch of crap from the guys when he'd shown little interest in the fairer sex. He'd been burned badly and wasn't anxious to do it all over again.

"One mistake. That's not all that bad in the big scheme of things."

"I'm sure I'll be laughing about this in my golden years," Wyatt replied, not wanting to delve into any emotional bullshit with his friend. When things didn't go his way he sucked it up just like his father and grandfather had. He didn't need a therapist or a tea party. He needed a good night's sleep. Several of them. Preferably in a row. Plus a good stiff whiskey. "But I can't seem to catch a break. I ran into Carla's sister in the hardware store and ended up having breakfast with her. She's got herself into some harebrained scheme and bought a haunted house."

Even when Toni had explained what she was doing and why, it hadn't made a hell of a lot of sense to Wyatt. Carla's younger sister had always been a little bit different than anyone else, her nose buried in a book and her heavy glasses sliding down her nose. She'd liked art and literature and she was a pretty damn talented painter from what he could remember. How she traveled from oil paintings to building monsters he didn't know or understand.

That's what was different. She didn't wear glasses anymore.

"A haunted house?" Jason echoed, amusement in his tone. "You mean like ghosts and goblins? She bought it on purpose?"

"She wants to turn it into some sort of haunted hotel," Wyatt groaned, wishing he'd never brought up the subject of Antonia Ross. She had a way of burrowing into a man's head and bugging the shit out of him when all he wanted to do was rest. "I hope I talked some sense into her but I doubt it. She's always been hard-headed, just like Carla."

When the check for breakfast that morning had been placed on the table, Wyatt had reached for it and had to practically wrestle it out of Toni's hands. She'd argued that she should pay because she'd asked him to eat but he'd countered that he was a gentleman and that meant he'd pay. For his trouble all he received in return was a snort of derision and more arguing. She didn't think that his gender was good enough reason to pay all of the check and at least wanted to pay her half. He assured her he could afford breakfast, which had obviously pissed her off since she took it to mean that she couldn't afford it.

In the end, he'd flung a twenty on the table whether she liked it or not.

"I hope she gives you a wide berth then, my friend. Thanks for being so cooperative and I'll speak to you next week. I promise there won't be any talk of ex-wives or sisters of ex-wives here. How does that sound?"

Like heaven on earth.

Wyatt had done his duty and tried to persuade Toni to give up her crazy idea so he was in the clear if something bad happened. Which surely would. Toni was a dreamer, not a savvy businesswoman reading *The Wall Street Journal* and having two martini lunches with bankers. The best thing she could do is go back to painting portraits of dogs like she had in high school and leave this monster and ghost stuff alone.

And the best thing he could do is stop letting Toni have free real estate in his brain. That family had taken far too many things from him already and peace of mind was on top of the list.

Chapter Four

THE SUN WAS beginning to dip in the sky when Toni gathered her papers and laptop, stuffing them into her messenger bag. It had been another long, dusty, and loud day at the estate and she was anxious for a hot bath and a glass of wine. Maybe two glasses.

The good news was they were on time and on budget, which was a miracle with all that needed to be done. The bad news was the house sparked her creativity and she spent many more hours than she should working on designs for next year's catalog line when she should be working on the house. Consequently, she ended up working in the evening when she went back to the hotel and not getting enough sleep.

Slinging her bag over her shoulder, she tiredly plodded down the front porch steps, her gaze trained on her phone. She had several texts from her second-in-command at the main office that she'd need to deal with right away.

She threw her bag onto the passenger seat and then slid behind the wheel, firing up the engine of her BMW sedan. Pulling out of the driveway, she spied a car parked on the side of the road with a flat tire. A man was kneeling next to it trying to loosen the lug nuts and she wished him the best of luck. If they had been air-tightened instead of hand-tightened, he was going to have a tough time.

She ought to know. She'd had a flat about six months ago.

Not one person had stopped to offer her help – despite it being a well-traveled street – and she didn't want the same to happen to this guy. She'd ended up calling the auto club who had sent someone out to change the tire for her but if he was trying to do it himself, he might need a hand. Worse case, she could use her auto club card and have someone help him. The hot bath and wine were going to have to wait.

She pulled in behind him and tucked her phone into her jeans pocket before getting out of the vehicle. He'd stopped what he was doing and had stood, watching her approach. She waved and smiled, wanting him to know she was friendly and intended to help.

"Hey, looks like you've had some bad luck there. Can I give you a hand?"

The man, probably mid-thirties with short, dirty blond hair, returned her smile. "That's very nice of you to offer but I've got it under control, thank you."

Toni held out her hand in greeting. "Are you sure? I can call the auto club, if you like. I'm Antonia Ross, by the way."

The man looked down at his hand, the palm smeared with grime. "Hold on one second there."

Reaching into his trunk, he pulled out a small red towel and wiped off his hands before reaching out to shake hers. "It's nice to meet you, Miss Ross. I'm John Dutton. I do appreciate the offer but I finally got the lug nuts loosened so it's only a matter of switching out the tires."

"It's nice to meet you, John."

A blonde woman stuck her head out of the passenger window, her face pink from the heat.

"Are you almost done? It's like an oven in here."

"Just a few more minutes," John assured his companion. "I promise."

The poor female looked miserable, sweat beading on her forehead. This was something Toni could help with. "I have some bottled water in my car. Would you like one?"

The woman sighed gratefully, her entire demeanor perking up. "I would love one. Thank you so much."

Happy to be of some assistance to the stranded couple, Toni reached into the backseat where she'd stowed her cooler earlier that day. The ice had melted long ago but the three remaining bottles of water were slightly cooler than the temperature outside. She grabbed two of them, walked over to hand one to the woman and then offered the other to John. The woman disappeared into the vehicle, her cell phone to her ear.

"We really appreciate this." John held up the bottle and grinned. "I didn't come prepared to sit out in the heat."

"No, problem. I'm glad I had a few left."

The sound of a truck engine had her swiveling her gaze toward the road where her foreman Bill was parking behind her vehicle. He hopped out of the cab and came over to check out what was going on.

Taking off his stained baseball cap, Bill scratched his head as he inspected the flat tire. "Look like you might have picked up a nail. Can I help you out?"

John shook his head and took a large gulp of the water. "Thanks but we're good. I'll have this finished in just a few minutes."

Bill nodded toward the east. "If you follow this road into town, you might want to stop at Larry's Auto Care. He can fix up that tire in just a few minutes. Good prices too. Tell him Bill sent you."

"I will, thank you." John finished the water and tossed the empty bottle into the trunk.

It appeared that he really just wanted to change his tire and be on his way. Toni gave him a big smile and a wave as she palmed her car keys. "It was nice meeting you. Have a good evening."

Bill shook the man's hand again and followed Toni back to their cars while John knelt back on the ground, tugging the tire off of the hub and tossing it aside.

"You didn't know them?" Toni whispered to Bill. "I assumed they were locals."

Shrugging, the foreman shook his head. "I guess they could be new in town but I've never met them."

"Then what were they doing way out here?"

"This road not only heads into town but it will also get you to North Pinemont. Or they could be here to look at the house. All those scary stories bring in the crazies. Everybody wants to get a selfie with a ghost."

Toni couldn't help the grin that spread across her face. She'd made the right decision. This place was going to be wonderful. In a way, she'd already had her first customers.

"That's what I'm counting on, Bill."

✦ ✦ ✦

TONI LEANED BACK against the headboard of the hotel bed and opened her email. She'd had a leisurely soak in the tub and now she was planning to enjoy a glass of wine while catching up with all the administrative tasks that had been piling up while she was here in Birchville. Luckily, she had a terrific second-in-command who was ensuring that orders were completed on time and budget, allowing Toni to concentrate on the creative side of things.

"Penis enhancement? Delete," she muttered under her breath as she sorted through her inbox, one by one. "A Nigerian prince? I'll pass. Delete. Shit and double shit. My mother. What on earth could she want? I was just there at the holidays four months ago. I'm not due until Thanksgiving."

Taking another fortifying gulp of the full-bodied cabernet, Toni opened the email from her mother that was dated today and sent only hours before. She had a difficult relationship with her parents and she thought of them like the dentist. They should be seen twice a year and with great trepidation along with something to ease the pain afterwards, preferably a strong vodka. In fact, she wished she had some now.

Toni,

Your father and I just got back home from our cruise to the Caribbean. We climbed a waterfall and swam with dolphins. I can't wait to show you the photos. Of course, your father is red as a lobster in all of them since he wouldn't put on any sunscreen. I told him he'd get a sunburn.

I bet you did, Mom. Repeatedly, over and over again until he thought his head was going to explode in a cascade of blood and gore. Note to self – create a monster that nags someone to death.

On our way back into town we stopped off at the gas station and saw that nice young man you used to date in high school, Mark Yates. Just as handsome as he was back then. He smiled when I mentioned your name so I definitely think you should look him up when you come home. I'm not sure why you two ever broke up. You were perfect for each other.

Perfect? Not sure what Mark's husband might have to say about that. And that's why we broke up, by the way. I was definitely not his type and we were absolutely not perfect for each other. He was a nice guy though and he still sent Christmas cards every year.

I need you to call me just as soon as you can. So much went on while we were on vacation and we really need to talk about it.

Love, Mom

There was no way Toni was going to call her mother tonight. She'd argued with first Wyatt Stone and then the contractor who was renovating the house, and she'd enough frustration for one extremely long day. Maybe tomorrow. Or the next day. Or better yet, Toni would wait for her mother to call back. Barbara Ross was known for blowing ordinary situations out of proportion and this could be exactly that. Better to wait and be sure that this was something that needed Toni's attention. Her mother was probably upset that she didn't win at bingo on the cruise ship.

The last exciting thing that had happened in the Ross family was when Carla had left Wyatt for another man. Toni had scrambled to stay out of that situation no matter how much her mother had tried to drag her into the middle of it. Unless someone had a serious illness or had died, she couldn't see that she needed to be involved in the family drama. Nothing good ever came from it.

She'd tried to be a good daughter but had failed miserably. These days she concentrated on being a good person instead.

Smacking the lid on her laptop closed, Toni breathed a heavy sigh. She would not allow her mother to pull her back into whatever nonsense she or Carla had found themselves in this time. She wouldn't give in to the passive-aggressive remarks and the backhanded compliments.

Stay strong. Hold her head up. Stand tall.

And if that didn't work, she'd avoid and ignore. She wasn't too proud to hide either.

Chapter Five

WYATT WASN'T A stupid man but the current decision to stop by the McMahon place to check on Toni certainly wouldn't be classified as the smartest thing he'd ever done. It had been almost a week since he'd talked to her and despite the little voice in the back of his head that practically screamed in his ear to stay the hell away, he was concerned about her and how she was getting along. He'd heard a few rumblings in town that the renovation was huge and expensive.

That's how he found himself on the long driveway in front of the house, staring up at the rundown monstrosity and wondering what in the hell Toni had been thinking when she'd purchased it. He'd readily admit that the grounds were expansive and the house was large enough to hold many guests but the effort it was going to take to put this place back together was mind-boggling.

"Did your curiosity get the best of you?"

Toni appeared from around the corner of the garage, clipboard and pen in hand. In deference to the temperature she was dressed in a pair of faded blue jeans with holes in the knees and an oversized light blue blouse. Her long hair was loose around her shoulders, strands blowing freely in the breeze, and her cheeks pink from the brisk weather. No worries though. Tomorrow the temperature was forecasted to soar to record highs.

"You could say that. You could also say that I needed the break from fixing fences."

Clearing her throat, she gave him a smile that said she didn't believe a word.

"Fair enough. How about the nickel tour? Or did you just come here to try and talk me out of my folly? You'd be wasting your breath and you always seemed like a man that hated waste."

He did but he'd never realized she'd noticed that about him.

Letting his gaze wander around the property, he nodded in agreement. "I wouldn't mind a look around. Is the work crew here today?"

Tucking her pen into her pocket, Toni chuckled and motioned for him to follow. "They're here every day but Sunday. With any luck they'll be done at the end of next month."

They traveled up the steps and to the front door, the scent of fresh paint hanging in the air. "What will they be done with? The kitchen?"

"Everything. I've got five crews here from four counties. I've learned that the best way to get things done is to use momentum. If you allow things to drag on, you lose that and then projects take so much longer."

He almost tripped over his own feet and choked on his spit. "Five crews? Holy shit, Toni, how much is this costing you? Have you lost your mind? Does Barb and Joe know you're doing this?"

At the mention of her parents, she abruptly stopped, the

smile disappearing from her face. Dammit, he'd forgotten what a strained relationship she had with her family. She had good reason to keep them at arms' length.

"Yes, although they aren't privy to the details since this business is mine and mine alone. They'd only discourage me and tell me that I'll never amount to anything so why bother them? As far as they're concerned I'm throwing away my life because I don't have a husband or children. Oh, and let's not forget the whole art and design thing. They really hate that."

Wyatt grimaced, remembering unpleasant family conversations he'd been present for. Barb and Joe favored Carla over Toni and they didn't bother hiding it or pretending in any way. "I'm sorry I brought them up. I guess things aren't any better there?"

Holding the clipboard against her chest like a shield, Toni shook her head. "I was an accident and they've never let me forget it. Then to add insult to injury I had the audacity to not be a blonde, blue-eyed prom queen. They're still not over that."

"I have vivid memories of the Goth phase when you were in high school. Glad to see you're getting some sun these days," Wyatt chuckled. "And wearing colors too. You've come a long way."

"That was fifteen years ago."

Toni pushed open the door and he stepped over the threshold. He didn't make it more than four of five steps into the foyer before he found himself stunned by the interior. It looked like a nightmare, and the smug-looking woman standing next to him didn't seem to have a clue. She was giggling, her eyes alight with happiness as he turned himself in a circle to take everything in.

"Woman, what have you done?"

✦　✦　✦

Toni loved the gobsmacked expression on Wyatt's face.

His eyebrows were almost to his hairline. His mouth hung open and he'd made several complete three-sixty turns to try and take everything in. He was acting as if he'd never seen a construction site before.

"We're down to the studs in most of the house so they can get to the plumbing and wiring. I'm bringing everything up to code. But once the drywall is finished the rest of the work should go very quickly. I have all the furnishings ordered and on their way."

In her mind's eye, she could see the finished product. The refinished balustrade and floors, the new rugs and lighting, and the gothic touches she had planned that would pull everything together for this haunted hotel. She'd learned early in her career that the look of everything was of utmost importance when it came to a scare attraction.

"You might have done better to bulldoze the damn thing and start again. This is going to take months."

Toni sighed and rolled her eyes at his dramatics. "You're kind of a glass half full kind of guy aren't you? It won't take that long. I have fifty men in here every day working on the house. They did all of this in a week. By the end of next week, the walls will be back and they'll be painting."

His back was turned to her but she knew he was wearing a scowl. Finally he turned around, that determined look on his face again that he'd worn at breakfast the other day.

Crap. Here he goes again.

"Toni, this is a huge undertaking. Are you sure you're up for something like this? I've known full time contractors with a decade or more of experience that wouldn't take on a job like this."

Apparently she had the word *imbecile* stamped on her forehead. She must remember to wash that off first chance she got.

"I've managed large projects before."

Toni didn't go into more detail. Wyatt wasn't her daddy.

He opened his mouth to speak again and she'd had enough. Raising her hand in a stop sign, she shook her head. "No, you don't get to do this. The fact is I do not have a problem. *You* have a problem. It's sweet that you are worried about me but we've had this discussion and it's over. I am a grown woman and I do not owe you any explanations for my actions. I don't question you and frankly, it's insulting that you question me. Was that your intention, Wyatt? To make me feel like a child that doesn't have the sense that God gave a goose?"

His mouth gaped open like a fish and he still managed to look handsome. If she wore that same expression, children would run screaming in terror.

But damn it felt good to shut him up. His cheeks were a ruddy shade and she didn't feel a bit sorry for what she'd said. How he was treating her wasn't okay.

His jaw snapped shut and his shoulders straightened. "No, that was not my intention. I was simply worried about you, that's all, but I can see it was a waste of my time. You don't take advice well."

"I do when I ask for it," Toni shot back sweetly, an innocent smile on her face. "I didn't ask for yours. Now, do you want to see the rest of the house and property or do you want to go back to your place and pout? I'm good either way."

The silence stretched between them but Toni refused to budge or back down. She liked Wyatt. He was a good man and her sister had been an idiot for driving him away, but that didn't mean he could come into her home and criticize how she ran her life and business. Putting up boundaries early in a friendship was one of the most important things she could do.

Of course that assumed she and Wyatt were going to become friends while she was in town. They'd never been friends before despite being in-laws, so perhaps she was being overly optimistic about any future relationship they might have.

His eyes narrowed and his body stiff, Wyatt turned on his heel and stomped toward the front door, his cowboy boots echoing on the hardwood floors. Before he hit the bottom front porch step, Toni quickly ran outside so he could clearly hear her.

"It was nice to see you too, Wyatt. It's always a pleasure. Drop by any time."

Sarcasm dripped from her words and he came to an abrupt stop a few feet from his truck. Looking over his shoulder, his serene smile might have scared a lesser woman but she'd tangled with her share of alpha males in the past. Wyatt Stone wasn't any different.

"I think I will take that tour after all. Lead the way."

Okay...maybe he was a little different. The asshole had called her bluff.

Point to Stone.

Chapter Six

WYATT WAS WELL aware that he had royally pissed off Toni. He also knew he'd surprised her by turning around and coming back to the house after stomping out like a diva that didn't get their way.

He'd pushed too far and he needed to apologize. And he would. Soon.

It was just that there was something about Toni that made him crazy and slightly irrational. Maybe it was her hellfire independence and her stunning control issues. Maybe it was how she didn't give a furry rat's butt what anyone else did or thought. She'd always been like that and he kind of admired her bravado. But he also knew that if she wasn't careful she was going to end up like Wile E. Coyote and make a human-shaped hole in a wall somewhere when she hit it at full speed.

It was insulting to her how he'd been going on and on and she'd done nothing in her life to deserve that treatment. He wasn't a man given to flowery words and effusive apologies but he'd choke out an *I'm sorry* if it killed him.

"That's a huge break in the cabinets," Wyatt observed as they toured the kitchen. She'd kept the solid maple cabinets but pulled the doors off. They were sitting on a table a few feet away being repainted a bright white. "Is that for a double door refrigerator?"

"No, that's for the fridge." Toni pointed to another large area on the opposite wall. "That's for the stove. It will have six burners and two ovens, plus a warming drawer. The spot needed to be big to accommodate it."

"Granite countertops?"

Toni didn't appear to be holding a grudge. She laughed and pulled a paper from her clipboard and handed it to him. "Stainless steel. This is a commercial kitchen."

She'd handed him what looked like a rendering from a computer program and he had to admit – at least to himself – that the kitchen was going to be impressive. Lots of countertops and bright light. He wouldn't mind whipping up a meal in a place like this. His own kitchen needed to be trashed and completely renovated.

The upstairs was much like the downstairs although not quite as extensive. There were going to be eight suites and one mammoth deluxe suite on the second floor, and an apartment on the third floor that would belong to Toni when she was in town. The rest of the third floor was unplanned and for now would be used for storage. According to Toni, she was also planning to renovate the guesthouse out back and turn it into some sort of Presidential suite.

"Do you want to see what I have planned for outside?"

Wyatt hadn't said much, not wanting to upset Toni any further, so he nodded his head in answer, following her downstairs and out the French doors off the dining area to the backyard.

The extensive patio area had already been cleaned up and the concrete scrubbed until it shown. There were a few gothic statues and bright green plants in oversized pots lining the walkway down to the lawn below.

"We installed colored lighting out here to give it a spooky air at night." Toni pointed up into the trees where he could just see twinkle lights nestled in the leaves. "I wanted the walk out of the house to start fairly innocuous but with each step becoming more ominous."

The pathway through the thick trees that had been shaped with blind turns would keep a guest on their toes. In the dark, the effect would only be magnified.

"I'll have haunted effects through this entire walkway, including monsters that jump out at you, ghost shadows that cross your path, and a clearing of witches brewing up an evil spell."

Toni went on to describe them in more detail, painting a vivid picture of not only a truly good scare but also great fun. She'd clearly thought this through which only made him feel even worse about earlier. That apology needed to come sooner rather than later.

They paused outside of a rustic barn at the end of the path. Toni pushed open the doors and the smell of hay made his nose twitch. "This will be the end of the haunted walkway where guests can get a drink or snack. If they want to continue the spooky fun, the haunted hayrides will leave from here. Those will go deep into the property and will contain much more elaborate scares including live actors dressed and in makeup. But I'll only run the hayrides in the fall around Halloween. In the winter it will be too cold and the summer too hot. I'll use the springtime to update the monsters and ghosts so each year will be a little different. I'm hoping for repeat customers. Oh, and I'm putting in a pool just over there for guests in the summer. There was lots of free space and I think every hotel should have a pool."

Sighing, Wyatt shoved his hands in the pockets of his jeans. "Listen, I need to apologize. I'm sorry that I acted the way I did. Obviously, you have an elaborate plan, and while I still think it's a huge amount of work and money, I see that you've thought this through. I don't understand the monster and haunted attraction industry but this certainly seems like it might be interesting to those that like this sort of thing."

Her lips were pressed together as if she was trying not to laugh or smile. It was okay. He was man enough to take some ribbing. He'd been in the wrong, after all.

"Thank you," she said solemnly, although her eyes were lit with happiness. "I can't tell you how much your apology means to me. Most men just can't say they're sorry and it's nice to be with one who can."

Wyatt knew quite a few women who couldn't say it either.

Like his ex-wife Carla.

He'd been trying not to let that woman ruin everything even when she wasn't around. She was the biggest ghost in this place but she followed Wyatt everywhere he went.

"You're thinking of my sister, aren't you? I don't think I ever heard her apologize in all the years we were growing up. Did she ever apologize to you?"

Wyatt's lips twisted and he gave a choked laugh. "That would be a no. But I'm guessing she still doesn't think she has anything to say she's sorry for. Last time I saw her she said everything was my fault."

Toni snorted and tossed her head. "Don't even get me started. I have stories that would curl your hair."

He raised one eyebrow. "You think I don't?"

"It's not a contest."

"I sure as hell didn't get any trophies. Is there anything else to see?"

Toni laughed and feigned insult. "Isn't this enough?"

"It is and I stand by my original statement. Damn, woman, this is a monumental amount of work. I have no doubt you know what you're doing after seeing your plans but who is running the day to day? Your contractor can't possibly keep track of all of the renovations plus this outdoor area too."

"Me," she sighed, rubbing her temple as if it ached. "I'm doing it. It's a lot of work but at least I know it's getting done right. I have a vision and I want to see it come to life."

She pulled out more renderings from her clipboard and handed them to Wyatt. Each one was more imaginative than the one before, although some were actually quite simple.

Simple but effective. People were going to pee their pants with fear and pay her for the privilege.

"You simply need someone you can trust, Toni. Someone who has your best interests at heart and shares your enthusiasm. And most importantly, someone who has a track record of delivering whatever they promise."

Her smile widened and she clutched the clipboard to her chest, clapping her hands together with glee. When she wasn't glowering at him or chewing him a new asshole, Antonia was a very attractive woman.

"Wyatt, that's the best idea ever. You're hired."

Wait. He was what?

Chapter Seven

TONI WAS PRACTICALLY bouncing up and down with joy but Wyatt looked much more dubious. And a little shell-shocked.

He held up his hands in a sign of surrender. "Now wait just a minute, little girl. I wasn't talking about me. I was talking about some other poor bastard. I already have a job."

She couldn't stop smiling even though Wyatt clearly wanted to run and hide. She wouldn't let him. He was perfect. He was detail-oriented, a stickler for perfection, and if she remembered correctly, he had a work ethic to be envied. In other words, he was the right man for the job. It was like she'd won the lottery.

After all, he'd said about the project being over her head and not being able to handle things…she owed him this one.

"A job you are on vacation from," Toni couldn't help but point out. "You told me you are free as a bird for the next month and this is a great way to earn some extra cash. I'll pay you very well, I promise."

Crossing his arms over his wide chest, he wasn't impressed. "You couldn't afford me anyway. The money I make consulting is just fine for my needs, thank you very much. Besides, I have projects around the farm that need to get done."

Think. Think. Think. There has to be an answer to this.

"I have a crew of fifty that can help you. You'll be in charge and they can do the work. I bet they can knock out whatever needs done in a couple of days. Tops. Can you start tomorrow?"

"No, I cannot. I can't work here. You should hire someone but not me."

"There is only you. I've hired every capable person between here and Salt Lake City. There's no one else left."

"I'd like to help you–"

"Great. You can be in charge of–"

"But I can't," he cut in, shaking his head and looking at her like she'd sprouted a few extra arms and legs. Maybe some stripes and polka dots on her face. "I have plans."

The way he'd said it was odd. Like he was planning to rob a liquor store or printing some counterfeit money and didn't want anyone to know about it.

"What kind of plans?"

Shrugging, his gaze wandered over her shoulder, not meeting her own. "Just plans. I'm on vacation."

She regarded him closely. The slight flush to his features. The flat line of his mouth. The way he wouldn't look directly at her.

"You don't have any plans, do you? Other than watching Netflix marathons, anyway."

"I don't watch Netflix." He sighed and his shoulders slumped. "I've got a stack of books I've been wanting to read. There, are you happy?"

"Deliriously so. What if I promise you that you'll be off

work every day by three o'clock? That would give you plenty of time to read. Deal?"

"No deal."

He was hard to convince but now that she'd pictured him in this role she wasn't going to let this go. He'd do an amazing job. She only wished she'd been the one to think of it.

She wasn't too proud to play a little dirty.

"So you came here to tell me that this project is too large, too difficult, and way over my head, then when I ask you to help, you turn me down flat? So much for family and friendship, Wyatt. I can see your concern wasn't all that real. It was simply an excuse to throw your alpha male weight around. But you never intended to really help me. Just point out the problem and then turn your back and walk away. Wow, that's not the Wyatt Stone I knew. I guess everyone changes."

Oh...oh...oh...she'd pushed him too far. A muscle was working in his jaw and his blue eyes were an icy gray. Her gaze quickly strayed back to the pathway that had led here and she wondered how much of a head start she'd need to make it back to the house and safely away from his wrath.

"Are you done talking?"

His tone was low and deathly, sending a shiver down her spine but not in a fun, scary way.

I am in deep shit. Must learn when to shut up.

Sucking in a breath, she nodded. "Yes. Yes, I am. And can I just say—"

"No, you may not." Wyatt stepped forward so he was looming over her short stature, close enough to feel the heat from his skin and smell the subtle tang of his body wash. "You will be quiet and listen. Are you listening, Toni?"

She nodded mutely, her gaze captured by the intensity in his face. She'd ripped him a new one and now she was about to get the tables turned.

"I'm going to help you."

Huh? What? I couldn't have heard that right.

"I–I don't think I understand."

"I said I'm going to help you."

Toni licked her suddenly dry lips, taking a few false starts before words came out of her mouth. "Why? What changed your mind?"

He straightened and a slow smile spread across his face. "You did. Your little speech. That's what it was for, wasn't it? You didn't say all that just to piss me off."

A niggling of guilt made itself known.

"Hey, I shouldn't have said that stuff but I knew I would get a reaction. I'm sorry."

He shook his head and chuckled. "Were you wrong?"

"Wrong? I don't follow."

"Were you wrong?" he repeated. "What you said, Toni. Were you wrong?"

She thought about everything that had happened between them today. "No, I wasn't wrong. You came to point out the cracks in the foundation but all you wanted me to do is give up and quit. You never intended to help me. You just wanted to be right."

He didn't contradict her or argue.

"And that is why I'm going to help you."

✦ ✦ ✦

WYATT HAD BEEN hoisted on his own petard.

He simply couldn't argue with Toni's logic. He had gone there to tell her she couldn't handle a project that size, but he hadn't had plans after that. The only "help" he was offering her was saying she was wrong and that she needed to quit.

That wasn't help. That was arrogance and plain mean-spirited.

It was no wonder she'd told him off. He'd offered nothing constructive, no ideas. Only that she needed to quit and walk away. Toni would never do that and he ought to know. He'd watched her persevere through school and then college when her entire family told her she couldn't do it. She wasn't going to pack up and go home just because he expressed a few doubts.

He tossed his keys onto the side table next to the front door and headed straight for the kitchen to grab a cold beer. He'd run several errands after leaving Toni's and now all he wanted to do was put his feet up and read one of the stack of books he had sitting by his favorite leather recliner.

But that wasn't where he ended up.

Instead, he found himself pulling down a shoe box from the top shelf of his closet and sifting through the contents piece by piece. A ticket stub from when he'd seen the Eagles during one of their reunion tours, a map of the city of Paris, a paper menu from a restaurant in London, a small rock from when he'd visited Yellowstone Park as a child. Each item brought a smile to his face as he remembered back to what now seemed like simpler times. Easier and much less complicated. He'd been young and naive and damn…that was a great way to live. He longed for that sometimes. The enthusiasm of youth and the wide-eyed optimism when everything in the world seemed possible.

Kind of like what Toni had shown him today.

She believed so deeply and because of his own cynicism he'd tried to shake that confidence, poke holes in her plans. She was right. His issues with her projects weren't her problem. It was his. He'd brought his life baggage along and battered her over the head with it.

Soon there was nothing left in the box but a stack of photos.

Pictures he should have thrown away long ago but for some reason had held on to. It wasn't because he still loved Carla. Fuck no, those feelings had died when she'd stabbed him in the heart over and over. She'd never truly loved him, and maybe he'd never loved her either. He wasn't even sure he knew what real love was. Other than his mother and father, he'd never been loved by anyone so he probably wouldn't recognize it if it smacked him upside the head and then kissed him on the lips.

He'd kept these photos because he'd wanted a reminder of what opening up and letting someone in could do. How much damage a human being could sustain when they made themselves vulnerable, when they put their heart on the line.

He picked up the top photo, one of himself and Carla sitting on his motorcycle. He had a stupid grin on his face and her smile was more smug than smitten. He'd purchased the damn thing to impress her and it had for awhile. But Carla's mantra had always been "more." More of something, more of everything, and on a soldier's salary and then a farmer he'd been ill-equipped to handle her demands. Her focus on material goods should have been a clue.

The next photo was on their honeymoon in the Caribbean. Carla was tanned and blonde in her bikini, holding up her hand with the best diamond he could afford on the ring finger. That should have been his second clue. She'd been much more interested in the "show" of the wedding and the ring than she had in her husband.

Carla had probably loved him in her own way, as much as she'd been capable of. After all, she'd known he wasn't rolling in dough yet she'd still walked down the aisle with him. But she'd quickly grown tired of being a soldier's wife. He was gone for long periods of time and there was never enough money. He couldn't really blame her for finding someone else.

The third picture made him chuckle and smile. Carla and Toni wearing blue checked aprons and slaving over pans of Christmas cookies in their parents' kitchen. That had been the first Christmas after he and Carla had married and Toni had still been in school. Her hair had been dyed black and she wore black eyeliner and lipstick but despite the Goth exterior, she still looked happy.

With all the gunk she'd worn and the strange clothes, he hadn't noticed but she'd been delicately pretty with a small chin and nose. She'd kept to herself quite a bit, hiding in her room so they hadn't spent much time together. But she'd been funny and spunky and hardworking even then.

So different than Carla. Yet…they were sisters. They had to have a few things in common although they didn't look or act alike. It was as if they'd been raised in separate homes with totally different parents.

Now he found himself in the position of spending every single day for the next four weeks with the sister of a woman he hoped to never see again for the rest of his life. Toni didn't remind him of Carla but she did keep the past alive to a certain extent. She kept the memories simmering on the back burner when he really wanted them taken out with the trash.

She made him think about all the mistakes he'd made in his life, the wrong turns, the might-have-beens. Frankly, he didn't want a stroll down memory lane. He didn't want to reminisce. He wanted to pretend he hadn't been such a fucking idiot.

And he did want to help Toni. Really. She couldn't have talked him into something he truly didn't want to do. He would have found some sort of excuse. Her ideas were fascinating and he wanted to see the fruition of her vision. In his line of work, he didn't create things.

It was four weeks. Not a lifetime.

This was Toni, after all. He wouldn't have to see or deal with Carla, or the past. He could live comfortably in the here and now.

Just where he wanted to be.

Chapter Eight

TONI SHOULDN'T HAVE been surprised that Wyatt was an early riser. They had pulled up in front of the estate at the exact same time, both carrying a coffee. Hers from the small shop in town and his in a metal thermos. She was also juggling her messenger bag, a stack of drawings she'd been working on the night before, and a piece of toast sticking out of her teeth. Thank goodness he wasn't a man she wanted to impress. He might be handsome and sexy but she wasn't interested. Too much history there and it wasn't even *her* history.

"Stupid sister," Toni mumbled under her breath and around the slice of toast as they crossed the threshold into the large foyer where a team of workers were beginning their day.

"Did you say something?" Wyatt frowned, lifting the messenger bag from her shoulder and placing it on an oak side table. Chivalrous bastard.

She had a bad habit of talking to herself and would need to curb it around him. He had keen hearing and unlike so many men, he actually listened.

"Nothing really. Just remarking on the weather. It's going to be another beautiful day."

Her plan had always been to do the renovation in the summer so she could open for the all-important Halloween season come the fall. So far, everything was on track to be done early. She'd have time for some trial runs before her bread and butter time of the year began.

"It's going to be warm today," Wyatt remarked and she wasn't sure why until she remembered she was the one that brought up the weather to begin with. "Where do you want me to start?"

He was wearing a pleasant smile on his face and didn't seem perturbed in the least considering she'd practically shanghaied him into the job. "You don't have to do this, you know. I appreciate it and all but I know that I cornered you and made it impossible for you to say no."

He twisted open the thermos and poured steaming coffee into the lid before he answered.

"Honey, if I didn't want to do this, I wouldn't. I'm a grown man and a little girl like you couldn't corner me in any way, shape, or form. I want to help you."

That was nice and everything but…wait…what did he say?

"I am not a little girl. I'm a thirty-one-year-old woman. Some might even say I'm past my prime."

She needed to shut up. Right now if not sooner.

"Thirty-one is young and you are little. You're a foot shorter than I am. How do you reach the upper shelves in the kitchen cabinets?"

"A utility step," she answered automatically. "Or I climb up on the countertops. Either works."

"Sounds dangerous. If you need anything up high while I'm

here just ask me and I'll get it for you."

He looked completely serious. "You're kidding, right? Every time I want something, you think I'm going to ask you to reach it for me? That's insane. Did you hit your head recently?"

He gave her a big grin and laughed, irritating the hell out of her. She hadn't been trying to be funny. "I have not, although I'm not sure you believe me from the look on your face. Helping you is not insane, by the way, it's gentlemanly behavior. A man shouldn't mind helping out a woman every now and then."

"That sounds very patronizing. What if she doesn't need help?"

He was amused by her and that pissed her off. It was yesterday all over again.

"Then this entire conversation doesn't apply. I was simply offering, Toni. I was not casting aspersions on your ability to care for yourself or do your job."

"I would hope not," she huffed, thinking maybe she'd overreacted. She normally didn't talk to people until she'd had her morning caffeine. "Honestly, I'm not at my best until I've had a couple of cups of coffee."

"And your toast." Wyatt indicated the forgotten and now soggy piece of bread in her hand. Sighing, she tossed it in the huge trash can the crew kept by the door.

"How about we start by going into the office and looking at the blue prints? You and I can review all the work that is going on now and what's planned. Then we can move on to the grounds. You can choose where you want to concentrate your efforts."

"I know little about scare attractions so I thought I might be more help on the home renovations, but it's up to you."

It would be a monumental weight off her shoulders to know someone had the work in hand for the home while she worked on the outside. "That sounds perfect. Why don't I show you the office and go through the drawings?"

"Sounds good. Lead the way."

Having Wyatt here was going to be a good thing. Sure, he was overly protective and a little too alpha but he was also a stickler for detail. She could trust him to keep the crews on their toes and moving forward. Once he learned to back off, everything would be fine. It looked like smooth sailing as far as the eye could see.

✦　✦　✦

IT WAS AFTER eight that evening and the sun was going down when Wyatt found himself staring at a battered and patched wall. A wall that according to the blueprints he held in his hand should be ten feet from where it currently stood. The walls surrounding this bedroom didn't make sense either which meant one of two things...

Either the blueprint was wrong or the walls were.

The safe money was on the blueprint being incorrect. Construction crews had to make adjustments at times and anyone might have made changes inside the house without taking the time to get a permit from the county. It was just one of the weird things he'd encountered on his first day. He'd been so engrossed in his work that the time had flown by which by his estimation was a good thing. He'd enjoyed himself today. The crew was mostly easy going and hardworking and it felt good to creating something that didn't exist before.

In the last twelve hours he'd been over almost every inch of this house and couldn't help but be impressed. At one point, long before he'd been born, this home and grounds must have been a beautiful sight to behold. He could see it in the little details that Toni was trying to preserve like the mosaic tiles on the back patio or the hand-sanded oak floors. The house needed more than elbow grease. It needed love and she was willing to give it.

"Are you still here?" Toni's voice carried from the end of the hall into the master bedroom. "I thought you left hours ago. I promised that you could leave by three every day."

Her face was shiny and pink with sweat, obviously from being outside all day. A few strands of sable colored hair had escaped the confines of her ponytail and were clinging to her cheek. He had to resist the urge to reach out and tuck them behind her ear.

No touching. Bad idea. So very bad. She might be cute, and funny, and talented, and smart but there were even more reasons – good reasons – to keep his distance, no matter how attractive she looked at the moment. Or all the time.

"It's okay. It's the first day and I've had a lot to do to catch up with everything that's going on. Bill finished the downstairs plumbing today so he'll start up here tomorrow, which is why I'm up here getting the lay of the land. so to speak."

"Yes," Toni hissed, doing a cute little fist pump. "That's awesome news and right on time too. You must have cracked the whip all day."

"Not really. They're good guys and they want to do a good

job."

"They want to do a good job *for you*. The way Bill was singing your praises this afternoon it sounds like they enjoy working for a man more than a woman. I'll try not to take it personally."

Wyatt placed the blueprints on the dresser. "I'm sure it's not that."

A corner of her mouth quirked up but she didn't look all that upset. "Maybe. It doesn't matter to me. If men don't want to work for me, they don't have to. There's always someone else who is happy to take my money. But it does look like you two bonded like brothers this morning."

Wyatt shrugged and reached for the water bottle he'd shoved in the back pocket of his jeans earlier but hadn't gotten around to drinking yet. "We're both former military and from this area. I know some of his friends and he knows some of mine." He held out the bottle, offering it to Toni. "You should drink this. You don't want to get dehydrated."

She blinked a few times as if she didn't understand what he thought sounded perfectly clear. "You want me to drink your bottle of water?"

"It's not *my* bottle of water," he explained a little less patiently than he would have this morning but then he was more tired now. "It's simply a bottle of water I grabbed earlier. It doesn't have my germs on it if that's what you're worried about."

She was clutching that clipboard – the one he was beginning to hate – to her chest again.

"I can get my own water."

That wasn't the point and she was smart enough to know that. She was also more stubborn than a mule.

Taking a deep breath, he tried to rein in his fraying temper. If they were going to butt heads like this every day for the next four weeks, this job was going to be a major pain in the ass.

"I know you can but you didn't. You're flushed, sweaty, and it was very hot out there today. When was the last time you had something to drink?"

Appearing to consider the question, she tapped her chin with her pen. "Maybe–"

"If you have to think about it, it's been too long. Take the damn water, Toni. I don't want to have to run you to the emergency room tonight."

He held out the bottle again and this time she snatched it from his hand, her lips pressed together tightly. "Thank you."

She didn't sound all that thankful but he decided to ignore that. She'd had a long, hot day as well, so if her answers were short and to the point it made sense.

"You're very welcome."

He also wanted to ask her if she'd eaten anything since lunch but she might actually explode into a million pieces if he did that. She made sure the crew had water and snacks all day long but he had a feeling she didn't take care of herself nearly that well.

"I admire your dedication but you can go home. I'm headed there myself. I need a hot soak in the tub and a glass of wine."

A vision of Toni covered in not much more than bubbles flashed through his brain but he ruthlessly pushed it away. She was practically family and thinking about her that way wasn't something he was proud of. Hell, he'd seen her off to the senior prom with some handsy, pimple-faced teenager boy. He couldn't go from the benevolent brother-in-law to panting male every time she talked about taking off an article of clothing.

Clearly, he'd gone too long without a woman. Too much solitude and perhaps a bit of loneliness had now manifested itself as a yearning for a girl – no, woman – that was completely out of bounds. He'd sworn off females and love after his divorce. It was better to be alone.

"There's a beer with my name on it as well. You lead the way and I'll follow, turning off the lights as we go."

He glanced at the blueprints on the dresser but decided to leave them there for the night. If he took them home, he'd be studying them when he should be sleeping. It was better to leave work where it was.

Toni led the way down the stairs and into the tiny office – which was not much more than a folding table and a few metal chairs – where she'd left her purse and messenger bag. Wyatt waited as she loaded up her laptop and paperwork, the still full water bottle, even that damn clipboard and slung the bag onto her shoulder.

"I guess I'm ready to go."

Wyatt reached for the light switch but before he could turn off the large and ornate chandelier hanging from the ceiling, it began to sway back and forth. Slowly at first, and then faster, the lamps flickering off and on creating a strobe effect.

"Again," Toni sighed, pulling his attention from the swaying light fixture to where she stood, lips pursed and hands on hips. She wore a thoroughly disgusted expression on her face as she watched the chandelier. "I almost hate to tell Bill to fix this. As much as it frustrates me, the guests would love it. But I doubt it's safe."

"Safe?"

"An electrical short, or whatever causes this. I don't want the house to burn down because I didn't get something dangerous corrected."

His gaze wandered back to the light fixture, which was now stationary, the bulbs burning brightly as normal. Wyatt rubbed his chin and smiled slightly. "You know that they finished the rewiring already?"

Toni turned and looked at him, her brow lifted slightly in challenge. "Then they didn't do it right." She pointed to the chandelier. "Obviously we still have a problem."

"Yes, and I'll tell Bill to look at this first thing in the morning. But there is a problem with your solution."

Toni exhaled noisily and crossed her arms over her chest. "What problem is that?"

Wyatt stepped closer so he could watch her expression. "Bad electrical wiring doesn't explain how the chandelier was swaying like that."

"So? It was the wind."

Chuckling, he indicated the closed windows surrounding them. "Wind from where? The air conditioning doesn't work and the windows in this room are painted shut. Besides, it would need to be a hell of a gust. That light fixture has to weigh over a hundred and fifty pounds."

"Don't tell me you believe in ghosts," she scoffed, tossing her long ponytail over her shoulder. "You always seemed like a scientific kind of guy to me. Do you believe in vampires and witches too?"

"No, I do not," he answered. "But I think it's funny that you don't. You're the one into all this haunted, scary stuff. You don't believe in ghosts?"

"Nope, only the ones I create in the factory. If ghosts really existed, don't you think that there would be irrefutable proof by now? But all we get are blurry photos and cold spots. Do you honestly believe?"

Wyatt thought about the question before he answered. He'd seen some strange things in his lifetime, things that couldn't be explained, but she was right when she pegged him for a scientific type. He liked to have proof.

"Yes and no. I don't believe but I'd like to believe if there was truly compelling evidence. Don't we all want to know what's on the other side? Everyone thinks about the afterlife." He pointed to the chandelier. "Just so we're clear, swinging lights are not sufficient proof. I'm sure there is a very reasonable explanation for it. Not ghosts or goblins."

"You wish there were ghosts? Really?"

"Hell, yes. Wouldn't it be interesting to be able to interact with a spirit from the past? Maybe from the Revolutionary War? Or even your Uncle Phil? You can't tell me that wouldn't be cool."

Toni shuddered and shook her head, clearly not liking that idea in the least. "No way. Dead people need to stay dead. I don't want to chat with George Washington's butler. I'll stay in the here and now."

Her complete distaste for anything paranormal was at odds with her chosen profession and Wyatt couldn't keep stop the laughter. This girl was a walking contradiction.

"I sincerely doubt we'll find any ghosts here, no matter what all the stories say."

Toni reached out and flicked off the dining room lights. "Of course not. There's no such things as ghosts. But there are such things as monsters, and that's what I'm going to be tomorrow if I don't get some food and sleep. Trust me, you don't want to see me in that mode."

It might be kind of cute. A tiny ball of growling female.

He trailed behind her as they locked up and headed to their cars, their footsteps loud on the steps in the silence. Everyone had left long ago and it was just the two of them.

"Good night, Wyatt. Thank you for today. I'll see you tomorrow."

She unlocked her car door and Wyatt helped her pull it open, waiting while she climbed into the vehicle. Once again, she was annoyed with his semi-chivalry.

Once again, he didn't care.

"Night, Toni. Be sure to drink that water or you'll feel nauseous and tired later."

He didn't let her reply, shutting the car door quickly but not missing the glare she shot his way. She started up the car and drove away without another look back. Her red taillights faded into the distance as he climbed into his own truck and pulled away, giving the house one last glance in the rearview mirror. In the dark, it looked every inch the haunted house, spooky and forbidding.

He hadn't been lying when he'd told Toni he didn't believe in ghosts. But she'd been right when she said there were monsters in this world, except she'd been joking. He'd seen monsters though. Real ones. He'd seen what they were capable of.

Death. Destruction.

All of that and more in the eyes of what passed for human beings.

He'd seen pure unadulterated evil. The house?

Wasn't even close.

Chapter Nine

"MOTHER, WHAT IS it exactly that you want from me?"

Toni unlocked her hotel room door, pushing it open with her foot while she juggled her belongings along with the cell phone she was cradling between her ear and shoulder. It had been a long day at the estate and she'd made the mistake of answering her phone without checking the caller ID. She'd been distracted and exhausted and now she was paying the price.

Punishment?

A conversation with her mother that was going in circles. She'd been talking to Barbara Ross all the way home and she still didn't know what the point of this was. Her mother never called just to chat. There was always a reason.

Toni could hear the harrumph from her side of the line. "Antonia Marie, you should speak to your mother with more respect."

She should but she often found it difficult.

"I'm sorry, Mom. It's just that I've had a very long, hot day at the construction site. I need a bath and some dinner."

More noisy sighing. Barbara wanted to make sure her daughter knew what a disappointment she was to her parents.

Trust me, I know, Mom.

"It's your own fault. We told you to go into teaching or nursing. A respectable profession for a woman. But no, you had to be creative. You had to express yourself. No one in my generation got to express themselves. Such indulgence in the youth today. That's what's wrong with the world."

Pollution. Wars. Violence. Inequality, just to name a few. But expressing one's self through the arts was what was wrong with society.

Right.

Toni was damn close to expressing herself in a way that would surely infuriate her mother but she managed to take a few deep breaths before speaking again.

"I love what I do, Mom. I never would have been happy doing anything else. Now, why did you call again? Are you planning Thanksgiving already? I think I'm going to be out of the country on business again this year. England doesn't celebrate Thanksgiving."

A shopping spree in London sounded better than turkey and dressing with her beloved family.

"This isn't about Thanksgiving," her mother replied sharply. "Are you sure they don't celebrate? I thought everyone did."

"I'm sure. Canada does, though, but in October."

Toni dumped all of her stuff on the dresser and fell into the inviting softness of her bed, closing her eyes and reveling in the cool air. Propping her feet on the mattress, she waited for her mother to get to the damn point. The conversation had gone off the rails again. As usual.

"Have you seen Wyatt in town since you've been there?"

Toni jerked at the abrupt question, her mind and body instantly on guard. She hadn't heard her mother mention Wyatt's name in literally years. Something also told her telling Barbara that Toni was spending all day, every day with him wasn't a good idea.

"It's a small town. Of course I've seen him."

Boy, had she. In the past four days since he'd began helping her, Toni had seen his t-shirt cling to a muscled torso that would make any woman sigh with longing. Coupled with soft, worn denim that cupped his perfectly shaped ass… It was a darn good thing the construction crew was all male. Otherwise, Wyatt would have a fan club by now.

He was also good at his job and hardworking. He had every detail under control inside the house, which left her free to oversee the outside construction in a divide and conquer strategy.

The only thing that drove her crazy was he worried about her like he was her nanny, constantly reminding her to eat or drink her water. He'd jump in front of her to open doors or clear a walkway in a cluttered area. He was trying to be a gentleman but what he didn't understand is that she didn't need him to be one. She could take care of herself.

"Did he say anything to you? No, never mind, of course he didn't. He wouldn't have the nerve after what he did."

"What he did?" Toni echoed. "I'm not sure I follow."

"He ruined your sister's life," Barbara declared, scorn in her tone evident. "She's never been the same since the day she met him."

It was all Toni could do not to burst into hysterical laughter.

Carla hadn't changed in the least, except perhaps she'd grown older and less able to manipulate people with her looks.

"I'm still not following you, Mom."

"Wyatt's parents died, you know, and left him everything."

She hadn't known but she remembered them from the wedding. They'd had Wyatt late in life so they'd already been gray-haired when he was in his twenties.

"They left him the farm. That's not a surprise, he was their only son."

Barbara snorted right in Toni's ear. "They had much more than that ramshackled farm. We found out recently that they were loaded and just lived that way for whatever strange reason. I don't understand it."

Wyatt inherited a fortune? Good for him. After everything he'd been through, he deserved it. Those around him would never know either. He appeared to lead a simple life just as his parents did. Commendable.

Dammit, that only made him more attractive. She admired down to earth men who didn't care about what other people thought about them.

"I'm sure Wyatt would rather have his parents back than the money. They seemed very close the few times I saw them together."

"He must care about the money, because he's holding onto it like a miser."

Toni officially had a headache. She stood and headed into the bathroom where she kept the ibuprofen.

"I guess that's his call. It is his money."

"Not all of it," her mother contradicted, her tone rising

slightly. "It belongs to Carla too, and he won't give her any of it. I wondered if he would say anything to you about it."

She shook two tablets out of the bottle and contemplated a third. "How is any of this money Carla's? They were his parents."

"But she was his wife. It's community property. Delores mentioned it when she got her divorce. She got half of everything Harry earned."

"While they were married. That's what community property is, Mom. Carla was entitled to half of everything Wyatt earned while they were married and vice versa. His parents didn't pass on until last year so Carla isn't entitled to anything."

Toni filled a plastic cup with some water and knocked back the two tablets in one gulp. With any luck, they'd begin working immediately.

"It's not her fault that they didn't die during the marriage. She shouldn't be penalized."

There wasn't enough alcohol and pain medication in the world to help Toni deal with her mother when she was like this.

Which was all the time when it came to her oldest daughter Carla.

Carla could do no wrong and deserved the very best in life. When Barbara Ross thought her precious baby wasn't being treated right, she could be downright nasty.

It was hard to believe that a woman that had given birth to Toni was now complaining that Wyatt's parents *hadn't kicked the bucket soon enough*. Sadly, her mother had passed these self-involved traits down to Carla who had then inflicted them on a nice guy like Wyatt. Toni hadn't been shocked when the couple had acrimoniously divorced after Carla had cheated on Wyatt and managed to get herself knocked up with his supposed best friend. Carla had been ruining friendships and relationships since kindergarten.

"That's not how it works, Mom. There are laws."

"I can't believe you're taking his side," Barbara whined on the other end of the line. "That's exactly what Wyatt's attorney said when we called him."

It wasn't all that shocking that Toni was siding with Wyatt considering no one on her family had taken her side in years.

Make that her entire life.

"You called his attorney?"

The one thing Toni could say about Barbara Ross was she had king-sized balls.

"We still had his name and number from the divorce. He actually had the nerve to laugh at us. So I'm having our lawyer draft an official letter to request Carla's portion. That should scare him."

Highly doubtful. There would probably be more laughing.

"Mom, I don't think that's going to work. Carla has no legal right to that money. None. I think you should just let this go."

There was silence on the other end. Toni's mother didn't take defeat well and she certainly didn't like to hear it from her youngest daughter. There would be some sort of punishment later. Toni didn't know what or when, but it would happen and it wouldn't be pleasant.

"Then you talk to Wyatt. Tell him to do the right thing."

And there it was. The real reason her mother had called.

And there went every bit of patience Toni had scraped together when she'd stupidly answered her phone. Gone. Poof.

"Wyatt is not stupid enough to give his money to his cheating, lying, and conniving ex-wife, Mother. In fact, I'm going to go out on a limb and say no one is. Carla burned her bridges and now she has to deal with that. She is not entitled to any money. If she needs money, perhaps she might think about going out and earning it."

Carla Ross Stone Wells had never had a real job in her entire life. Even her child was raised by her second husband's mother for the most part.

Strangled breathing sounds came through the phone and Toni wondered for a moment if she'd actually given her mother a stroke. She'd been close a few times but this might be the day.

"I can't believe how hateful you are being, Antonia. I don't know what happened to you as a child that made you this warped and cruel."

I do.

"The world doesn't owe Carla anything just because she's beautiful, Mother. She has to work for what she wants just like everyone else."

"Carla is not like everyone else."

Barbara made Toni's words sound like the worst insult in the world.

"You do have a point there. I'll give you that one."

She could practically hear her mother's fingernails digging into the plastic of the phone. Barbara Ross was not a happy woman.

"Are you going to talk to Wyatt?"

"I am not."

Surprisingly, there were not explosions or fireworks.

"We're not done talking about this." Her mother's voice quivered with barely suppressed anger but this wasn't the first time Toni had pissed off her parents. They pretty much hated every decision she'd ever made in her life.

"We are for tonight. I have to be up early in the morning. Some of us work for a living. It was lovely to talk to you but I do need to go. Good night, Mother."

She didn't even have a chance to hang up. Barbara did it first, before Toni had finished her sentence. Sighing with relief, she tossed the phone down on the bed and fell into the pillows.

"I want a DNA test. And a vodka."

Chapter Ten

THE GUEST HOUSE felt like a pottery oven, nary a cool breeze to break up the unrelenting heat. Sweat trickling down his back and making his shirt stick to his skin, Wyatt took another long swig of water from the bottle while it was still cold. It wasn't anywhere near the heat he'd dealt with in the Middle East, but for this part of Wyoming it was hot.

Even the workers seem to be feeling the uncharacteristic heat wave today, their usually quick steps slowed and their enthusiasm dampened. Bill, the foreman, had even bandied about the idea of working a split shift where they came in before dawn, rested in the middle of the day, and came back around dinner time until this brutal weather passed. What they needed was a good bout of rain, maybe even a thunderstorm. The grass was beginning to yellow and the plants to droop.

"Holy Mary, Mother of God that smell is getting worse with the heat," Bill groaned as he entered the master bedroom in the guest house where Wyatt had been sizing up the wall that still bugged him. He kept coming back to it every now and then over the last three days and finally he was going to talk to Toni about it. "It's also hotter than hell in this house. It's hotter inside than it is outside."

"I'd argue that point," Toni retorted, stomping into the bed-room with a sigh. Dressed for the stifling heat, she was wearing khaki Bermuda shorts and a yellow t-shirt paired with the steel toed boots she favored on the construction site. A white plastic hard hat was perched on top of her head, slightly askew from the ponytail that kept her long hair off of her neck. Somehow she managed to make that hat look delicate and feminine as if she was decked out in an expensive bonnet for the Kentucky Derby. "It's like the surface of the sun out there. It's beating down like we're working in the Sahara. I called the pool guys to see if they could come and get the swimming pool going so at least we'd have a cool place to drown ourselves when we can't take it anymore."

Wyatt frowned and checked the project schedule that had become a permanent part of his arm, trying not to picture Toni wet and dripping as she rose from the pool like Venus. This whole fantasizing thing was becoming a real issue. The more time he spent with her, the more he admired her. She challenged him and she was smart. That was a lethal combination for his libido. He spent most of his time avoiding her. "They aren't scheduled for a few weeks."

Toni swiped at her face with the sleeve of her t-shirt. "I don't care and I wasn't above begging. They'll try to fit us in this week."

"By the time they get here, the weather will probably be cold again," Bill joked. "That's the way it always is."

"Summer isn't over yet. We could get another heat wave. This way we're prepared," Toni pointed out. "Now why am I here again? We were installing zombies on the pathway."

Wyatt pointed to the wall. "Since we're taking these all down to the studs anyway, I want to completely remove this small dividing wall between the sleeping area and the sitting area. I think it cuts off the room and makes it look much smaller than it really is. Plus the best windows are out here and the sitting area is too dark. No way would anyone want to relax in there and read. There's no natural light."

Toni peered around the short wall into the sitting room and then back into the bedroom. "You're right. It's tiny, cramped, and dark, almost like a cell. I don't see anyone enjoying hanging out there. It's kind of claustrophobic. Plus this wall would need major work anyway. It's been patched with plywood."

"It's not original to the house." Wyatt indicated the blue-prints spread out on the dresser. "It must have been put in by a subsequent owner. They didn't even bother to match the original paint. You'd do better to take out the wall and if you wanted privacy add in a decorative screen or something."

Bill eyed the wall top to bottom. "Wyatt's right. We could put in sliding panels, the frosted kind. It would let in light but give the guest the option to close them."

Toni frowned and checked her clipboard. "How long would that take?"

"A day, but we'd need that time anyway if we simply pulled the wall down. This gives you options."

One of the things Wyatt had learned about Toni was that she was decisive. She didn't dither back and forth about an issue, worrying it to death. She understood no decision was actually a decision in itself.

"Do it. I like the idea. Good call, Wyatt. This suite will be much improved because of this and I want this guest house in particular to cater to an upscale clientele."

Bill grinned and reached for the pencil he kept tucked behind his ear. "I'll get right on it, boss." He scratched down a few notes and then motioned for two men with sledge hammers who had been waiting patiently in the hall. "Come on in, guys. Let's take her down."

"I might have been hoping you'd say yes," Wyatt laughed when Toni raised her brows in amusement. "I was ready to spend more time convincing you."

"It was a good idea. I didn't need convincing." Toni licked her lips and fidgeted slightly, moving the clipboard from hand to hand. "Listen, do you have a few minutes? I really need to talk to you."

She looked nervous which was unusual. Maybe she was going to fire him. For some reason the thought didn't make him as happy as he thought it would. They moved into the living room, settling down on two folding chairs the crew used when eating lunch. The guest house had become something of a hiding spot for the men to get away from the construction noise but now it was going through its own renovations.

"So?"

"So," she replied, seeming to have trouble figuring out what she wanted to say. Wyatt stayed quiet as she drummed her fingers on the metal seat of the chair. "I guess I just want to say I'm sorry. You're a nice man and you shouldn't have to put up with shit like that."

Wyatt rubbed his chin as he ran over every interaction he'd

had with Toni in the last week. Sure, she was stubborn and ornery and wouldn't take his suggestions about keeping hydrated and fed. She also bristled when he opened doors for her or tried to do anything else to help her but she hadn't said anything about it. If he were honest, he liked that she was independent, standing on her own two feet. He simply wished that she allowed someone to care for her a little more. She worked hard and she deserved it.

"You've done nothing to be sorry for," he finally said, watching her reaction closely. He didn't want her to think he wasn't grateful for the apology but it truly was unneeded. He was having fun and the work was rewarding.

Her eyes widened slightly and the corner of her lips turned up. "I know. I'm apologizing for my family. For what they've done. You don't deserve it."

"Thank you but that was five years ago. I hope I'm not still holding a grudge."

It was her turn to frown, her forehead wrinkled. "I'm not talking about before. I'm talking about recently when they called your lawyer. That's what I'm sorry for. I just found out about it last week and honestly, I'm mortified. I can't believe they did that. But good for you that you shut them down right away. They need a dose or three of reality."

"They called my lawyer? When did this happen?"

Wyatt searched his memory for any email, text, or call from Brent Hammond but he hadn't spoken to the man in months.

Toni's cheeks had turned a bright red and her fingers were massaging her temples. Wyatt remembered that feeling well from when he was married. Headaches. Lots of them.

"I—Well—Shit. Mom called and said that she or Carla or maybe Dad called your lawyer to ask about Carla's share of the inheritance."

Wyatt wished he could say he was shocked. Instead, he simply laughed at the mere suggestion. "Carla's share? She doesn't have a share."

Toni groaned and rolled her eyes. "That's what I told Mom but she went on and on about it. She even wanted me to talk to you about giving Carla money. She said she's going to have her lawyer draft an official letter to your lawyer. I told her that he'd just laugh because they don't have a legal leg to stand on."

Wyatt quickly sobered, the situation suddenly not so funny. "I'm sorry you got dragged into this. How did she even know about the money?"

"I don't know but she does." Toni leaned forward and grimaced, clearly embarrassed by her family. She needn't be. She was nothing like them. "I don't think they're going to give up, Wyatt. You should lawyer up or whatever it is they say. They're convinced that Carla deserves some of the money and that you ruined her life or some bullshit like that. That's why I'm so sorry. I wish I could make this go away."

"I'll call Brent," Wyatt assured her, patting her hand where it rested on her thigh. "It sounds like he already has this in hand though but I'll just make sure he's clear. She already signed a settlement that basically took everything. She got the house, the car, the savings and checking accounts, even my retirement savings. All I walked away with was my clothes and truck. I just wanted out of that marriage so I was willing to give her everything to do it."

"I don't know why she is acting like this. Her husband can easily support her."

"Can he?" Wyatt laughed. "She runs through money like water. He might not have any left."

"So she's going to start back in on yours?" Toni stomped her foot on the floor, the sound echoing through the empty house. "Over my dead body. She needs to be stopped before she ruins everyone around her."

Carla was a formidable woman but if the two ever scrapped, his money was on Toni. She had the fire and the grit that made her a winner. He also felt very grateful to be someone she respected enough to defend, although he could handle himself just fine. Her loyalty in a situation where she had to side against her own flesh and blood meant the world to him.

"Honey, I can deal with this. I know how your sister operates, remember? You have enough to worry about without adding me to your list. Let me handle this."

His fingers found hers, tangling together. Her skin felt warm to the touch and a zing of electricity shot straight to his chest, squeezing his heart painfully. If only they were two different people. If she wasn't Carla's sister and he wasn't done with women and love.

In another world and time they might have had a shot. But in the here and now they didn't stand a chance. He wasn't any good to anyone and he'd do well to remember that.

"She's just...such a...I don't want her to make trouble for you. Again."

"I'm a big boy, Toni. I'm serious about this. Don't add my troubles to your plate. You've got plenty."

She nodded, their faces close together, their gazes locked. Her brown eyes, flecked with gold, were currently dark with anger and frustration. He could smell the floral fragrance of her shampoo and this time he didn't resist the urge to run a silky strand of hair between his fingers before tucking it behind her ear.

Awareness crackled between them, the tension and electricity hanging in the air like a neon sign. They both knew what it was but neither one made a single move toward the other.

A throat clearing had both their heads whipping around toward the entrance to the room where Bill was standing. Shifting from foot to foot, his skin had a greenish cast and he looked as if he might boot his lunch any minute.

Wyatt jumped to his feet. "Are you okay, man? What's wrong?"

"You need to come. Both of you. We started knocking down the wall. Bad. It's very bad."

"Damn, is it a bearing wall?" Toni groaned, covering her eyes with her hands. "Tell me it's not a bearing wall."

Bill swallowed hard, his Adam's apple bobbing in his throat. "It's not a bearing wall."

Wyatt didn't like the feel of this at all. Bill was usually cool as a cucumber. "Then what is it?"

Scraping a hand down his face, Bill made a few false starts before he answered.

"It's a body."

Chapter Eleven

THE SMELL WAS the first thing that hit her long before Toni actually laid eyes on it.

There was a sickening aroma that had been trapped in the wall along with the body. It curled around her nostrils before clutching her intestines and squeezing until bile sat in the back of her throat. To think they'd assumed there was a raccoon or squirrel carcass in the walls or attic space.

Wrapping her arms around her middle as if she could ward off the burgeoning nausea, she steeled herself to look. With her love of all things haunted and scary, she'd never thought she would react in this manner but real was miles from fake. Fake she could handle. Fake was easy.

Toni had seen many things in her life that grossed her out but this topped them all. She'd never given much thought as to what an actual real dead body would look like so there was a part of her that was intrigued while the rest of her wanted to vomit and run. She'd seen all sorts of fake dead bodies, covered in red paint and even lit from within by LED lightbulbs. This was something altogether different.

"How long have they been here? Sweet baby Jesus."

Barely paying attention to Wyatt's hoarse query, Toni couldn't drag her gaze away from the desiccated corpse that looked like something she might have whipped up in her factory to scare unsuspecting guests at a haunted house. The skin, papery and wrinkled, pulled tightly on the emaciated skeleton, and the dead man or woman wore a toothy grin that seemed grossly misplaced considering their current condition.

Dead and all.

"I guess this was the smell?" Bill asked, leaning forward to take a closer look. The body was nestled in the wall between the two by fours, only the torso and head showing from where the crew had bashed a hole in the plywood patch with their sledge-hammers. The dust still hung in the air and tickled her nose. "You'd think it would have been stronger."

Someone was going to have to pull him or her out of there. It wouldn't be Toni.

Wyatt studied the lounging corpse with surprising dispassion. "Maybe the body has been there for a long time."

"Not much left," Bill grimaced, shaking his head. "Should I call the sheriff?"

"Yes." Toni finally found her voice. "Call the sheriff."

Stumbling through the house, she hit the front door as fast as she could, sucking in a lungful of fresh air on the front porch. She took several cleansing breaths as she felt a large, steadying hand on her shoulder.

"You okay? Are you going to throw up?"

Of course it was Wyatt, holding up another one of those water bottles he was constantly pushing her way.

"I am not—"

She never finished her denial. Her stomach heaved and twisted, acid flooding her mouth. Her hand flew up and she snapped her lips tightly closed but it wouldn't be enough. Wyatt quickly led her to the side of the front porch where there was a railing to lean over and bushes to baptize. Every bit of her breakfast and lunch made another appearance in reverse order.

Her eyes watered, tears leaking down her clammy cheeks as her stomach and intestines cramped painfully, over and over, long past the point there was anything to expel. When it was over, she slumped into Wyatt's strong, comforting arms and let him carry her to a lawn chair in the shade. His handkerchief dried her tears and then wiped her mouth. He twisted open the water bottle and handed it to her.

"Rinse and spit, honey. You'll feel better."

It was humiliating enough to puke in front of him, and now he wanted her to spit too?

"I'm fine. I'm okay."

"Christ, Toni, you are not okay. Can you just for five minutes let someone take care of you? Just a little? I promise nothing bad will happen."

Trying to stand, her legs shook badly and her stomach tightened ominously again. Wyatt shot to his feet and wrapped an arm around her waist, guiding her back into the chair. He didn't scold her again. He didn't have to. His pissed off expression said it all.

Her mouth did taste like she'd licked a dumpster so she took a large drink of water and swished it around her mouth before spitting it out as discreetly as possible. She took some small sips of the water while she allowed him to dab at her face with the soft cotton of the handkerchief.

Every move he made demonstrated a gentle care that had been sorely missing in her childhood home. Her boo-boos hadn't been kissed when she scraped her knee nor had stuffy noses been fed chicken soup and cartoons. She'd quickly learned to fend for herself but she had to admit it was kind of nice to have someone who worried. But it was nothing to get used to.

"Thank you," she said, her throat still raw and sore, the words coming out gravelly. "I feel much better."

"Good. Is there anything I can get you?"

"Brain bleach and a box of saltines?" she replied, trying to lighten the atmosphere which was quite dark at the moment. "I'd settle for one or the other if I can't have both."

She felt his warmth breath on her cheek and the rumble of his chuckle. "I'm fresh out of both, I'm afraid. How about we sit here until the sheriff shows up? There's no reason to go back in there."

Because there was a dead body.

"It's ironic, isn't it?" Toni sighed, slumping down in the webbing of the lawn chair and running the cool bottle over her forehead. Even in the shade it was hotter than hell now that her body temperature had returned to somewhat normal.

Wyatt levered off the ground and into another chair, pulling it close so they were knee to knee. "What's ironic?"

"I scare people for a living." Toni gave him a bitter smile. "Now I've found a dead body in the guest house of what was supposed to be my haunted hotel. And I couldn't even deal with it. I puked in front of you and the crew. That's irony."

"The crew doesn't care and neither do I. I'll bet a few of

them are tossing their cookies behind the barn right now. There's nothing to be embarrassed about. You deal in making something ordinary feel scary but no one is truly in any danger. This is a whole other deal, honey. Seeing a dead body for the first time will change you. Seeing one that's been dead for awhile...well, shit...that's going to be something you won't forget for awhile."

Toni knew he'd been in the Middle East. He'd been in combat although he never talked about it. She'd asked him questions once but he'd brushed her off.

"You must have seen this before."

"Yes," he answered but didn't elaborate which was so like him. "Do you need to talk about it?"

Almost ready to say no, she changed her mind at the last minute. "It was actually less creepy than things I've designed but it affected me more. Isn't that weird?"

He pressed his fingers to her knees so she had to look up at him. "It was real. That's the difference."

She wrinkled her nose in distaste. "It was the smell. To think we thought it was a coyote or something. A body never crossed my mind."

"It's not the first thing I would think of either. Now drink a little more water so you don't dehydrate."

She'd let him care for her for a few moments but she was feeling much more human. "We're both out in the same heat. If I need water, so do you."

Wyatt smiled and stood, patting her shoulder. "Point taken. I'm going to get something to drink. Are you sure I can't get you anything?"

The mere thought of a morsel of food passing her lips made her sick to her stomach. "Nothing, thanks. I don't think eating is a good idea right now. I'm going to take your suggestion and wait for the sheriff. Maybe I should send the crew home too."

"Not yet. The sheriff may want to question them."

He'd probably want to question her as well. What would she say?

"That's true. Geez, I just can't stop thinking about that poor person. How did they die? Was it painful? Did someone they love kill them? I doubt it was suicide since they couldn't close themselves up in that wall."

Images of some serial killer stuffing the body in and then patching the drywall made her shudder.

"Honey, you wouldn't be human if you didn't have thoughts like this," Wyatt said gently. "Death is traumatic and you've been up close and personal with it today. Don't expect to be unaffected by this."

Toni sighed and looked up at Wyatt. "I want to know who it is and what happened to them. This is so tragic and sad. I bet they had family and friends, people who loved them. It's not fair."

She'd always known about the fickle nature of fate but today it had been brought abruptly and violently home. On her property, in her wall. There was a human being whose life was cut short and it was wrong. Someone did this on purpose.

Even if the death was an accident, the hiding of the body wasn't.

Toni's gaze moved from Wyatt to the imposing structure of the house and grounds. Minutes ago it had looked shabby and rundown but completely innocuous. Now it was something totally different – dark and foreboding.

What other secrets would they find?

Chapter Twelve

TONI SAT BACK in the steaming hot water and sunk down to her neck, slowly letting the tensions and horrors of the day recede. After the sheriff and coroner had shown up at the house, the events passed so quickly they all seem to run together. Now yellow crime scene tape blocked off the guest house and the body had been taken to the morgue for an autopsy.

It had been a long, hot, terrible day and she'd been glad to come back to the hotel but then she'd quickly realized that being here was no better. Every footstep in the hall, every closing door, or creak of the building made her jump with fright. In the last two hours her heart hadn't stopped racing and her stomach was twisted into knots that made it impossible to eat dinner.

There was a very real possibility that there was a killer out there somewhere. He or she looked like everyone else but they weren't. They'd taken a life and then covered it up. How many other lives had they ended? Were they sorry? Did they think about it every day? Did the deceased have a family that mourned? Did they wonder what happened to their loved one?

The whole situation was morbid, sad, and a little scary. If a person takes a life, are they more or less willing to do it again?

Toni imagined it might become easier after the first time. Especially if the person hadn't been caught. Of course, she didn't know for sure that the killer wasn't in jail now. They could be behind bars for something completely unrelated to the body in the wall.

The slamming of a door that seemed much too close made her pulse jump as she sucked in a breath. Sitting up in the bath, she sat as still as possible, straining to hear anything else. That bump hadn't sounded like it was from the hall. More like her own room.

This bath wasn't relaxing her in the least. Every tiny sound simply sent her anxiety spiraling higher. If hot water wasn't the answer, perhaps cold wine would be.

Carefully Toni levered herself out of the tub, water sluicing down her torso and legs. She grabbed a towel, quickly dried herself off and then threw on her robe, her ears perked to pick up any tiny movement from the other room. Her imagination had taken control and visions of crazed clowns hiding under the bed and wielding knives made her shudder with revulsion and fear. Most of the time her overactive imagination was a good thing. It was the reason she was so successful but tonight it was her undoing. She could clearly picture every bloody and horrible thing she'd ever read or seen.

Belting the robe, she padded into the bedroom and headed straight for the mini-fridge where she'd stashed a half empty bottle of Riesling. There was also some leftover tiramisu from dinner last night but she didn't think her stomach could handle it at the moment.

She poured a glass and walked over to the large picture window, pulling back a corner of the drapes to peer out into the darkness. She was on the second floor of the hotel but her only view was the side of the bank next door plus the empty street below. This town rolled up its streets by eight o'clock.

Settling down on the bed, propped up by several pillows, she reached for her phone and thumbed through the contacts. Someone had to still be awake at nine-thirty on a Thursday night. Talking to a friendly voice would calm her down, make her less jumpy.

Her family was off that list then. They'd only make things worse.

Tasha? No, the baby still wasn't sleeping through the night and she might be catching some much needed rest.

Lana? No, she was on a business trip to Paris and that was at least five or six hours ahead. It would be the middle of the night there.

Dan? No, no, no. Calling an ex was a stupid thing to do. They'd somehow managed to stay friends after their breakup mostly because they hadn't had many tender feelings for one another. They should have kept their relationship platonic but their friends had been rooting for them to become a couple. Toni didn't want him to think she was calling because she missed him or the sex. Neither had been all that memorable.

Her thumb hovered above another contact and she contemplated the name for a long time.

Wyatt.

Would he even be awake? They'd had a long day at the site and he'd appeared tired and hot when they'd finally called it quits around eight. But she had vague memories of Carla complaining that Wyatt was an insomniac and he slept at the strangest times.

If he did truly have trouble resting and was asleep now and she called him, waking him up…? That would be awful. But if he was also awake and not sleeping, maybe he was bored?

It wasn't a conscious decision but somehow her thumb had pressed a few buttons and she could hear the metallic ring as she waited for him to answer.

Shit, this was stupid. She should hang up right now. But the longing to not be in this hotel room all alone overrode her good sense and instead she placed the phone against her ear, holding her breath. He might be furious when he answered. If he answered.

"Hello? Toni?"

Letting out the breath she'd been holding, she attempted to sound casual. "Uh, yeah. Did I wake you?"

"Not at all. I was just reading." A pause before he continued. "Is everything okay? Is there more trouble at the site?"

She hadn't thought he would jump to that conclusion. She should have thought this through a bit better but she wasn't even sure why she'd called him in the first place. There was something solid and dependable about Wyatt that made her think of security.

She hated that. She was a grown woman who shouldn't need a man to make her feel safe.

"No," she replied quickly. "Nothing like that. I was hoping we could talk about what adjustments we might need to make to the schedule, that's all. But I guess we can talk about it tomorrow since you're busy."

"I'm not busy, Toni. I'm just reading. We can talk about that if you like but since we don't know how long the police are going to hang onto the guest house I'm not sure we can make too many plans. I was thinking we would move the crews back into the main house and the pathway until we know more."

It only made sense and if she'd been thinking at all clearly she would have known that without having to discuss it.

"Oh, good idea. That sounds like a plan."

She sounded like an idiot.

"Honey, are you okay? You don't quite sound like yourself."

That's because she wasn't her usual self. She wasn't feeling all that brave and bold, loving all things blood, gore, and horror. In fact, her chosen profession at the moment seemed like a stupid move. She was a wuss.

"I'm fine. It's just been a long day, you know? I'm a little keyed up, to be honest."

There was more silence Toni wanted to fill but she didn't have any words that wouldn't reveal how rattled she was about the turn of events today.

"You can't sleep."

It wasn't a question.

She sighed in defeat. "I can't. I keep seeing it. Him. Her. Hell, you know what I mean. I can't get that image out of my head."

"I'm not surprised. Why do you think I'm reading? So I won't think about what happened today."

She'd never thought about Wyatt being sensitive to death but it was brave – and kind of cool – of him to admit it. She felt less alone.

"I don't want to feel like this."

She heard his soft chuckle on the other end of the line. "You don't like anything you're not in charge of, in control of, and isn't written down on a project plan or to do list. Cut yourself some slack. You're not a block of ice."

"I know you're right. I just feel so incredibly stupid. Here I thought I was immune to stuff like that and just because I've seen *Texas Chainsaw Massacre* twelve times. I didn't think anything could unnerve me."

"It was you that explained it. What you create puts people in a safe place to be scared. They can experience the adrenaline rush feeling secure that they are never in any danger. Not really. This is different."

Toni fiddled with her wine glass. "Do you think he's still out there?"

"I don't think it's wise to put too much thought into this until we have some idea of what happened. We don't know who our John or Jane Doe is or what killed them. Once we do, I might have more thoughts on the matter."

Toni rubbed the back of her neck and grimaced. "At the rate I'm going, I'll make myself crazy before dawn."

"Maybe we can both howl at the moon," Wyatt responded. "I'll be there in ten minutes. Be out front in the lobby waiting."

Why would he come to her?

"What? I don't understand."

"Neither of us should be alone tonight. Pack an overnight bag and be waiting in the lobby in ten minutes. You're coming home with me."

Massive relief. Plus something else. Excitement?

Toni wouldn't deny she was curious and wanted to learn more about him. She'd heard about the small farm he lived on but she'd never been there. He and Carla had always come to her family, not the other way around.

She wouldn't be alone either. That was a huge benefit. But it was too much to expect.

"You don't have to do this."

"I know, but I probably won't sleep either. I'm a terrible insomniac and this will mess up my sleep for days. Might as well have some company. Do you really want to be by yourself?"

No, she did not.

"That's not the point."

"That's exactly the point. You don't want to be alone and neither do I. Let's not be alone together. Unless of course you hate my guts. Then I can understand you turning me down."

From the amusement in his tone, he knew quite well she didn't hate him.

"I don't hate you."

I like you too much for that, even though I shouldn't.

"There we are then. Ten minutes. Don't make me wait."

She doubted many women did.

Chapter Thirteen

TONI CLIMBED INTO Wyatt's truck with her messenger bag slung over her shoulder, a small duffel in one hand, and a pillow tucked under one arm. If she'd been in her pajamas when she called, she wasn't now. She'd pulled on a pair of sky blue shorts and a white eyelet t-shirt. She looked young, fresh-faced and innocent. All her makeup had been scrubbed off at some point and he felt like a dirty old man as his gaze raked her head to toe and then back again.

"Right on time."

She shoved her two bags in the small back seat but kept her pillow clutched to her chest.

"You said not to make you wait. So I didn't."

He smoothly pulled onto the deserted street and headed for his place. The only business establishments that would be open was the local watering hole and the pizza parlor. Everyone else was ensconced in their homes and preparing for a good night's sleep.

"I didn't think you'd actually do it. I'm used to waiting on women."

He couldn't see her expression in the dark of the truck cab

but he heard her delicate snort of derision. "What did you think I was going to do? Put on a cocktail dress and do my hair and makeup? I did change out of my pajamas though. I wasn't sure what the attire for this slumber party was."

"It's not black tie and thank you for being so efficient. It's a lovely quality."

"In a woman."

"Pardon?"

"You said half a sentence. That it's a lovely quality. I finished the sentence for you. It's a lovely quality in a woman. That's what you really meant."

Wyatt shouldn't be enjoying the verbal sparring as much as he was but he had to admit he liked it. Toni gave as good as she got and he had to be on his toes at all times. He couldn't ever remember a woman who challenged him the way she did. But he was damn tired tonight and he might not be able to keep up with her.

"Actually that's not what I meant. Which makes me wonder why you feel the need to tell me what I meant. I just think being on time and efficient is a good quality. In anyone, for the record."

"It is."

Toni didn't say anything else and he should have relished the silence but he was a glutton for punishment apparently.

"You didn't comment on why you felt the need to clarify what I meant."

She sighed heavily and he had the feeling she'd rather talk about anything – including the murder – than this topic. "It's been my experience that men don't have the highest opinion of professional women. They hold them to a different standard than males. If a woman is assertive she's a bitch but a man is forceful and in charge. If she's late then she must have been in the ladies' room touching up her lipstick but the man must have been in an important meeting or call. I've had to fight hard for my company and the attitudes some males bring to the table. You don't know how many times someone has asked to speak with the *man in charge*."

Wyatt whistled in disgust. "It's the twenty-first century and some men are still embarrassing themselves. I don't blame you for getting pissy. You shouldn't have to deal with shit like that. But just for the record, I'm not threatened by a successful and smart woman."

"You—"

Toni started to speak but then abruptly stopped, turning her head to start out the window instead. She obviously had something to say.

"Spill it, honey. I can take whatever you were about to dish out."

Her gaze swiveled back and he could see the outline of her face by the dashboard lights. He was once again struck by how different she was than Carla. They didn't have anything but an X-chromosome in common.

"It's just you're so condescending to me sometimes. You're constantly reminding me to drink my water or have a snack. You worry about my health more than I do. It's disrespectful to think that I am incapable of taking care of myself and that hurts, Wyatt. It makes me feel like you see me as less than you."

Christ, how had he created that impression? He certainly

didn't feel that way and his intentions were good but the results were bad. He needed to fix this. Now.

"I do respect you, Toni. Very much. I'm sorry, so very sorry, that I've made you feel this way and I apologize. I have great admiration for what you've accomplished and I know that you are capable of wonderful things."

"Then why do you do it? All the fussing and reminding? It doesn't make sense."

To her it didn't but to him it was perfectly logical.

"I do it because I have so much respect for you. I respect you to such a degree that I hold you in high esteem and want to make sure you're healthy and happy. You work so hard, Toni, and you're so kind to everyone but yourself. I simply want you to treat yourself in the same respectful manner that you show to others. You deserve it."

"I–I–Heck, I don't know what to say," she finally said, her words halting and unsure. He'd surprised her with his answer. "We're looking at this from completely different places aren't we?"

"As long as we're open-minded I think we'll be okay. I can see how you would think what you did. Can you see my side too?"

One of the hands that had been clutching the pillow came to rest on his arm, the skin warm on his own.

"I can see it. I never in a million years would have thought of it like that though." Her fingers slipped away and he felt their loss acutely. "But that doesn't mean you can go around telling me what to do."

He chuckled at her militant tone. "I expect nothing less,

honey. We'll find some middle ground. In the meantime, we're home."

✦   ✦   ✦

"Do you have any…fours?"

Toni eyed Wyatt over the playing cards in her hand, giving him a suspicious look. He had to be cheating. No one won game after game like this out of pure luck. He'd kicked her ass at Blackjack, Hearts, and now he was winning at Go Fish. If she wasn't so grateful to not be by herself in that lonely hotel room she might have been upset.

But between the frozen pizza he'd baked and the ice cream, she was feeling quite content. He'd almost managed to make her forget the horrors of the day. Now they were playing cards on the floor of his living room, perched on oversized cushions, with the television playing softly in the background. No one was watching it but it made her feel better to have the low hum of voices when the two of them were quiet.

The house was decidedly masculine, decorated in browns and blues except for the kitchen. Toni had a feeling that his mother had created the homey vibe with white and blue checkered curtains and a big farm sink with rooster dishtowels.

"I do not," she finally replied, keeping a close eye on him. "I told you that before."

"That's true but you've drawn from the deck since then so you could have one or two."

"I guess you need fours then?"

"That's the only reason I would ask for them."

Maybe.

"You could be trying to throw me off. Fake me out."

A devilish smile played on his lips. "I could but I'm not."

Toni tapped her cards on the coffee table. "I'm not so sure about that. You don't think it's funny how you've won every game? What are the chances of that?"

"Fairly high when I'm playing someone who is as bad at cards as you are. You don't pay attention and you don't think ahead. That's why you're getting your ass handed to you, honey. Nothing nefarious is going on here."

Slapping her cards face down on the table, she leaned forward and poked Wyatt in the chest. "I am paying attention. You're cheating."

"That's a serious allegation. Can you back it up?" He didn't look perturbed with her. "Never mind, don't bother. The fact is I could cheat but I don't have to. You're that bad. It's like this is the first time you've played cards in your life."

Toni shrugged and picked up her cards. "I don't have a lot of practice. I work all the time."

"What about when you were a kid?"

Her mouth turned down as she thought about her childhood. "Not really. I wouldn't say we were the kind of family that did all that much together. I didn't learn to play cards until I was in school."

"Sometimes I want to kick your mom and dad in the ass. They have a shitload to answer for."

Toni didn't dwell on her childhood. She wasn't a victim and wouldn't allow herself to delve into that mentality. But she appreciated his enthusiasm.

"It is what it is. Carla was their favorite and I wasn't. Whining about it isn't going to change anything. The best thing I can do is be successful in spite of them."

"You're nicer than I would be," Wyatt groused, drawing a card from the deck between them. "They should be proud as hell of you and what you've accomplished, and without any help from them, I might add."

Toni didn't normally like to bring up her sister but she couldn't resist. "Did they interfere in your marriage? It kind of looked like they might have."

His lips twisted and he laughed, although it sounded bitter. "They did but it wouldn't have mattered either way. By the time Carla and I married, she was already spoiled rotten. Sure, it made things more difficult when she ran to her parents every time I wouldn't give her what she wanted. Then I had to listen to your parents give me a lecture about all the things Carla deserved in life. But we were doomed from the beginning. Nothing was going to save us."

The question she always wanted to ask but never had the guts came tumbling out of her mouth before she could stop it. "Why in the hell did you marry Carla in the first place? Was it the sex or something? Were you thinking with your dick?"

Realizing what she'd just blurted out, she slapped a hand over her mouth as heat suffused her cheeks. She needed to learn to watch her tongue. She didn't even have the excuse of alcohol, and ice cream didn't make you stupid.

If she thought he was going to be angry, she was sorely mistaken. Instead, a grin spread across his face and he threw back his head and laughed. Not just a titter or a guffaw. A deep belly laugh that had him holding his stomach and rolling on his back onto the area rug beneath them.

"Honey, that's the most honest question I think I've ever been asked."

"I didn't mean to say it," she muttered, watching him in fascination. He wasn't mad; he was amused. "Forget I asked."

He sat back up and wiped at his eyes where tears were beginning to leak. Her mortification was hilarious, apparently. "I don't think I can. Besides, I'm going to answer your question. Anyone who has the balls to ask that deserves an answer."

He really was the most confusing, nice, wonderful, aggravating man on the planet.

"So answer it then," she snapped. She didn't want to think he was the kind of male who took divorce lightly. She'd thought he was more serious than that.

He sat crisscross and leaned his elbows on his knees, the amusement gone from his expression and in its place something far more somber. "Carla made me feel like the most important person in the world. She has a way about her. When she listens to you it's like there's no one else in the room and you're saying the smartest, most fascinating things she's ever heard. When we kissed, she told me I was the best kisser she'd ever experienced. Every idea I had was pure gold. When I cooked, it was an epicurean delight. I felt special, Toni. That's why I married her. But of course after the vows things changed. Suddenly, everything I did was wrong. For the longest time I couldn't understand it. Then I realized it was just who she was and it didn't have a damn thing to do with me."

Toni shifted uncomfortably on the rug, his words affecting her more than he knew. Toni had never understood the power her sister wielded over not only men, but people in general.

"Were you angry?"

Wyatt gave her a lopsided grin. "Sure, at first. But then I realized I was just mad at myself for being so fucking stupid to buy into all that. I was dumb and gullible and I should have known better. But when someone wants to believe, very few things can talk them out of it."

"And now you know better?"

"I'm one cynical son of a bitch so yes, I know better now. I've barely dated in the last few years and I think that's the smart way to be. Love and relationships are off my radar and I'm much happier."

His reasoning shouldn't bug her but it did. "You can't let her win like that. If you stay alone then she's won."

"It isn't a contest, honey. I've moved on and I'm in a different place in my life. Frankly, with my job there isn't much room for a woman and a relationship. It wouldn't be fair to her when I work all the time and travel."

It sounded like a huge excuse and she should know. She'd spent the last several years using her career as a shield between her and men. She honestly didn't know much about being in love.

"The right person wouldn't care."

"If I ever meet them. I don't expect to."

Wyatt should have a nice woman in his life. He was a good man and he'd treat her well. He'd worry about her water intake and whether she'd had a snack or enough rest. Toni's chest tightened at the thought of him doing those things with someone else.

Wyatt is out of bounds. Not for you. He's Carla's ex.

She picked her cards back up and composed her features as if the entire intensely personal conversation had never happened. There was nothing left to say.

"Do you have any jacks?"

At first he didn't say anything, simply regarding her with that steady gaze that saw way too much. He arranged his cards and picked through them, looking for her request. Finally, he lifted his head and shook it.

"Go fish."

He didn't have what she needed, and he never would.

She'd do well to remember that every day that they worked together from here on out.

Chapter Fourteen

OPENING HER LIDS a mere slit, Toni groaned as bright sunlight pierced her skull. She snapped her eyes shut and covered them with her hands. Ever so slowly she opened them again, filtering the light with her fingers until her ice cream fogged brain could deal with the morning sun.

They'd eaten too much pizza and mint chocolate chip gelato and she'd fallen asleep with a too full tummy and too much sugar coursing through her veins. Now she had a Ben and Jerry's hangover. At thirty-plus years old, she ought to know better.

Slightly disoriented, she looked around and found she'd never made it out of the living room. Playing cards were strewn around her along with a lovely blue and white quilt Wyatt must have thrown over her last night that she'd kicked off at some point. Yet, she was still toasty warm and comfortable.

Wyatt.

Her body stiffened and she sucked in a breath, holding it for dear life. Her mind and body were beginning to wake up and realize just where she was. Holy crap on a cracker. What had she done?

She'd fallen asleep on Wyatt, that's what she'd done.

Her head was pillowed on his bicep and his body was spooning hers protectively, keeping her warm despite the blanket around her ankles and the air conditioning blowing directly on them full blast from not three feet away.

Letting the air out of her lungs slowly, she tried to shift without waking him but his left arm was laid over her body and as heavy as an anvil. Toni wrapped her fingers around his wrist and lifted his arm to wriggle out from under it but it only served to make the situation a million times worse. She'd rubbed against…holy hell…

He might not be awake but certain parts of him were at full and impressive attention.

Stifling another groan of sheer embarrassment, she attempted once again to squirm free but to her surprise his arm tightened around her waist like an iron band before completely releasing her, the weight disappearing as he rolled to his back.

"Woman, what are you doing?"

Good question. Bad question. No, very bad question. Ignore it.

"I need coffee."

Keeping her back to him, she dared not look him in the eye. She'd been close enough to feel him in all his glory and she wasn't sure she'd ever be the same again. Funny how it changed everything. Toni wasn't sure she was capable of being casual friends with a guy after being pressed up close and personal with his equipment. Impressive equipment.

"I'll make some. You can use the bathroom first, if you want."

Way too gracefully for this early in the morning, Wyatt

hopped to his feet and padded into the kitchen without a backward glance.

Toni sat there for a long moment watching him walk away, his shoulders straining the material of his t-shirt in direct contrast to his loose sweatpants. The back of him looked just as fine as the front.

Shit, she didn't have many filters before she'd had her caffeine. With her luck, she'd blurt out how attractive she found him. How sexy and smart. Kind and protective. And she didn't even want him to fuss over her. It was simply kind of nice that he wanted to.

It wasn't her usual modus operandi but retreat was the only valid option. Straight into the bathroom and away from temptation. She'd wash her face, comb her hair, and then apologize for falling asleep on top of him. Or on the side. Whatever, she'd make sure he was aware that wasn't her plan when she'd called him last night. She was no booty call girl.

She didn't want to make things any weirder between them than they already were.

Fleeing to safety and her toothbrush, she locked the bathroom door wondering whether she was keeping him out or her in.

✦ ✦ ✦

WYATT HEARD THE click of the bathroom lock, which meant Toni was safely on the other side. Sagging with relief against the kitchen counter, he scraped a hand down his face and wondered how one man could be so incredibly stupid.

He'd had the best wakeup call this morning that he could

remember in a long time. Toni's delightfully pert and round derriere had been pressed up against him, her long silky tresses tickling his cheek, and her soft scent so like vanilla and something lightly floral wrapped around him like a comfortable blanket. It had felt so right to have her tucked into his embrace, her head resting on his arm. An arm that had gone numb in the middle of the night but he hadn't wanted to move it and wake her. After yesterday's events, she looked peaceful and almost angelic.

Of course, he knew better. She was stubborn, independent, and ornery as hell. But when she let down that brick wall and showed her softer side, she damn near took his breath away.

If he had a lick of sense – which he clearly didn't – he'd make up some excuse and run away. Far and fast. With every passing day, he was feeling more and more territorial, like she was his to worry about and protect. His to hold and care for.

His to…?

Fuck no. No.

She was not his and he was not hers. He didn't even want to be in a relationship, least of all with the sister of his ex-wife. Dear God, what if they got serious and ended up getting married? Those crazy people would be his in-laws. Again. He wasn't a glutton for punishment and he wasn't a masochist.

And why in the hell am I thinking about marriage?

He needed a woman like he needed a hole in the head.

Wyatt wiped the cold sweat on his brow with a dishtowel and then began making the coffee. Toni was simply a woman and he'd known plenty of women over the years. She wasn't any different, or special. He'd just been too long between bed partners and it was skewing his perception of attractiveness. In any other circumstances, he wouldn't give her a second look.

Everything was going to be fine. He could handle this, and her.

He was completely in control.

✦　✦　✦

WYATT HAD MADE eggs – scrambled with cheddar cheese – and bacon and toast to go with the coffee. Sitting across the table from one another, they hadn't said much during breakfast and that was fine with him. He didn't want a discussion about how they'd fallen asleep on the floor, tangled together.

He had vague memories of it being about four in the morning and they were both exhausted, half-delirious with fatigue. Whether it was her idea or his didn't matter. It wasn't something he was going to repeat.

"Did you want to go to the estate today?" he asked, face buried in the newspaper. In a tiny town like this the body found was front page news. "Maybe you should take a day. I can keep the crews busy in the main house and the pathway."

He waited for her to chew him out for even suggesting that she stay away, but instead she stared off into space as if he hadn't spoken a word.

"Toni?" he pressed, his hands reaching for hers that lay on the table. "Are you with me or off somewhere else?"

Head swiveling forward, her normally light brown eyes were almost black with emotion. She must be thinking about the body again. He wished he could help her through this but there wasn't much he could do or say other than be there for her when she needed it.

"I'm here." She sounded tired and a little sad. "I was just thinking."

"About what, honey? You shouldn't dwell on yesterday if you can help it."

Her lips turned up at the corners and she propped her chin in the palm of her hand. "Good advice and I'll try to follow it. Actually, I was thinking that maybe this project has been ruined. Maybe I should cancel all this and cut my losses. The universe might be trying to send me a message."

Things were much worse than he'd thought. Toni's usual swagger and confidence had disintegrated, leaving one unsure businesswoman who wanted to be anywhere but here. Funny how a few weeks ago he would have wholeheartedly agreed with her and encouraged her to walk away. Now? Absolutely not. Her plans and designs were amazing and he had no doubt that she'd make this endeavor a total success. First, she needed a little tough love. Last night had been all about comfort but today she needed a dose of something far different.

"That's the dumbest thing I've heard in a long time."

Her head jerked up and she gasped in shock, her mouth hanging out at the audacity of his statement. Good, he now had her attention.

"Fuck you, Wyatt Stone."

Even better. She was feeling feisty and less defeated. He just needed to stoke that fire into a blaze.

"If you expected me to feel sorry for you, you are quite mistaken."

Her eyes narrowed and her lips pressed together. Anger. That was progress.

"I don't expect anything of the sort. I was contemplating a complex business decision out loud. I won't do that again."

Wyatt snorted out a mouthful of coffee. "Honey, you were not contemplating a business decision, for crying out loud. You were feeling sorry for yourself and thought I might join in. Admit it."

A fork slammed down on the table. "I will do nothing of the sort."

Shrugging, Wyatt stood to refill his coffee, acting intentionally nonchalant. "Fine. But I find it hard to believe that this woman sitting at my breakfast table this morning is the same one who has been running this project on budget and on time for the last few weeks. The same woman whose designs are cutting edge in the industry. That same woman who has a vision of a place where scare enthusiasts can come–"

Toni groaned and tossed her crumpled up napkin away. "Stop. I get it. I'm a big wuss now that something bad has happened. There, I admitted it. You win."

He refilled her coffee cup and placed the carafe back on the warmer. "No. I get that yesterday was traumatic and it would be enough to shake the strongest human being, but you can't let this deter you from your dreams. This is your dream, isn't it?"

"Yes," she sighed, giving Wyatt a dirty look. "It is. It has been for years. Did anyone ever tell you how annoying you are?"

"On occasion."

"You're a real pain in the ass."

He leaned down, bracing one hand on the table and the other on the back of her chair.

"Likewise, I'm sure."

"So we better get to the site then, hadn't we?"

Toni stood, carrying her coffee with her. She loved her caffeine and he wouldn't dream of separating her from it, especially not today.

First, he was sweet and supporting, then tough and mean. Once they returned to the estate, it was back to supportive and caring.

It was no hardship at all.

Chapter Fifteen

THE ESTATE WAS eerily quiet when Toni and Wyatt arrived. She'd become used to the constant sounds of hammers, saws, and drills, along with the workers yelling to one another over the din. The absence of it was jarring to say the least.

Too quiet.

"This is spooky," she heard herself whispering. "Where is everyone?"

As if hearing her, Bill stepped out of the front door and loped down the front steps, a roll of blueprints in his hand and a guarded expression on his face. Something was very wrong.

"Bill, why is it so quiet? Did the cops run everyone off?"

If they did, she'd call everyone up to the governor. She didn't mind handing over the guest house and surrounding grounds but the entire estate was asking too much.

The foreman's gazed was riveted to the ground. "Not exactly. The cops were in the guest house early this morning. They left about fifteen minutes ago, but they didn't release the crime scene."

She hasn't expected them to. Wyatt had warned her it would be a few days minimum.

"That's fine. But where are the crews? I wanted to work on the pathway today."

With every passing moment, her heart sunk lower into her belly. She had a bad feeling.

Bill lifted his gaze, conflict in his eyes. "They're not here."

"All of them?" Toni raced up the steps and stuck her head in the front door expecting to see a few people drinking coffee and eating donuts. No one. Empty. "How can that be? Where is everyone? Did you give them the day off? We didn't talk about that, Bill."

The men had followed her and they were now all standing in the foyer. She was about to head deeper into the house when Wyatt placed her arm over her shoulders, his fingers squeezing in a silent gesture of support.

"They didn't come today, did they, Bill?" Wyatt asked, his voice soft, yet it still echoed in the large empty space.

"They're afraid," Bill admitted, studying his shoes again. "They think this place is haunted, Toni, and it was tough enough to get them to work, but now? There's a dead body and they're freaked out. No one wants to work on a cursed construction site."

Anger and frustration sizzled through her veins. "It's not cursed. Dammit, the weird stuff that happened before was all a coincidence. There are perfectly logical explanations for everything. There are no such things as ghosts."

Bill shook his head, his neck red with embarrassment. "Some of the men don't think that way. The men that don't believe this place is haunted still don't want to work on a site where there might be dead bodies buried. They're all a little spooked after yesterday and rightfully so."

Tugging away from Wyatt, Toni paced the area, emotions simmering on a low boil.

"I was freaked out and I'm here." She poked a finger to the middle of her chest. "This is crazy. The chances of finding one body are astronomically low. Do they honestly think there are more?"

Wyatt stepped between her and Bill, shaking his head before turning back to the foreman.

"Thank you for sticking around to talk to us, Bill. I appreciate it and I know Toni does too. We'll be fine here on our own. You can go."

Bill couldn't get out of the house fast enough, practically tripping over his own feet. Toni sunk down to sit on the stairs while the foreman gunned his engine and sped down the driveway.

"Thanks a lot," Toni groaned, rubbing her aching temples. Tiny hammers were pounding against her skull and she didn't even have a hangover. "Now we have no crew and no foreman. Why did you send him off like that? You were the one giving me a pep talk this morning about how I needed to continue this project."

Sitting down next to her on the step, resting his elbows on his knees. "I still believe that you should. The reason I let him was that there was no point in keeping him here. He clearly wanted to leave so torturing him with more questions he'd answer exactly the same didn't seem like a productive thing to do."

Tears of frustration squeezed through her lashes and she

leaned over and rested her head on his shoulder. She needed some outside strength at the moment and he was the perfect candidate.

"I don't suppose you had a plan when you told him to go?"

His arm came around her and he ran his fingers through her hair soothingly. If he massaged her scalp she might marry him. It wasn't easy but she had to admit having him to lean on and talk to was helpful, comforting. Like a giant, good-looking teddy bear.

Never tell him that comparison.

"Yes and no. I think we should look out of town for a crew but I have a feeling once the news gets out that we're continuing and plan to hire from outside the area, the men will come back. They might be afraid of ghosts but they're more afraid of not paying their bills."

"How can they honestly believe that there are more bodies?" she marveled. "They're imaginations are more macabre than mine is, and that's saying something."

He was rubbing his chin in that way she was coming to know. Damn.

"Say it," she sighed. "Tell me why I'm wrong. I'm getting used to it."

"There are such things as serial killers, Toni. I'm not saying that's what we have here but it's not out of the realm of possibilities."

She called herself a scare expert. Clearly, she hadn't thought this one through.

"Ugh. I didn't even think of that. Ewww, I might own some kind of body dumping ground. Like for real and not pretend.

Jesus, what is wrong with the world?"

"There's no reason to believe that's what happened here," he reminded her. "Just that they had a reason to think what they did. I'm going on the assumption that the body found yesterday is an isolated case. I think you should too."

Toni stood and descended the stairs to stand in the middle of the foyer, looking right and left. "Now what? I'm open to ideas."

Wyatt smiled and rubbed his hands together in excitement. "You and me. We work on the pathway. There's lots we can get done with just the two of us. What do you say?"

What could she say? She only had one employee left and he liked to boss her around.

"I say yes. But let's make another pot of coffee."

She was going to need it.

✦   ✦   ✦

WYATT WIPED THE sweat from his brow and then reached down to adjust the motion sensor for what felt to be the hundredth time. Logically he knew it hadn't been that many but in the unforgiving heat it felt that way. All they needed to do was get this motion detector working and he and Toni could knock off for the day. He could already taste the cold beer waiting in his refrigerator.

"Okay, try it one more time," he called to Toni who was waiting down the pathway. She'd walked by the sensor several times and hadn't tripped it once. Hopefully this adjustment would do the trick.

"I'm walking." From where he was standing, he couldn't see Toni but he heard her voice and the crunch of her footsteps on the gravel path. "I'm almost there."

His fingers curled into a tense but hopeful fist and he held his breath in anticipation. If it worked…

Fuck, yes. The witch figure that had been hidden in the foliage swooped out and flew right in front of Toni, causing her to laugh in delight and even jump for joy with an added fist pump. It worked, and with the spooky lighting at night, it was going to be awesome.

"We did it." Toni ran to him, their bodies colliding in an excited hug as she danced around, singing at the top of her lungs. "We did it. We did it. That was great and scary. We did it."

Somehow his arms closed around her, every curve of her figure pressed close. He could feel the heat of her skin penetrate the thin cotton of his shirt and it sent a jolt of arousal straight to parts in a southerly direction. He'd been aware of her all day long and it was beginning to make him crazy. Her sweet smile. Her stubborn nature. Her innate honesty. Her flair for the creative and dramatic. Her warm and sultry scent that seemed to emanate from her every time she was within a few feet.

This wasn't fucking fair.

Toni must have felt that same shot of awareness because she was staring up at him, her eyes wide with surprise and more than a hint of desire. Her tongue snaked out to wet her lips and that was pretty much all she wrote for him. He couldn't take the tension that had been building between them the last few days. He'd hate himself later, but right now he was going to stake a claim to those full, pink lips.

Nothing could have prepared him for the rush of pleasure

that ran through his veins when their mouths finally touched. The kiss started soft and gentle, his tongue sweeping her lower lip until she opened for a more thorough exploration, but became more passionate as the rest of their bodies joined in the action.

One of his hands cupped the back of her head, his fingers tangled in her long ponytail while the other sat at the base of her spine stroking the strip of silky skin above the waistband of her shorts. Her hands clutched at his back, her torso smashed up against his so he could feel the pointed tips of her breasts.

He didn't know how long the kiss went on but when it was over they were both breathless, stunned, and even more sweaty than they were previously. Antonia Ross was dynamite in a tiny package and he'd just been blown to smithereens, never to be the same again. The teenage geek Goth had turned into a sexy siren in pink Chuck Taylor tennis shoes.

"That was..." Toni's voice trailed off, her gaze still soft and unfocused. They were both reeling from their mutual attraction.

"Yeah, it was..." The words came out hoarse and gravelly but she nodded as if he'd actually said something that made sense.

Taking a step back, she took a deep breath before speaking. "That was a surprise."

"It was," he agreed, the blood still rushing in his ears. "I suppose I should apologize for taking advantage of you."

"You didn't. I mean, I may have taken advantage of you. I was the one who hugged you but I was just so excited."

She was looking everywhere but at him, hands stiffly at her sides. He didn't want her to think this was her fault. It was all him.

"No, it was me. I was excited too and I took it too far. I'm sorry. I've complicated everything."

Her shoulder lifted and her gaze came back to rest on him. "It doesn't have to be that way. We're both adults and obviously there's some attraction here…"

Toni seemed to run out of steam when he didn't respond. He didn't know what to say without sounding like a total asshole but he had to try. None of this was her doing. He'd created this mess and it was his to clean up.

"There is but I think we both know this can't go anywhere. I don't expect anything, Toni, so you can rest easy. I won't be one of those jerks who can't take no for an answer."

"Good. I can't stand when that happens."

He couldn't seem to stop the verbal diarrhea that spouted from his lips. Here he was aroused and wanting and she was standing there like she didn't have a care in the world. It hurt and it shouldn't. It wasn't right to put her in this position when he wasn't going to do anything about it anyway.

"It's just that since the divorce I've been laying low when it comes to relationships. I've barely dated and the few times that I did, the women knew what they were getting into. They knew I wasn't looking for a commitment."

"A commitment," she murmured, crossing her arms over her chest. "Never fear, Wyatt, I'm not looking for that."

He gave a nervous laugh that sounded like a choked coyote. "I'm sure you're not and even if you were I would be the last guy you'd go for. I have a history, after all."

"I guess you do."

"I mean, look at the fiasco of my marriage." He was still talking, for fuck's sake. "Obviously I have lousy judgment when it comes to women. It's really for the best that I avoid dating and relationships. I don't want a repeat of the past. I'd rather be alone than have that again."

Lips flattened into a line, Toni's eyes narrowed. "Excuse me? What did you say?"

"I don't want a repeat of the past. I don't have good judgment when it comes to women."

He heard her suck in a quick breath as she stepped forward and poked her finger in his chest, her expression fierce. "Are you trying to say that you think I'm like my sister? You think that a relationship with me would be like your marriage to her? What the fuck?"

Had he said that? He hadn't meant to. Panicked, he immediately began to backpedal.

"No. No, I don't think you're like Carla. I'm just saying that I don't trust myself. This is about me."

Whirling around, she walked a couple of steps away, her back firmly turned to him so he couldn't see her face. "About you? You can't trust that you think I'm not like Carla? So you think that maybe I might be like her but you're not sure? You can't believe that I might be different?"

When you find yourself in a hole, stop digging.

"That may be what I inadvertently said, but that is not what I meant. I know you're not like Carla."

Toni turned to him, tears glistening in her eyes. Shit, he'd really hurt her feelings. This was the reason he avoided relationships. He didn't know the right things to do or say.

"But you can't trust yourself to be sure?"

He stepped closer and reached out to take her hand, but she jerked it away and tucked it behind her back. "I know you're not anything like her, Toni."

Ignoring his outstretched hand, she bent to pick up the toolbox sitting on the pathway.

"You know, we're not so different after all. It turns out I can't trust my judgment about men either. I thought you were a good and decent guy but it turns out you're an asshole, just like all the rest. Thanks for your help today."

With that parting shot, she strode back down the pathway toward the main house leaving Wyatt standing there like the idiot that he was. He wasn't sure how he'd managed to get himself into this predicament but he knew he needed to find a way out. He needed to make this up to her; he just didn't know how to fix it.

Chapter Sixteen

THE SOUND OF Wyatt's footsteps pounded on the dry earth behind her but Toni didn't bother to turn around, instead hurrying up the path and bounding up the back patio steps, her anger and pain driving her as far away from him as she could get.

He'd hurt her and she hated that he could. His opinion had become that important to her in such a short time and it made her weak. If it had been anyone else, she would have laughed off the words but with him she found she simply couldn't do it.

He'd hurt her heart.

That surprised her most of all because she hadn't realized how close they'd grown in the last week. He was her friend and when he'd kissed her she'd seen the opportunity for them to be more. She'd seen the possibility but she'd been alone.

She was almost in the house when his hand stayed her progress and stopped her in her tracks.

"Toni, I'm sorry."

Rounding on him, she looked up into his eyes, wanting to see if he was truly sorry or just sorry she hadn't taken the brush off well. He appeared contrite and remorseful but it didn't assuage the very real damage he'd done to their burgeoning relationship, even if it was simply friendship.

"What exactly are you sorry for?"

Frustration passed over his features then resignation, an acceptance that he'd started this painful conversation all over again. She would have been happy to drop it and never speak of it but he'd chased her down and now here they were. Pissed off, hurt, and ready to kick the other person in the shins.

"I'm sorry for hurting your feelings. I do not in any way, shape, or form think you are like your sister. God, are you not like your sister. In fact, I think one of you might have been switched at birth. You cannot be blood relatives."

She tugged her arm away, wrapping them both around her torso as a shield between him and her already battered heart. Letting him hurt her again was something she couldn't allow.

"Okay."

He blinked in confusion. "Okay? What does that mean?"

Toni sighed, fatigue beginning to set in. She just wanted to get some rest.

"It means okay. It means fine."

"Fine, you're an asshole or fine, I forgive you?"

Swallowing the lump in her throat, she shook her head sadly. "I forgive you, Wyatt, but I haven't forgotten. What you said was really mean." She held up her hand when he opened his mouth to defend himself. He didn't need to; she wasn't attacking. "I know you didn't intend for it to come out that way but it did and it hurt. So I can forgive but it's going to take some time to forget."

His shoulders slumped and his gaze dropped to the concrete patio. "How can I make this better? I need to fix this."

If she only knew. "I don't know. I do see that you're sorry and remorseful and that means the world to me but I don't take being compared to Carla very well as you can tell. I'm not even sure why you were comparing us."

Red stained his cheeks and he shifted on his feet. "Because of the kiss."

Men were funny sometimes. They seem to be under the impression that women were prowling the streets looking for a man to tie down and marry. Nothing less would do. Commitment or bust.

"I didn't expect you to ask for my hand in marriage. The only thing I was thinking was that the kiss was great and I wouldn't mind doing it again. I wasn't thinking about us settling down in a three-bedroom ranch with a two-car garage, three kids, and a dog named Fluffy. I'm not even sure I want to get married, to be truthful. It sounds like a hell of a lot of work and I'd have to share the bathroom."

"I'm kind of fucked up, if you hadn't noticed. Because you're Carla's sister, well, my mind made some jumps in logic that it wouldn't have otherwise."

Fantastic, although she ought to be used to it. She'd had plenty of high school teachers that compared the sisters and Toni had often come out the loser.

"So we put the kiss in the past and I try to pretend you didn't mix up Carla and I. Is that what I'm getting from you?"

He exhaled noisily; she was clearly trying his patience. "I know the difference."

"When your eyes are open," she shot back, hands on hips. "But when they're closed, not so much."

He acted like the kiss was a huge mistake. True, it had been a surprise but she couldn't have been the only one to feel the heat between them.

"Can we go back to when we were celebrating getting the witch up and running?"

She didn't have a time machine so the answer was no.

"I doubt it, unless we both get hit on the head and lose our memories."

Wyatt rubbed the back of his neck, his jaw tight. "Let me say I'm sorry again. My intention was never to hurt you. You're a wonderful woman and I have a great deal of respect for you. I was trying to express my own doubts about my ability to be in a relationship but I think doing that seconds after we kissed maybe wasn't the best idea."

She had to give it to him…he knew how to apologize.

"On second thought, you probably shouldn't be in a relationship. If you doubt yourself that much you wouldn't be doing the female any favors. Stay single, Wyatt. We'll all benefit."

She sounded like a royal bitch but was far past caring.

"I am sorry, really sorry."

They were going in circles and it only made her dizzy.

"Let me give you a hint. Once you have been forgiven for something you don't have to keep apologizing. You have said you are sorry and I've accepted that apology."

She could see that he felt badly and she did want to let him off the hook for what he had said but dammit, it hurt that he felt that way. She thought they had moved beyond the past. Clearly she'd been mistaken.

"Our friendship means a lot to me and I don't want to lose

it. I have screwed up but I hope that we can salvage something here. Getting to know you again this week turned out to be the best thing about this vacation."

"I appreciate that but please see this from where I'm standing. We run into each other, we spend time together, we have some fun, and we kiss. Then I get the speech about how it's not me it's you. Except that it is me because you were married to my sister. A woman I haven't seen in almost two years, by the way. I don't like her any more than you do."

She didn't know why she was bothering to explain. It was one kiss and it wasn't her first, but she'd thought… Heck, it didn't matter what she'd thought or hoped.

"I think we're done here for the day," she finally said. "I'm tired and I'm going back to the hotel."

"Will I see you tomorrow?"

His expression was so earnest and regretful she found it difficult to keep being snarky. She wanted to say no and ask if he would care but she wasn't sure she was ready for his answer.

"Yes, I'll be here."

Because ultimately, men and relationships and even Wyatt didn't matter. It was the work that was important. It was what she knew and where she felt the most confident. She'd gotten kicked in the ass today and all because she'd stepped out of the box and tried for something she'd known would never work.

Tomorrow it would be all business, all the time.

Chapter Seventeen

DESPITE BEING FORGIVEN by Toni, Wyatt didn't feel much better. The fact was he felt like a big old shit-head and he deserved to have her pissed off at him. He should have known better but his brain had been scrambled by the kiss.

The kiss...

That shouldn't have happened either but he simply couldn't help himself. Toni's irresistible charm was far too potent and he'd been defenseless against it. Then afterward, all his doubts and fears had crowded in, confusing him and making him blather like an idiot. He'd said hurtful things that he didn't mean but he was sure he couldn't convince Toni of that. He didn't think she was anything like Carla but somehow he'd managed to make her think he did, and of course she'd been wounded.

A dozen times tonight he'd picked up his phone to call her and apologize again but what else would he say? He wasn't dealing with the attraction between them well, and he didn't want to screw up even more than he already had.

He grabbed a beer from the refrigerator as his phone dinged with a text. Pressing a few buttons, he had Jason on the line within seconds. Talking directly to him was easier than texting back and forth, plus Wyatt could use a friendly voice and maybe even some advice. Jason sure as hell hadn't been looking for a relationship when he'd found Brinley.

"I hope you have some good news because I could use some."

Jason laughed on the other end of the line. "It depends on how you define good news. I have the information on the estate that you asked for."

Just to be on the safe side, Wyatt had requested that Jason pull the history of the house and grounds to look for anything that might give a clue about the crime.

"Thanks, man. I do appreciate it. Anything of interest?"

"First, I want to ask you something. Are you investigating this dead body? Should I send Logan down to help?"

"That's a damn good question," Wyatt sighed, lowering himself into the leather recliner. "I'm not planning on inserting myself into this investigation unless the police can't come up with anything. They haven't had a murder in this county in over twenty years so the sheriff isn't experienced in running a case of this type."

"That was an interesting answer."

"I wasn't trying to be evasive. Toni is upset, and rightly so about this and wants to know who the victim is and to see justice done. I don't want to start sticking my nose into things unless they really need me. So, the answer is not yet. I'm just…interested in the details of the case."

"Do you know the sheriff personally? Is he the kind of guy that would be okay if we looked over things?"

Harvey Sullivan was a new, young sheriff and a good man. He'd asked Wyatt a myriad of questions about his job with Jason and had never seemed anything but open-minded.

"I do, although he's a little younger than I am. He's a decent cop and I think he'd be okay with it. He doesn't have the kind of ego that would get in the way of things."

"That's good. I asked because I wanted to let you know that I'm fine with you offering our consulting services if they get bogged down. Logan has a little time in his schedule and you're technically on vacation. It sounds like this is pretty important to your girlfriend."

Holy fuck. Girlfriend? I'm too old for that.

"Thanks but she's not my girlfriend. She's a girl that's a friend." Jesus, he sounded lame. "Hell, after the argument we had today I'm not sure we're even friends anymore but I still want to help her if I can."

"What did you do?" Jason chuckled.

Wyatt took a fortifying drink of his beer before he answered. "I hurt her feelings. I kind of compared her to my ex-wife. I didn't mean it to come out that way but I wasn't thinking all that clearly and I said some stupid things. Anyway, she's upset and hates my guts."

"Why would you compare her to your ex-wife? Does she look like her or something?"

He realized he hadn't told Jason all the details. This was going to be fun.

"Not in the least. They're like night and day. But she is Carla's little sister."

"You have got to be shitting me." Raucous laughter from his

supposed friend and boss. Nice. "All the women in the world and you fall for your ex's sister? She must be one hell of a woman."

She was. Too good for him.

"First off, I did not fall for her. Second, she is not my girl-friend. Third…shit, I don't remember what my point was, except that I hurt her feelings and I'm an asshole."

"Just who are you trying to convince? Me or yourself? You keep telling me that she's not important in your life and that you don't have feelings for her but your actions say something far different. You've been helping her out on your vacation. You're worried about how much you've hurt her. And you said yourself you're not thinking clearly. That sounds like love to me, you poor bastard. Another one bites the dust."

"Love isn't the reason I wasn't thinking clearly. It was–"

Wyatt stopped talking before he revealed too much but Jason smelled blood in the water. "It was what? What happened? Heat stroke?"

Wyatt wished Jason was right in front of him, if only to punch him right in the gut.

"We kissed, okay? I knew I shouldn't have done it but I did and then I regretted it."

"Because it was bad?"

"No," Wyatt explained patiently, "because it was good. Very, very good. But Toni is Carla's sister and that's eight kinds of fucked up. I don't need that kind of complication in my life and neither does she. I'm not looking for a relationship."

"Because?"

Now he was wondering why he thought Jason would have

anything helpful to say in this situation.

"For the same reason you weren't looking for a relationship not that long ago. I'm not in the right place in my life."

"Hold on, I'm going into another room." There was some banging and then the sound of a door closing. "Listen to me closely, my friend. Few people are in the right place when the love of their life decides to show up. I know I wasn't but Brinley didn't let me give in to my petty fears. She was there and made it clear she wasn't going to be scared away. She knew what she wanted and could see that I wanted the same thing but was too afraid to do it. I see the same thing in you. You're scared, just like I was, but for a different reason. I was certain I had nothing to give a woman and you're scared you'll give too much. Ironic, isn't it?"

This was why Wyatt had called Jason. The man had a blunt but effective way of summing up a situation. After being held prisoner by a drug cartel, he felt that life was simply too damn short to beat around the bush. Jason was a firm believer in the old adage, *Speak the truth, but speak it with love.*

"I hate it when you're right."

Jason would remind him of this for the rest of his life.

"Is she the type to take and then ask for more?" Jason queried. "Is she like her sister? Only out for herself and what she can get?"

Not in the least.

"No. She's one of the good ones. Toni is generous and caring and quirky. She'd never take advantage of someone the way Carla would."

"But you don't trust her? No, you don't trust you," Jason

guessed. "You think there's this sliver of a chance you might be wrong and you'll end up hurt again. There's always a chance but is that the plan? Stay alone for the rest of your life so you never have to deal with people. It might work if you were anyone but who you are."

"Who I am? I don't understand."

Jason chuckled and Wyatt could practically see the other man leaning back in his office chair, cowboy boots propped up on the desk. Brinley hated when he did that, muttering something about mahogany under her breath.

"I've only known you for a little while but from what West said you like taking care of a woman, spoiling her a little. You want her to feel special and cosseted. That's not the type of man who is going to do well spending his life alone."

"I think I'd be just fine on my own."

Wyatt might miss having company every now and then but that didn't mean he couldn't be alone. Sometimes it was good to have peace and quiet after a long day.

"There's nothing wrong with wanting to take care of a woman. I wasn't criticizing. I like to spoil Brinley every now and then too. I'm just saying that it seems like you're the kind of man who needs someone to nurture. The right woman, of course. A female who would appreciate it and want to return the favor. Is that Toni? Because if it is, do yourself a favor and smooth over whatever it is you've done and make it work. You owe it to yourself not to die a lonely, crotchety old man. Soon you'll be yelling at kids to get off your lawn."

He didn't want to be that guy either but that meant taking another chance, and he'd been safely tucked away from that side of life for five years now. The first step toward Toni was a doozy.

They had a ton of baggage to deal with. Was it worth it? Better question, was he worth it? Toni didn't even like it when he tried to take care of her.

"I will not yell at kids to get off my lawn. Hell, they'd have to drive a mile down a dirt road to get to my lawn."

"That's what you got out of my little speech? I was laying down some serious wisdom there."

Jason had the nerve to laugh. Wyatt couldn't let that pass.

"Wisdom? I could have got the same thing from a Hallmark card." They were men and this entire conversation was getting way too touchy-feely for his comfort. "In fact, now I feel like watching a romantic comedy and eating chocolate. Thanks a lot, asshole."

"From your reaction I can see my work here is done. If I'm making you that uncomfortable then this girl might mean more to you than you're admitting. Now do you want to hear about the history of the house?"

Anything as long as they left his personal life behind.

"That's why I called you back. What did you find out?"

Work was what Wyatt needed to concentrate on. All that personal bullshit simply made everything more difficult. Work was simple, straightforward, and there was always plenty of it.

"The estate has a fascinating history but that's not what you want to know. You want to know if anyone has ever died there."

"And?" Wyatt prompted, pulling a pen and notebook from a side drawer so he could take notes. "Has there?"

"There has. More than once, actually. I'll start from the beginning."

Chapter Eighteen

LISTLESSLY, TONI PUSHED her scrambled eggs around her plate, her usually healthy appetite missing in action this morning. Even the cafe waitress was giving her concerned looks but Toni instead concentrated on her laptop, sightlessly staring at her email. She'd barely slept last night and exhaustion didn't mix well with bacon and eggs. Instead she sipped at the strong coffee, almost burning her tongue in her haste to imbibe the caffeine.

An email from an old college friend. She'd answer that tonight when she could take her time and write a good long update.

One that promised a larger penis. Again. They were persistent. Delete.

A long diatribe from her mother as to all the reasons she was such a disappointment to her parents. Typical. She skimmed through the same old whiny and emotionally manipulative drivel until she was at the last paragraph, hoping her mother would sum up what this was about. Barbara Ross had instigated more contact than usual lately and Toni wasn't naive enough to think it was because they yearned to be closer to their younger daughter.

There it was.

Smacking her forehead, Toni let out a choked sound of shock. She shouldn't be surprised but she was, which said more about her than her parents. It meant that she was still too stupid to live and that optimism was overrated.

Maybe Wyatt had a point. She'd spent last night cursing his name but he was cautious and aware, not letting himself fall back into a position of vulnerability. She, on the other hand, walked through life with rose-colored glasses – okay, not really, she was too cynical for that – inviting anyone to take a swing at her. Perhaps she owed him an apology. She'd been pretty hard on him last night.

That was one of the reasons she hadn't slept well. She'd ripped him a new asshole when clearly he was simply bad at expressing himself. He'd apologized about a million times and had been completely sincere. She needed to cut him some slack. If she'd been married to her sister, she'd be wary of getting involved again too.

Rereading the last lines over and over until she could have recited them from memory, Toni chugged down the last of her coffee and signaled the waitress for more. It was too early to start drinking alcohol so coffee was going to have to do the job. She needed to wake up but stay calm, all at the same time.

Her mother wanted Toni to give Carla money.

Technically, Barb had used the word "loan" but Toni wasn't dumb enough to think she'd ever see a dime from her sister after writing the check. If she gave Carla any money, and she hadn't decided to, she had to be willing to write it off completely.

According to the email, Carla's husband Trevor – who owned a construction company – was having a hard time. Between the economy and the state of commerce in general his income was down significantly. So instead of tightening their belts, the answer apparently was to get Carla's mother to ask Toni to start financing their out of control lifestyle.

Since they couldn't squeeze the cash out of Wyatt.

"You're scowling at your laptop." A deep voice jolted her from her reverie. "Are you okay?"

Sighing, Toni didn't know whether to laugh or cry. Somehow Wyatt managed to be there when she was feeling low or lost. It was becoming a habit and she didn't want to get too used to it.

"Not really," she admitted, thanking the waitress as her cup was refilled. "I think today is going to be a lousy day."

Wyatt slid into the booth opposite her and quickly ordered his usual breakfast. Unlike her, he didn't appear to have missed any sleep last night. She wanted to kick him under the table.

"Want to talk about it?"

Toni shrugged and shook her head. Carla was the last topic she wanted to discuss with him. "Not particularly. I'd rather just concentrate on the estate if you don't mind."

"Fine with me. In fact, I had a friend do some research into the history of the house. I thought it might give us a clue as to who our victim might be or why they were dumped there."

"I know the history of the estate. It's been empty since 1981 and before that the McMahon family owned it. They were in the mining business. The mine closed and they moved but were never able to sell the house because of the haunting rumors.

People say that a McMahon daughter died there by falling down the stairs and now walks around scaring the shit out of everyone."

Wyatt fiddled with his coffee cup, a smile playing on his lips. "There's much more to the house than that, although none of it helps with our current mystery. Do you still want to hear about it?"

She did but she needed to say something first or she wouldn't sleep again tonight.

"I do but first there's something I need to say." She took a deep breath and looked him right in the eye. "I'd like to apologize for last night. I was out of line. I took something you said out of context and overreacted. You wouldn't have agreed to help me with my project if you thought I was anything like Carla. Heck, I doubt you'd even be sitting across from me now. So, that's what I needed to say. I'm really sorry for how I acted and I hope we can put this behind us."

She didn't mention the kiss, not wanting to open that can of worms. If they were going to move forward, she needed to put that in the past. It wasn't going to happen again.

Just watching her and stroking his chin, Wyatt appeared to be ruminating on her words. When she couldn't take the silence much longer, she opened her mouth to speak only to be beaten to the punch.

"Apology accepted but you didn't need to do it. I understand where you were coming from and I don't blame you."

"And I don't blame *you*," she replied swiftly, wanting him to know that she was willing to put this entire episode in the rearview mirror. "Being married to my sister must have been hell. I would imagine it's hard to trust your instincts about anyone."

"But I know better—"

She waved away his explanation. "It's okay. Let's just get back to where we were. Friends."

He looked like he might argue but then his expression relaxed and he smiled. Or maybe it was the steaming hot plate of food the waitress placed in front of him that made him so happy. Wyatt was a man with a large appetite.

Did he have other appetites that were unsatisfied?

Toni inwardly slapped herself across the face. She'd sworn this morning that she wasn't going to dwell on the kiss and by God she was already doing just that.

Cleansing breaths. Think of innocent puppies and kittens. Fluffy bunnies.

"Friends," he agreed, digging into his hash browns. "Now let me tell you about the history of the house. It's fascinating."

✦ ✦ ✦

"So the daughter did die but not from a fall down the stairs?"

Wyatt patted his full stomach and pushed his now empty plate away. "Amelia McMahon died of the flu. She'd never had a strong constitution in the first place so when she got sick, she had no energy to fight it. Not that unusual at the turn of the century."

"I wonder how the other story started."

"Twisted and embellished over the years." Wyatt shrugged. "Also not that unusual. People like to make things more exciting than they are, add drama. Once the house began to fall in disrepair I'm sure lots of stories sprung up to give the local kids a scare and keep them away from the estate where they might get hurt from the crumbling building."

"And the other death?"

Wyatt signaled for the check. "Amelia's mother died in childbirth while birthing Amelia's brother. I don't want to repeat myself too often but once again, not unusual for the nineteenth century."

"Nothing violent. Nothing creepy. I hope this doesn't get out to the general population. I need the house to keep its air of mystery."

"My lips are sealed although I'm sure someone else is going to dig up the dirt so to speak on the estate once you open. Maybe you can spin a tale about the lonesome souls of the McMahon women or something like that."

Toni gave him a smile that had his stomach flipping in his abdomen. "You're getting good at this. Next thing you know you'll be drawing zombies and hellhounds for my company."

"No one wants me to draw. I can barely manage a stick figure. I'll leave the hard stuff to you."

The bell over the door rang and Sheriff Sullivan strode into the café. The young man looked around the room and his gaze landed on Wyatt.

The sheriff quickly came over to the table and rested a hand on Wyatt's shoulder.

"I'm glad I caught you here this morning. I was hoping we could talk about this case. I'd sure appreciate any help you could give me."

Wyatt had been planning to stop by and talk to the sheriff as well. "Of course I'll give you any help that I can. I'd like to take a look at any evidence you may have collected from the scene. Would that be possible?"

The sooner the better.

"Come on by the station and I'll give you access to anything you need. I really appreciate this. You don't know how much. I want to make sure that we give ourselves the best chance to find whoever did this."

"It's not a problem. I've got plenty of time on my hands these days. My boss is supportive of me working on this too."

Wyatt made a mental note to text Jason that he would be spending some time on the murder case.

"Well, I am grateful. I know you came home to take some vacation time, and I normally wouldn't ask you to give that up, but something like this is out of my element. I could ask the state police for help but honestly I'd rather it be you."

It was then that the sheriff seemed to notice Toni sitting across from Wyatt. His cheeks went a ruddy shade and he tipped his hat nervously.

"I'm sorry, Sheriff. I didn't introduce you to my friend Antonia Ross. She's the new owner of the estate, and as you'd expect she's very interested in seeing whoever did this brought to justice."

Toni nodded and extended her hand, which the sheriff accepted.

"It's my pleasure, ma'am. I heard that someone had purchased the house and grounds but I haven't had a chance to come by and introduce myself. I'm sorry that it had to be under these circumstances."

"Me too. But I'm glad to hear that you'll be investigating this case vigorously. Since the victim was found on my property, I'm curious as to what happened."

The sheriff shook his head sadly. "I think we all want to get to the bottom of this." He turned back to Wyatt. "Before I forget, there's going to be a gathering at the Roberts place at five o'clock tonight. Just a way for the town to say goodbye and pay their respects. It's potluck if you and Miss Ross would like to be there."

The Roberts farm was right next to Wyatt's and he knew them well. Good people. Honest and hard working.

But did that mean...? Damn.

"It was one of Helen's girls?"

Ken and Helen Roberts had three daughters who had all moved away after college. Wyatt had been older but he'd known all of them before they left.

The sheriff's brows shot up in surprise. "You hadn't heard yet? It was Mandy, the oldest. She'd disappeared about five years ago without a trace but everyone thought she'd left on purpose due to some issues she was having."

Mandy had always been level-headed and down to earth in addition to being a nice girl. It was a damn shame that her life had been cut short so tragically. It made him twice as determined to help solve the case.

"I'll definitely be there this evening. This has to be a nightmare for Ken and Helen."

"They might have expected something like this to happen to Arlene but Mandy? They're in shock."

"Have you talked to them yet?"

There was never a good time to question a grieving family but it had to be done. At least he actually cared about them as friends while some anonymous cop might not be as sensitive.

"Briefly when I informed them of the identification. I didn't ask too many questions and they were in no shape to answer them. Mandy's been gone a long time so I figured another day or two wouldn't make much difference."

Yes and no.

"I'll come by the station in a few minutes to look at your report and evidence. That will be a good place to start."

"Sounds good. I'll let my deputy know to expect you. Thanks again."

The sheriff nodded to Toni and exited the cafe, leaving Wyatt to contemplate what he'd learned. The Roberts family would be devastated by this turn of events and he'd do well to be careful while working this investigation. They deserved all the respect he could give them.

"You knew her?"

Toni's question pulled his attention back to her. There was curiosity in her eyes but she didn't ask anything else, letting him decide what he wanted to tell.

"I did. The Roberts family lives on the farm next to mine. They have three daughters—Jenilynn, Arlene, and Mandy, who are all younger than myself but I did know them as they were growing up."

Her hands wrapped around her coffee cup. "So she wasn't an old flame?"

Toni had a vivid imagination, which made her successful in her chosen profession but it also sent her on flights of fancy.

"Not in the least. Mandy was several years younger than me. I don't rob the cradle. But she was a nice person and something of a friend. The whole family, really. This has to have hit Ken and Helen hard."

"Can I go with you tonight? I'd like to pay my respects too."

He'd had a feeling she would. "Of course. That means you have to help me make the potluck dish though. Can you cook?"

Her lips twisted into a crooked smile. "I can microwave like nobody's business."

Wyatt didn't really need her to help. He enjoyed cooking and found it relaxing but he also liked to tease her a little bit. "You can chop the garlic and onions. Or maybe not. That would require the use of a knife. How about you stir the sauce? That should keep you out of trouble."

But for how long? Toni was going to want to know what he was doing regarding this investigation. He needed to make sure she stayed close so he could keep her out of trouble but also hold her at arm's length so she didn't get in the way.

Because now the case had become personal and failure was not an option. The Roberts family were friends and neighbors, and the Mandy he'd known would never do anything to deserve the end she'd been given. Nobody should be entombed in a wall and forgotten for years.

His first call would be to Jason. They needed to dig up every detail about Mandy Roberts.

Chapter Nineteen

THE NEXT STOP after the cafe was the sheriff's station and Wyatt had made Toni sit in the waiting room while he disappeared in the back, supposedly reviewing the case file and evidence. She would have been more annoyed with him but she was well aware that she wasn't a cop, a consultant, or even an amateur sleuth. She didn't even read mysteries, enjoying horror stories instead.

She'd kept busy reading her emails and playing games on her phone until he finally reemerged, his lips a grim line and his expression shuttered. It must have been quite ugly in there. He'd probably looked at graphic crime scene photos. Suddenly she was glad he'd made her sit out here.

She opened her mouth to question him about what he saw but he shook his head, and pointed outside to where his truck was parked. "We'll talk out there."

He helped her into the passenger seat and then slid behind the wheel, firing up the engine.

"Do you want to go back to the cafe and pick up your car?"

"I want to hear what you learned," she replied, impatiently tapping her fingers on the leather seat. "I don't care about my vehicle."

It was safely locked and there was nothing of value in it.

"You will later," he countered. "I'll drop you at your car and we'll head to my place. We can talk there."

From the set of his jaw, Toni knew not to argue. She'd seen that expression before but of course, Carla had never heeded the warning, which always led to a huge, loud argument.

Stop thinking about her. You're not like her, and he's not thinking of her. Probably.

Did he think about Carla from time to time? Remember the good times in the beginning when he'd fallen in love? Did he wish they hadn't ended?

Way to torture yourself. Why don't you just picture them having sex?

Except that she couldn't picture them doing that. Carla always seemed too fussy to get naked and sweaty and Wyatt would definitely get down and dirty. For all his quiet restraint, Toni just knew there was the heart of a wild man underneath the veneer of civilization.

Don't even think about it. He doesn't want that. You. Forget it.

When they reached his farm, he insisted they start the ziti and get it in the oven first thing. She'd sighed long and loud to let him know she wasn't amused but it was clear he wouldn't be rushed. Perhaps he needed the time to organize his own thoughts. She'd give it to him – grudgingly.

"This kitchen smells amazing," she sighed as she gave the bubbling tomato sauce another stir. Wyatt was draining the al dente pasta and the steam billowed upwards, hot enough to open her pores. "I love Italian food."

He dumped the pasta into a huge glass bowl along with a generous amount of ricotta cheese mixed with egg and parmesan. "This is one of my favorite recipes. It tastes good reheated as well."

She sniffed at the pan, the aroma of garlic and tomatoes making her stomach growl. "This may not even make it into the oven."

Laughing, Wyatt turned off the burner and picked up the pan, stirring the sauce into the pasta and cheese mixture. "I promise it tastes much better when it's baked. Besides, I thought you wanted to hear all about the case. We can do that while it's cooking."

"As long as I get to eat it at some point, I'll be happy."

"You should eat a bigger breakfast."

She'd been too nauseous this morning to eat much of anything.

"I can't eat until my digestive tract wakes up."

"From the gurgling of your tummy I think it's alive and kicking. Let's get this in the oven."

He divided the mixture into the two pans, sprinkled generous amounts of mozzarella and basil on top, covered them in foil, and slid them into the hot oven. He set the digital timer next to the stove and then reached into the refrigerator, pulling out two sodas.

"How about we relax in the living room and I'll tell you everything I know?"

About damn time. She'd been extraordinarily patient which wasn't her usual style at all, but she'd come to the end. He needed to start talking.

He popped open the can of root beer and handed it to her. "I'm not sure where to start."

"At the beginning is usually the best place. Pretend I don't know anything."

She didn't know anything, not really, so it wasn't a stretch.

Wyatt settled himself on the couch while she curled up in the chair to his left, tucking her sock-covered feet underneath her.

"Mandy was killed by blunt force trauma to the head. Her skull was cracked in two places. From the shape of the wound, the medical examiner thinks it might have been a pipe or a bat."

A shudder ran through Toni's body as an image of that poor girl being beaten and then lying in a pool of blood appeared before her eyes. "Or maybe a piece of wood? There's a lot of that around the house. Or was she killed someplace else and brought there?"

"Could be," Wyatt grunted. "They combed the scene for the murder weapon but didn't find anything. It does appear that she was killed elsewhere and brought there. There was no blood pool or sign of a struggle."

"And no one noticed she was gone?"

That was the strangest thing about this case. Even with all the angst with Toni's parents, they'd be haunting the police station if she suddenly disappeared.

Wyatt leaned forward, resting his elbows on his knees. "They noticed but they thought they knew the reason why. They thought she disappeared on purpose."

"Why would anyone do that?"

"That's what I want to find out tonight. According to the

few questions the sheriff was able to ask, Ken and Helen weren't worried when Mandy vanished. They never reported her missing because they didn't think she was."

"I know these are friends of yours but I have to say that their explanation doesn't make much sense. How could she be missing but not missing? Even if they thought she was going off for awhile on her own, wouldn't they start to worry after a year or so? I'm not sure I'm buying this. Are you?"

"That's why I'm going to talk to them tonight. I've known them all my life so I think they trust me."

"What if you don't get the answers you want?"

A corner of his lips turned up. "I'm prepared for that too. Just so we're clear I don't think Ken and Helen had anything to do with this. They were good people who loved their kids."

She couldn't help what came out of her mouth next. "For someone who doesn't trust his judgment regarding people, you're depending on yours pretty heavily here."

From the shocked look on his face, it was clear he hadn't even thought of it that way. He was sure his neighbors were completely innocent but he wasn't sure that Toni wouldn't break his heart.

And that hurt.

Chapter Twenty

S TANDING OUTSIDE OF the Roberts' home it reminded Wyatt why he hated funerals in any shape or form. Technically, this wasn't one, Mandy's service had been scheduled for next week, but it felt the same. People dressed in dark clothes, bringing covered dishes, and the family sitting grim-faced as they received their visitors. The front door was wide open and guests milled back and forth, coming out for a smoke and then going in for a drink.

For once, Toni had toned down her outfit and instead of the usual bright colors, she was wearing a short-sleeved navy blue shift dress that skimmed her curves and showed off her lovely tanned legs, and a pair of high heels that gave her a slight lift in height. She'd left her hair down this evening and the chocolate tresses reached all the way to the middle of her back. When he'd picked her up at the hotel, he'd struggled not to tell her how gorgeous she looked and how good she smelled. How much he wanted to kiss her again.

Focus, man.

"Are you ready?" he asked her in a low voice. Once they crossed the threshold, she'd be committed for however long he would be there. She didn't even know these people but it was clear she felt empathy for what they were going through. Toni might act like a hard-headed businesswoman but she had a soft side as well.

"I was born ready," Toni whispered with a smile, taking his hand in hers. It didn't feel strange or pushy, just warm. It felt just the way she probably meant it. Supportive and caring. What any good friend would do for another when faced with the death of someone they'd known since childhood.

"Then let's do this."

He led the way inside the house, the smell of food the first thing he noticed. The dining table to his right was groaning under the weight of dish after dish, although there seemed to be several trays of pigs in a blanket along with two giant bowls of potato salad. He added his baked ziti to the collection before moving deeper into the home, looking for Ken and Helen.

"Should I get us a couple of drinks while you look for her parents?"

Wyatt made a mental note to smack himself across the face when he returned home. He deserved it. Toni wasn't anything like her sister and tonight only underlined that fact. She'd made this all about him but Carla would have somehow made it all about her.

I need to stop feeling sorry for myself. It's getting fucking old.

"That would be great. A beer. Or water. Hell, I'm not fussy."

She gave his hand a squeeze. "I'll come find you."

Or he would find her. He was finally waking up out of a five year long stupor that had kept him frozen in place. He'd been so busy looking over his shoulder at the past he hadn't seen all the possibilities up ahead.

Drifting from his side, Toni vanished in the crowd of bodies leaving him to find Mandy's parents. With height and luck on his side, he tracked them down in the family room at the back of the house, both of them perched on a loveseat, holding hands. Her eyes red and swollen, Helen looked much older than the last time he'd seen her which had only been about six months ago. Ken's lined face was as stoic as ever although his hand trembled slightly when he reached for his iced tea.

Helen looked up and her eyes widened. "Wyatt, how kind of you to come. We'd heard you were back in town for awhile. Come sit down and tell us what you've been doing."

"Thank you," he replied as he settled himself into a chair. From this angle, he could see family portraits lined up on the mantle. One of those smiling and happy photos was of Mandy graduating high school. Ken and Helen had thrown a big cookout in the backyard to celebrate but they'd been rained out and everyone had ended up soaked to the skin. "I'm so sorry about Mandy."

Clasping her hands together, Helen nodded, her eyes watery. "She was a good girl but in a way it's a relief to know she'll be at rest soon. She'll have peace now."

"She didn't have peace before?"

Wyatt hated probing but Toni had a point. How could Mandy be missing but not missing? Why didn't they report her disappearance to the police?

Helen looked like she was going to burst into tears again and Ken reached over, placing his hand over hers in comfort. "Our little girl had a lot of trouble in her life. Trouble she didn't deserve."

Leaning forward, Wyatt's gaze darted around the room making sure that no one was listening in. They all seemed to be absorbed in their own conversations.

"I'm trying to help the sheriff," Wyatt revealed. "Anything you could tell me would be of help. I want to do right by Mandy."

The couple hesitated but some unspoken understanding must have passed between them because Ken cleared his throat. "Someone was stalking Mandy. He sent her threatening letters and gifts. She was terrified and the local authorities couldn't really do anything when the guy hadn't actually hurt her. Cole, her husband, even hired a private investigator to track down this lunatic."

A few tears had slipped down Helens' face. "Mandy used to say that if they couldn't find this man she was going to just vanish. You know, fake her own death and assume a new identity. She'd often talk about how she'd go about it. I never thought she was serious but when she disappeared we just thought..." Helen swiped at her damp cheeks. "And we were happy for her. We thought she'd finally done it and outsmarted that maniac. Until now."

The older woman's voice broke and her shoulders shook with sobs. Wyatt's own throat tightened with emotion as he watched a mother mourn the loss of a child. No one should ever have to bury their progeny but Ken and Helen would be doing that now. It brought up too many memories of fallen comrades in the service, not to mention the passing of his own mother and father.

Ken wrapped his arm around his wife, his own expression tortured. "It's okay, bluebird. She's with the angels. No one can hurt our girl now."

"I'm so sorry. I'm going to do everything I can to get whom-ever did this."

His own words came out choked and he pushed to his feet, knowing the couple wasn't in any shape to answer more ques-tions. Wherever Mandy was living at the time would have a police file. Wyatt also wanted to have a conversation with that private investigator.

"Mom? Dad? Are you okay?"

A man stepped forward and put his hand on Helen's shoul-der before leaning down to whisper something in her ear. She nodded and sniffed, dabbing at her eyes. "We're fine. Cole, this is Wyatt Stone, our friend and neighbor. Our families go way back. Wyatt, this is Cole Hoskins, Mandy's husband."

Cole was probably a few years younger than Wyatt with shaggy, dark blond hair and a medium build. He vaguely resembled Mandy's high school sweetheart Vance Armell, who was now married to the woman who owned the local cafe. Mandy must have had a type that she liked.

"I'm sorry to be meeting you under such sad circumstances. I'm so sorry for your loss."

"Thank you. Mandy will be missed more than you can imag-ine. She was a wonderful wife."

Cole already looked like he'd been crying and his eyes were tearing up again as he grabbed a handkerchief from his pocket.

"Damn, I'm sorry. I can't seem to stop myself. I just can't believe I'll never see her smiling face ever again."

"She had a beautiful smile," Wyatt replied, taking in the husband's disheveled appearance. His skin was pale and his clothes were wrinkled as if perhaps he had curled up in a corner to sob in private. The man was almost shaking in his shoes, clearly distraught. Without a thought, Wyatt clapped a hand on Cole's back. "How about we get some air? Let's just step outside for a minute. Will you excuse us, Helen and Ken?"

The poor bastard needed space and a place to fall apart that didn't have witnesses. He was probably trying to be strong for his family and friends.

Guiding Cole out onto the back porch, he let the younger man pull himself together. Several deep breaths and some muttering under his breath, Cole leaned against the railing looking over the quiet backyard, the sun fading in the sky.

"Thanks, man. I didn't want to lose it in front of Ken and Helen. I'm trying to comfort them, you know. They shouldn't have to worry about me."

"No problem. Are you going to be all right? Is there anyone I can get for you?"

Cole shook his head, his eyes sad and his lips turned down at the corners. "Thanks, but there really isn't anyone. Just give me a minute and I'll be okay."

So many questions were on the tip of Wyatt's tongue but he wasn't a complete heartless asshole. Asking a grieving spouse probing questions about his wife's disappearance and subsequent murder seemed the height of insensitivity.

"This must have come as a shock to you," Wyatt said instead. "Helen told me that you all thought Mandy had vanished due to her stalker."

Cole blew his nose and then shoved the handkerchief in his pants pocket. "We did, although I always wished that she had taken me with her but I know she did it to keep me safe. That's the way she was, always thinking about others. There hasn't been a day that's gone by that I haven't thought about her. She was one of a kind."

"I'm really sorry. I hope I can help bring whomever did this to justice. Mandy deserves that."

Brow knitted, Cole shook his head in confusion. "Are you a cop or something? I don't live in this town so I don't know too many people here."

"I'm a law enforcement consultant and I work for a firm that specializes in helping small towns with limited resources solve cases just like this. The sheriff has asked me to help out and I want you to know I'm committed to do whatever I can to assist."

Cole smiled slightly. "That's the first good news I've got all day. I feel better knowing there is someone on the case that really knows what they're doing,—plus you care. You did care for Mandy, right? You were childhood friends?"

"I was a few years older but yes, we were friends." Wyatt pulled a card from his pocket and handed it to Cole. "I know today isn't the day but when you think you can, I'd like to talk to you about Mandy. You never know what might help. You could know some small detail that could make all the difference."

Cole nodded and slipped the card into his shirt pocket. "I'll call you. I want to help all I can too."

"Thanks." Where was Toni? She could have fetched a dozen drinks by now. "I lost my companion somewhere in there. Are you sure I can't get you anything?"

"I'm good. I'll just take a few more minutes. No one knows me here anyway. I came for Ken and Helen."

Letting the grieving husband have some privacy, Wyatt entered and scanned the crowd for Toni. He'd driven and the keys were in his pocket so she hadn't left. She wasn't in the kitchen or around the bar.

Had she wandered off to the barn? He wouldn't put it past her to want to see if the darn thing was haunted. Or to check on the cows.

He needed to put a tracker on that woman, the way he spent his time trailing after her.

But she was worth it. And he intended to tell her later tonight.

He'd apologize one more time and then kiss her. With any luck, she'd kiss him back.

Chapter Twenty-One

"**W**HAT ARE YOU doing here?"

Toni stopped dead in her tracks, just a few steps from the bar and her ultimate goal. But that voice. She'd heard it before and she'd honestly hoped not to hear it again for a very long time. No such luck. She whirled around and found her older sister standing there with a very unbecoming scowl on her face.

"Careful there, Sis, you're going to get wrinkles if you keep making that face."

Carla's eyes widened and she leaned in closer, her perfectly painted red lips in a tight line.

"I do not have wrinkles," she hissed. "Take that back."

If Toni was going to have to see and speak to her sister, she was at least going to have some fun.

"I didn't say you had wrinkles. I said that if you kept scowling you would get them. Didn't Mom always tell you to smile?"

That had been the mantra in the Ross household. Be happy, perky. A veritable ray of freakin' sunshine.

Carla took a deep breath and forced a smile to her carefully made up face. "Now, I'll repeat the question. What are you doing here?"

It was really none of her sister's business, although Carla thought she needed to know everything about everybody. She didn't need to know her ex-husband was in the same house. Toni wouldn't put it past her sister to corner Wyatt about the inheritance money. At a wake, no less.

Toni tapped her chin, pretending to think it through. "On second thought, you shouldn't smile. It shows off those lines around your eyes. Resting bitch face is the way to go."

All she received for her trouble was a finger wagged in front of her face as if Toni was a naughty child. "You think you're funny but you're not."

"I think I *am* funny, Sis. Did I ever tell you the one about the horse that walked into the bar?"

Purple. Carla's face was turning purple. They hadn't seen each other for a few years and clearly she'd lost her ability to take a joke.

"At least I know how to dress. My God, what are you wearing? I wouldn't dress my dog in that."

Toni glanced down at the simple, straight dark navy dress. She'd paired it with a pair of pewter high-heels sandals and a slim jade bracelet around her left wrist that she'd purchased in a funky shop in Chinatown a few years ago.

"I would hope so. He'd never be able to walk in these heels," Toni giggled, giving her sister the same once over she'd received. Per usual, Carla was in some floaty creation with pink flowers that was designed to make her look vulnerable and waif-like, although Toni thought her sister at thirty-six was pushing the boundaries. It might have worked at twenty…

"What are you doing here?" Carla asked between gritted teeth. "I thought you were in Denver."

Toni turned toward the bar and ordered a beer for Wyatt and a screwdriver for herself. She wasn't going to talk to her sister without pulling out the hard liquor.

For her part, Carla was waiting almost patiently although her toe tapped on the carpet as she stood there and fumed silently. She could wait. Toni wanted her vodka. The orange juice was merely a decoration.

A drink in each hand, Toni stepped away from the bar for the next guest and took a sip of the cool drink, a happy sigh escaping her lips at the pleasant but subtle burn. "I was in Denver and now I'm here. I'm working on a scare attraction and the unfortunate woman was found in the wall of my property so I came to pay my respects. What's your story?"

She made no mention of Wyatt's presence. No way would she out him.

"I knew Mandy several years ago. She lived in our town for a short while."

Toni took another needed sip of her drink. She needed to be nicer to her sister or she was going straight to hell. One hand basket required.

"It was nice of you to come then. Had you seen her recently?"

Carla looked away and then back, shaking her head. "No, she left town suddenly and we lost touch."

This was interesting. Did Toni's sister know anything about this disappearing stuff? Perhaps running into Carla wasn't the tragedy she thought.

"Did you know much about her life?"

"Not really," Carla replied before her eyes narrowed suspiciously. "Why do you ask?"

It wasn't an out of line query. Toni and Carla hadn't spent any time voluntarily chatting since they were in school and even then they hadn't done it often.

Toni rolled her eyes. "I was making conversation. Did you want to talk about something else? We could talk about how Mom is bugging me to lend you money because you're broke."

Carla's mouth fell open and she grabbed Toni's arm so hard a small amount of liquid splashed over the side of the glass in her hand. "Keep your voice down."

Staring down her sister, Toni then moved her gaze to where Carla's fingers were still wrapped around her upper arm. "You might want to let go of me. I can be mighty clumsy with these drinks if I'm not careful."

Stepping back, Carla freed Toni's arm but her expression was still stormy. "I am not broke."

Shrugging, Toni gave her sister a sunny smile. "That's good news. You should tell Mom. Now, if you will excuse me I haven't spoken to Mandy's parents yet. It was lovely to see you. Let's do this again soon."

Turning to go, Toni was home free. Wyatt had to be wondering if she'd wandered into another state by now.

"Why do you have two drinks?"

Well, crap. So close.

Toni held up the bottle of beer and the cocktail glass. "A screwdriver with a beer chaser. Haven't you ever heard of it? It's the hot thing in Manhattan nightclubs these days."

Making a face, Carla shook her head. "It sounds disgusting."

"It's fantastic. You should try it. Bye, now. Give Katie a kiss from her aunt."

She hightailed it out of the dining room like she had a knife-wielding clown on her heels. There wasn't much time. If Wyatt didn't leave now he was going to run into Carla. Toni wouldn't let that happen if she could help it.

Going around the corner to the family room, she almost smacked right into him, another slosh of her drink landing on her shoe. She was going to be sticky before this was all over.

"We have to leave. Now."

His brows pulled together, Wyatt plucked the ice cold beer from Toni's now numb fingers.

"Relax for a minute. I learned a few things–"

Christ on a cracker. He didn't get it.

"Hush." Grabbing at his sleeve, she tugged him back into the hallway where she knew Carla wasn't. Yet. "Listen to me careful-ly. Your ex-wife is here. Probably Trevor as well. In this house. We need to leave. Unless of course you want to talk to her about her share of your inheritance and how you ruined her life. I wouldn't stand in your way if that's what you want."

Wyatt's jaw had gone slack and his skin had taken on a green hue. Not good.

"Fuck. Let's get out of here."

Casting a glance over her shoulder, Toni nodded in agree-ment. "She was near the bar a few minutes ago. I don't suppose you know another way out of here?"

"We can sneak out through the backyard. I saw a gate when I was outside." Wyatt turned to lead the way but paused, leaning down so his lips were close to her ear and his warm breath tickling her cheek. "And Toni? Thank you."

You are very welcome, Wyatt. Stick with me. I'll protect you.

Who was going to protect her from him?

✦   ✦   ✦

WYATT HAD NEVER left a building so quickly in his life. He didn't want to see or speak to Carla. He didn't even want to share the same space if he could help it. Their breakup had been nasty, bitter, and filled with vitriol. It was all best left in the past.

Then there was Toni.

Carla's sister but nothing in the world like her. The little miss had even taken his side and helped him sneak out of the wake, ducking down below the window line as they walked through the side yard to his truck parked outside. He'd said thank you but it wasn't enough. His apology hadn't been enough either.

He was crazy and the whole situation was insane but the rush of emotion he'd felt as they'd bolted out of that house hadn't anything to do with Carla. It had everything to do with Toni.

They were both giggling as they stumbled into his house, tears leaking from Toni's eyes. She was recounting her conversation with Carla and the part about "resting bitch face" had made him laugh. He was certain, however, that his ex hadn't appreciated it in the least.

"I don't remember you two sniping at each other like this. Did I repress the memory?"

He headed straight to the kitchen to pop the second ziti pan into the oven. Stealth mode always made him hungry. Toni trailed behind him, dropping her shoes onto the floor with a relieved sigh. How did women walk in those things?

"She always behaved in front of you and the parents but when we were alone she'd unload pretty viciously. I learned to give as good as I got. You know, the whole a good offense is the best defense."

He pulled two beers from the refrigerator and twisted the tops off before handing one to her.

"I know I thanked you in the truck a few times but let me do it one more time. Thank you. I did not want to get into an argument about the past with Carla. Even after all this time, I still don't think she and I remember our marriage the same way."

A smile played around Toni's lips. "They say there are three truths. His truth, her truth, and the real truth."

"I can't argue that," he conceded. "I'm sure I've blown some things out of proportion and I don't have the greatest memory. But she did get pregnant by another man while I was in the Middle East so I know I didn't conjure that out of thin air."

"That was real," Toni sighed, her smile wiped away. "I'm so sorry she did that to you, Wyatt. You sure didn't deserve to be treated that way."

His put the bottle down on the kitchen counter. "Hey, don't get all sad. I think I'm over all that crap, to be honest. I'm past it. Walked through hell and come out the other side."

Toni gazed up at him, her whiskey-colored eyes bright with unshed tears. Things had turned on a dime. Moments ago they'd been giggling like kids and now she was looking at him so intensely as if he held a deep, dark secret.

"Have you? Are you past it? Because it wasn't so long ago

you said you couldn't trust your own judgement." Her voice choked and he reached out to pull her into his arms, not wanting her to feel a moment of sadness. Toni was too alive and happy for that. "You said you couldn't trust me."

Pressing her cheek to his chest, he ran his fingers through her long tresses, the silky strands slipping through his fingers. She had the most beautiful hair and it felt as good as it looked.

"It wasn't you I didn't trust. Sometimes I have doubts, Toni. Carla knocked me sideways and then kicked me when I was down. I'm not in a big hurry to do anything like that again so I'm cautious. I'm so sorry that I hurt you before with my big mouth running off like that. I trust you more than you can imagine."

He must have said something right because her arms slid around his waist and she burrowed deeper against his body. "With your life?"

Now she was pushing him but it was cute. "Now, honey, a little bit like you shouldn't ever be in the position of saving my life. But if it did happen, I know that you would do everything you could. Just like I would."

"You'd save my life?"

With two fingers, he tilted up her chin so she had to look into his eyes. "Absolutely. Never doubt it."

Their gazes caught and held, Toni's eyes turning a darker shade of brown, the pupils blown. His own breath caught in his throat and his chest tightened painfully. He hadn't felt this much emotion and longing for a woman in…years? Decades? It didn't matter how long because doing math was an impossibility when all the blood in his brain was rushing to locations south.

The voice in his head that reminded Wyatt to keep his distance was nowhere to be found, probably tied up and gagged in some dark closet by his baser instincts. They were currently running the show and had one goal in mind.

Make love to Antonia Ross.

More than once if given the opportunity.

The kiss before simply hadn't been enough and she'd intimated that she was willing to try for more between them until he'd talked too much. Sex was more, right?

The problem with Wyatt was that he was too analytical. He worked over a problem or issue to death until he'd looked at every angle and thoroughly confused himself as to what he should do. He wouldn't make that mistake today.

With one hand cupping her jaw and the other still tangled in her hair Wyatt lowered his mouth to hers, letting his tongue glide over her lips until she allowed him entrance. She tasted of beer and mint toothpaste and everything he'd ever wanted but didn't think he'd have.

Sweet and wild.

Chapter Twenty-Two

ALL THE PENT-UP longing and denial inside of Toni could no longer be contained. Like the rushing water over Niagara, her arousal and desire overtook all rational thought. There were so many reasons to stay away from Wyatt but they all disintegrated into powder, blowing away on the wind, when he kissed her. She might regret it tomorrow but she would live today.

Splaying her hands on his back, she could feel the bunching of muscles under her palms as he lifted her off the ground, their lips still fused like molten metal. She wrapped her legs around his lean middle as he carried her back to the bedroom, kicking the door open so that it rattled on its hinges. He was as anxious as she was.

He never let her feet touch the floor. Instead, he laid her gently on the bed, finally tearing his mouth from hers with a groan. His fingers flexed on her hips but he didn't make another move toward her.

It was her decision.

Sliding her fingers up his neck and into his short, silky hair, Toni smiled at his somber expression. He was worried. For real. She'd practically thrown herself at him after the last kiss and he still had concerns that maybe she didn't want him.

Her finger traced his jaw, rough with stubble, and a shudder ran down her spine. Everything looked good on this man, even when he needed a shave. It felt even better.

"Yes."

She didn't elaborate, letting that one word speak volumes. She didn't want a verbal cascade ruining this moment and her mouth was always getting her into trouble. Better to err on the side of caution and simply say what she meant.

"Yes," she repeated when he didn't move. Then a slow, sexy smile mirrored her own and those rough hands that had been resting on her hips were now gliding up her bare thighs, creating a delicious friction that had her writhing on the mattress.

Oh hell yes.

Her fingers went to work on the buttons of his shirt, but she was clumsy in her haste, cursing when she fumbled and pulled off a button. She stared at the offending item sitting in the palm of her hand wondering if he might be pissed that she was tearing apart his garment one piece at a time, but he simply laughed and plucked it from her hand, tossing it on the nightstand. Before she could react, he'd stood and stripped off the shirt, throwing it to the floor before popping open the button at his waistband and lowering his zipper. Too damn slow.

Let's get this show on the road.

Levering up, she reached for his pants but he was already pushing them down his powerful thighs. He kicked them away before wrapping his hands around her wrists and pressing her palms to his warm, bare flesh. Taking the hint, she ran her fingers up his ridged abdomen far enough to glance over his flat, male nipples, drawing a tortured moan from his lips. Eager to feel him inside of her, her hands slid down his ribcage to the elastic of his boxers, struggling to tug them over what appeared to be an enormous erection until he came to her aid, tossing them aside and revealing his perfectly proportioned body.

Gifted. Beautiful.

Not an inch of spare flesh on his bones, he was all muscle covered in golden tan skin. Like a statue made of marble, he stood there for her inspection, a smile playing on his lips.

More like a smirk. He was well aware she was enjoying the view. Their gazes locked as her hands explored everywhere she could reach until they came to settle on the hardest part of him, velvet over steel. He'd tried to remain still but not quiet during her sensual foray, but now as her fingernails traced the red and blue veins that pulsed under her touch, his large hand cupped the back of her head, a thumb brushing tenderly at her cheek.

She'd never been one to resist a taste of sin and temptation.

Toni leaned forward and ran her tongue around the head of his manhood, chuckling inwardly when Wyatt let loose a torrent of curse words and his fingers tightened almost painfully in her hair. Running her tongue up and down his length, she paused every now and then to swirl at the sensitive underside.

Every moment she gave him pleasure ramped up her own and soon she was squirming restlessly, the mattress too soft to give her the friction she needed to send herself over. The desire built between them, his flesh hot to the touch, and the air steamy, raising a fine sheen of sweat on her skin. From the sound of his breathing, he was close.

So lost in the sensation, she was shocked when he pulled her off with a loud *pop*, stepping back so she couldn't reach him with her mouth. She felt oddly bereft but it didn't last long. Those big hands were already burrowing under her dress and tugging it over her head, a cool breeze caressing her newly bared skin. She knew a moment of panic as her brain scrambled to remember what lingerie she'd put on earlier, but then she relaxed when she realized it was one of her better sets – a baby blue satin and lace shelf bra with matching boy shorts.

From the glint in his eyes, he liked what he saw.

She'd always been a little self-conscious about her body, like most women she supposed. Unlike Carla who was tall and willowy, Toni was on the petite side but with generous curves that if she wasn't careful when she dressed could make her look dowdy and on the heavy side.

With Wyatt everything seemed different...safer. She'd known he hadn't wanted them to get involved so he must really be attracted if he was making love with her. He also wasn't a casual kind of guy. Women threw themselves at him all the time and he barely showed them a flicker of interest.

If they were in bed together that meant he wanted her.

It was that knowledge in her heart and head that allowed her to relax, lying back onto the sheets and luxuriating in his admiring regard. His gaze first swept her head to toe before he knelt on the floor next to the bed, lifting her right foot and pressing a kiss to her instep.

Holy hell, that felt good. Who knew the sole of the foot was an erogenous zone? Why, Wyatt Stone, of course.

What else did he know?

He took his time, not hurried along by her moans and murmurs of pleasure or entreaty, running his tongue along her arch and then tickling the tips of her toes. He blazed a trail of kisses up her calf and along the sensitive skin of her inner thigh, his teeth nipping at the flesh before his tongue soothed the small hurt. Pleasure and pain collided in a maelstrom of arousal and she couldn't have articulated her own name if her life depended on it.

A white hot heat swept through her veins as he continued his pathway but skipping over the part where she needed him the most. His lips nibbled at her rib cage before capturing an already rock hard nipple in his mouth, scraping it lightly with his teeth until she was writhing underneath his big, heavy body, half begging him to stop and half urging him to keep doing it forever and ever.

Thank goodness neither one happened. Wyatt turned his attentions to the other rosy tip, worrying it between his lips, sending arrows of pleasure straight to her center. His mouth then found that special spot at the place where neck met shoulder, his tongue painting circles on the skin. Her nails dug into his muscled shoulders and she lifted her hips off the bed, grinding urgently against him.

Wyatt chuckled against her skin, the vibrations setting off a cavalcade of sensation all the way to her toes. "Impatient, honey? I just got started."

"You're a bad man, Wyatt Stone."

Unfortunately, the words didn't come out all that indignant. They came out breathy and soft, slightly hoarse and no deterrent to the alpha male currently hovering above her, wearing a playful smile.

"The worst. I think you like it."

No, she loved it, reveled in it. At some point during the haze of pleasure, he'd crawled down her body and pushed her thighs farther apart with his wide shoulders, exposing every intimate inch to his heated gaze. She felt the warmth of her blush travel from her chest to the roots of her hair but he didn't give her opportunity to close her legs or twist away in shyness. His hands held her hips in place as his head bent closer...and closer. His warm breath caressing the wet flesh and making her quiver with anticipation.

She wanted it, needed it, but had never been able to express her desire for this one act. Sure, there were men who had performed it either just because she wanted them to or because they thought they had to, but she'd never seen the look of pure carnal desire on any male's face that she saw on Wyatt's at this moment. It was out there and he didn't try and hide what he wanted.

To devour her.

Her legs shook as his tongue lapped at the swollen button, and she mewled in frustration when he teased her, never quite giving her the pressure she needed to climax. He held her there on the edge until she thought she might be consumed by the fire he'd fueled.

"Now."

She almost thought she'd imagined his voice, rough and raw, but then he was right...there. His skillful mouth and tongue exactly where she needed him to be and that was all it took. Her legs shaking violently, she cried out his name as she tumbled over the edge, wave after wave sending her into a star-spangled pleasure spiral. When she could breathe normally, he was hovering above her, a sinful smile on his too gorgeous face.

"Are you ready for me?"

Still too overcome to string actual words together, she instead answered him by wrapping her legs around his waist and her arms around his neck, pulling him closer. She must have been lost in her orgasm because she could feel that he'd rolled on a condom at some point but she'd completely missed it. It had been that good. Hard and ready, he pressed at her entrance slowly, letting her feel every delicious inch until he was in to the hilt.

He paused and she watched as he sucked in a sharp breath, his head thrown back, exposing the cords of his neck. It was simply too tempting and she lifted her head to swipe her tongue on the rough skin under his chin, the tang of salt bursting on her taste buds.

His first movements were slow and deliberate but quickly built to a hard and fast rhythm as she urged him on in hoarse, desperate pleas. She wanted no gentle coupling; hopefully there would be time for that later. No, what she needed was a claiming and he seemed to understand that fact as he pounded in to her, each thrust bringing them closer to completion.

Reaching between their bodies, she stroked her clit a few times, needing the friction to send her over, but Wyatt lightly slapped her hand away.

"My job."

Toni wasn't in the mood for his macho antics. He could beat his chest and play caveman later.

"Then do it," she growled, pulling his head down so their lips met, hot and wet. His open mouth slid down her neck and bit the sensitive flesh of her shoulder. "Asshole."

He chuckled but didn't argue, his thumb making circles on the swollen pearl until she was arching underneath him, her climax making her shudder and tremble with its intensity. He followed right behind her, her name on his lips, as his entire body went taut. He looked beautiful in that moment and she allowed herself the luxury of drinking in the sight of him, sweaty and sexy.

The aroma of sex hung in the air as he rolled onto his back, bringing her with him and tucking her into his side. After a few minutes, he pressed a kiss to her forehead and levered out of bed. At first she was going to object but then realized he needed to take care of the condom. When he returned, he pulled the covers up over the two of them as he spooned her from behind.

Toni didn't want to fall asleep but she was fighting a losing battle with exhaustion. She wanted to stay awake and savor the closeness, a luxury she rarely allowed herself. Her life was all about being in charge and in control at all times. Now she simply wanted...

She didn't really know what she wanted, if she was honest. Maybe she was looking for love or some reasonable facsimile. Or perhaps passion and companionship were what she craved. Or it could be commitment. The feeling that she belonged to someone and he to her as they built a life and even a family together.

What she did know was that the question wouldn't be answered tonight and it couldn't be answered without Wyatt. He had a vote too in what this was going to be. Only the morning light would reveal if he was in it or ready to run.

If he tried to make a break for it she could always stick her foot out and trip him.

Chapter Twenty-Three

WYATT DIDN'T HAVE to open his eyes to know that the early morning light was beginning to peek through the windows. The sun wasn't quite up yet but years on the farm had ingrained him with an internal alarm clock that wasn't swayed by how much sleep he might have missed the night before. He could go to bed at ten at night or three in the morning and his damn brain would wake his ass at five-thirty, rain or shine.

He let his gaze wander over the sleeping woman who was snuggled into the curve of his body, her bottom pressed against the only part of him that was wide awake. Nuzzling a softly scented shoulder, he dropped baby kisses on the soft skin, drawing a small moan from her lips.

He ought to let her sleep.

Carefully, he extricated himself from their tangled limbs and slid off the edge of the bed, freezing when she wriggled around trying to find a new comfortable position. Luckily she stayed fast asleep and he grabbed a set of work clothes from the top of the dresser, pulling them on in the dim light. He'd let her stay in bed while he went out and did the morning chores. Physical exertion would help keep his overheated libido in check. If he didn't have responsibilities, he might think about keeping her in bed all day.

It was hot and sticky outside despite the early hour. Wyatt went about each chore as efficiently as he could, wanting nothing more than to return to Toni. He'd done an about face from his stance before but she'd been the true catalyst. She was as different from her sister as possible and he didn't need to be a genius to see it. Anyone could and he'd be a fool to try and run from something this good.

Sure, he still had reservations. He wasn't certain he was long term relationship material but he was willing to try – for the first time in years. There was also the little issue that Toni wasn't planning on settling here in town once the renovation was complete. She had a business and a life back in Denver; sticking around a backwater town wasn't exactly her style.

Last, but certainly not least, was the fact that her family would have a fit when they found out she was involved with him. Her parents blamed him for his divorce from Carla because they were blind to what their oldest daughter was really like. That they believed every word out of her mouth was stunning considering she lied to them as much as she did everyone else.

Carla wasn't going to let Wyatt and Toni live in peace either. She'd always been spiteful and he'd need to be extra vigilant to ensure that Toni didn't get hurt by her selfish sister.

Then there was the whole *what if they made Toni choose?*

Wyatt couldn't expect her to side with him if her parents threatened to pull out of her life because of their relationship. He didn't know for sure if they'd do that but he wouldn't be shocked. If Carla shed a few crocodile tears, Mom and Dad wouldn't hesitate to ruin Toni's happiness. When push came to shove, they'd always favor Carla.

So where did that leave him?

Happy but cautious. He wanted this to work between them but he wasn't blind to the obstacles they'd need to overcome. And due to his nature, he wasn't one to keep something like this quiet. When it came to his relationships with women, he was a simple, straightforward man.

Whether it was a good idea or not, he'd talk to her about it. If this was just for now and there was no future, he'd like to know up front. But if she was willing to give it a shot, hell, he would too.

Chuckling to himself, Wyatt wondered if the planets had aligned or some shit like that. He'd been vocal and adamant about never falling for another woman ever again. But then again, Toni wasn't just any woman and last night hadn't been simply a roll in the hay. She'd given as much as she'd taken and that was something he hadn't experienced. He wanted to do it again.

When he returned to the house, he heard the shower running and couldn't suppress a grin of mischief. He'd thought he was going to slip between the sheets with Toni but he wasn't a fussy man. The shower would do nicely.

Shucking his clothes off as he went, he tested the door to see if it was locked but it swung open easily, letting out a billow of steam. Damn, she liked her water hot. When it was warm and humid outside, he kept the temperature a little cooler.

No problem though. If he did his job right, she wouldn't be aware of how hot or cold the water was. She'd only be thinking about what he was doing to her. He had a few ideas that he wouldn't mind giving a try.

"Honey, I'm coming in. Make room."

He hadn't wanted to scare her but if anything, she surprised him. The shower curtain ripped back and there she stood in all her naked glory, rivulets of water running down her perfect curves and crying out to him to touch and caress.

"I was wondering where you were. Get in here and wash my back."

"Yes, ma'am," he laughed, loving the way she didn't play coy. She'd been a little shy last night but clearly that wasn't her natural state. She was a go-getter and if she wanted to come get him that was certainly fine. "I was outside taking care of the chores. I let you sleep thinking that you didn't want to feed the chickens. I might be wrong though."

Stepping under the steamy spray, he wrapped his arms around Toni and pulled her flush against him. There was no hiding that he was already aroused, his erection pressing into the softness of her belly. She gazed up at him, looping her arms around his neck.

"I do not have the urge to feed chickens but if you had asked me I would have helped. Are you all done?" She ran her tongue up the middle of his chest to his Adam's apple where she gave him a nip with her teeth. "I'm all dirty and I need someone to help me get clean."

Chuckling, he kissed a spot beneath her ear that elicited a wanton moan from her full lips.

"Are you certain you want to get clean? It's more fun being dirty."

Whatever her answer was going to be he didn't let her reply. Instead, he captured her lips in a long, hot kiss that had his heart pounding against his ribs as if a marching band had taken up residence in his chest. Blood pumped furiously through his veins and with a simple kiss he was already on the edge. He felt like a teenager again who only thought with his dick.

His hands roamed up and down her body, stopping to give a pert butt cheek a little squeeze before coming to rest on her breasts. Cupping them in his palms, he ran his thumbs back and forth over the hard nipples until her fingernails dug into the flesh of his biceps.

"Do you want me to stop?"

Her head back and eyes closed, Toni shook her head, arching her back to offer herself up even more. He didn't hesitate to accept, lifting her up in his arms so her back was braced against the wall and his arms under her bottom so that his mouth could easily reach the rosy peak begging for his attention. He ran his tongue in circles before sucking it into his mouth. Her fingers tangled into his hair, pressing him closer and he moved to the other side giving it the same lavish attention.

Toni wrapped her legs around his hips and he positioned himself at her entrance but the first sane thought he'd had all morning had him pausing. Fuck a duck, he wasn't thinking straight at all.

"Honey, I don't have a condom."

Her face was pressed to his wet chest but she looked up at him, her long dark hair slicked back and shook her head. "I'm on the pill and clean. I haven't been with anyone in awhile and I'm healthy."

Wyatt could have sworn he heard angels singing.

"I haven't been with anyone in a long time either and I'm clean. Are you okay with this?"

Nodding, she nipped at his shoulder and wriggled her hips impatiently. "Get to it, we have a lot to do today."

He adored a woman who knew what she wanted.

Not hesitating, he grasped her hips tightly and drove deep inside of her until they both gasped with the sensation. Reveling in her snug channel, Wyatt allowed himself a moment to simply savor the pleasure before beginning to thrust, slow and deliberate as if they had all the time in the world. He wouldn't be hurried and instead lazily pumped in and out while he pressed his forehead to hers, their gazes locked intimately. There was something scary but intense when he looked into her eyes, a connection that went further than their physical connection. It was more and at the moment, it was everything.

Hot water beat down on their skin as their arousal rose, building with each stroke until they were both panting and breathless. Toni only needed a nudge to go over the cliff, so he reached over his head and plucked the massage showerhead from its cradle and brought the spray down between their bodies.

She screamed his name as she flew into the stars, tightening on his shaft and taking him along for the ride. His muscles tensed painfully and he came up on his toes, gritting his teeth as powerful waves surged through him. When it was over, they clung to one another as he carefully lowered her feet to the tile floor below, steadying her when her knees would have given way.

Giggling like kids, they quickly washed each other and rinsed off, still smiling from a pleasant morning wake up call. Everything seemed better with Toni than without her. Showering, meals, work, even watching television. She'd thrown open the windows of his stodgy, closed-off life and cool, fresh wind was blowing through.

He could fall for her.

If he let himself.

Chapter Twenty-Four

WYATT DRANK DOWN the last of his coffee and signaled the waitress for the bill. He and Toni had dragged themselves out of the shower this morning with sated libidos and growling stomachs. After a quick stop at her hotel for a change of clothes, they'd stopped at the cafe for some breakfast and a much needed caffeine injection.

"I need to go into Harper Falls today and talk to the police there in town about Mandy's stalker. See if they ever got close to finding the guy. Right now, he's suspect number one, whomever he might be. What do you have planned?"

He was thinking they might be able to have dinner together, and then maybe he could convince her to spend the night.

Toni's brows were furrowed and she was stabbing at her cellphone, clearly frustrated with the other person. "I'm going with you. Dammit, Mother. Leave me alone."

Reaching across the table, he snatched the phone from her white-knuckled fingers. "You can't go with me. This is official business stuff. Now tell me what has you so pissed after I spent so much effort relaxing you this morning."

Turning a lovely shade of pink, Toni rolled her eyes and gave him a kick in the shin under the table. "What do you mean I can't go with you? I want to hear what they have to say too."

"I'll tell you when I get back. Now who were you texting?"

"You're like a dog with a bone." Toni went for the phone but he shooed away her hands. He wanted his answers first. She sighed and slumped in the booth. "It was my mother, of course. She's still on this kick of me lending money to Carla. You know, because I'm rolling in dough at the moment."

They'd had a small conversation regarding Toni's finances not long ago when Wyatt was so concerned about the estate purchase and she was doing extremely well. But she had tied quite a bit of cash up in this project. A year from now, she was probably going to be a very rich young woman. He'd seen the number projections and it was impressive, whether the hotel was a smashing success or not.

"Why did you answer the phone?"

She stared up at the ceiling for a long beat before looking back at him. "I don't know. I try to avoid her calls but every now and then that little girl inside of me that wants mommy and daddy's approval does something stupid. Today it was answering the phone. I should know better, I really should. She only calls me when she either wants something or to tell me how disappointing I am as a daughter. I'm so done with this."

He should definitely keep his mouth shut but he didn't want to start a relationship with Toni that wasn't completely honest. He needed to say something and she desperately needed to hear it.

"I'm going to tell you something that might make you mad. Hell, it might make you march out of this restaurant and never speak to me again, but honey, it needs to be said."

Fiddling with her coffee cup, Toni nodded, her lips twisted in a half-smile. She had to have some idea what was coming. "Go ahead. I'm listening and I doubt I'll go off in a huff unless you say you don't like my outfit or something."

Finesse wasn't his strong-suit. This was going to be brutal and blunt.

"Your parents are idiots."

Not a tinge of surprise showed on Toni's face. "I see. Go on."

"They don't deserve you. They have a wonderful, successful daughter and all they can see is the other one that they've ruined by spoiling and coddling her. Carla has a tendency to destroy or at the very least damage everything she touches, yet they can't see past their own prejudices."

He paused, wanting to gauge her reaction. She didn't appear angry, her expression more sad than anything with her mouth drooping and the sparkle gone from her eyes. He wasn't a man who railed at the world when it wasn't fair but this situation sucked.

"I see you trying to reach out to them and make something of the relationship, but Toni honey, it won't work as long as it's more important to you than it is to them. They should be scrambling, begging to be around their youngest daughter but I've seen them barely acknowledge your existence. I'm suggesting for your own peace of mind that perhaps you should pull back for a little while. Make them come to you for a change. Don't chase the crumbs of love they toss your way." He reached across the table and squeezed her hand. "You deserve a hell of a lot better than what you're getting. So there. I said it and I'll shut up now."

Her eyes bright with unshed tears, she shook her head. "You're fine. It's okay. You're not saying anything that I haven't said to myself in the wee hours of the night when I'm lying in bed wondering why mommy and daddy don't treat me the same as my sister. I do deserve better than running after them, trying to win their love and approval. Which, by the way, I'm not ever going to get."

"Maybe, or maybe not," he said gently. "Time can change things."

"It sure has," she laughed, but it came out dry and choked. "If anything they've built Carla's pedestal taller than it ever was. I'm so damn tired, Wyatt. Tired of trying to be the person that I am but somehow still be someone they can love. I'm not sure I can do it anymore. I just want to be me."

Next time Wyatt saw her parents he was going to kick them in the ass. They didn't have a clue the damage they'd done and if he told them he wasn't sure they'd care.

"I think *you* are just fine, honey. If they can't love all the terrific things you are, they don't deserve you as a daughter."

Toni's gaze wandered out the front window of the cafe and he stayed quiet as she seemed to gather her thoughts.

"That's why I'm the way I am," she finally said as the waitress dropped off the check. He grabbed it before Toni got her hands on it. This was a daily battle. "It's why I'm so ambitious and independent. What if I get used to someone taking care of me and then they're gone? I'll be in worse shape than before."

Placing his fingers under her chin, he turned her to face him.

"What if that's how they express their feelings? What if fixing you soup when you're sick and making sure your car has gas is their way of saying they care?"

Toni blinked a few times as if she'd never had thought about the question. "I don't know. I've never had anyone who wanted to be there for me like that. What would that look like?"

Time to man up. He wasn't ready to use the "L" word but he was ready to say that this relationship was something he'd been looking for.

"Do you see me?" She nodded, her brows pulled together in confusion. "This is what it looks like."

Her mouth fell open and her eyes went wide. She was honest-to-God surprised.

"You want to be there for me?"

"All the time. How do you feel about that?"

Toni simply stared at him for a long time, perhaps trying to figure out if he was serious. Eventually a smile spread across her face and the tears that had been threatening to fall looked far away.

"I'm terrified. I've never been any good at this, and we have the added complication of Carla and my family. How about you?"

Smiling right back, he didn't play games or beat around the bush. They understood each other perfectly.

"Scared within an inch of my life," he confessed. "I said I was done with relationships but here I am with the one woman I shouldn't want. But I remember someone telling me that people pay good money to be frightened."

"Throwing my words back at me?" Toni laughed, a real one

this time. "We must be in a relationship then. Next thing you know you'll be complaining that I make spaghetti for dinner too often or that you hate my friends."

"It won't be easy," Wyatt warned. "We both like being the boss a little too much and we're going to butt heads."

"I know. I also know that you scooped up the breakfast check a moment ago. Are you going to let me pay my share?"

"No, are you going to complain about it? Maybe you should relax and let someone pick up the check now and then."

Toni huffed and shoved her phone in her purse. "It's not now and then, it's every time. I swear, Wyatt Stone, you are the most stubborn, mule-headed man—"

"I sure am." He cut off her diatribe knowing she wasn't mad in the least. "You are too. Now I'll go back to the original question. What are you going to do today because you are not coming with me, honey."

Wrinkling her nose, she made a mean face that didn't fool him. She was laughing but trying to hide it. "I guess I'll head to the estate then. There are some things I can work on by myself for the pathway. It's not much but it's something."

"Those boys haven't made money in a few days and they might be getting mighty nervous. I have a feeling you might see one or two of them wander back to the worksite today or tomorrow. Have some faith."

"It isn't easy."

No, it wasn't but he was going to try.

✦　✦　✦

THE TOWN OF Harper Falls hadn't changed much since the last

time Wyatt had been there over five years ago. There was a new fast food place on the edge of town and a stoplight near the school but other than that it was exactly the same. Which of course brought back too many memories, both pleasant and ghastly. But in a way it was good that he was here. If he was going to have any sort of future with Toni, he needed to deal with his past.

Parking in front of the sheriff's station, Wyatt hoped that Sheriff Sullivan had called and warned them he would be coming to talk to them about Mandy's stalker case. If not, he was going to have to do some fancy talking to get them to share any information.

He pushed open the front door and was immediately greeted by a young woman, apparently the receptionist, who gave him a big smile as he approached her desk.

"Hi, how can I help you? I'm Cindy."

Cindy was blonde and buxom, probably in her early twenties. She looked a little too much like Carla and she was already giving him a flirtatious look. For all she knew, he was a criminal who had come to turn himself in.

"I'm Wyatt Stone and I'm here to see Sheriff Bickham. Is he available?"

Cindy tossed her hair and shifted in her chair so her blouse showed a little more cleavage.

"He is here. Is he expecting you?"

"Sheriff Sullivan should have called yesterday letting him know I was coming."

Cindy lifted the receiver of the phone on the desk to her ear. "One minute. Sheriff? There's a man named Wyatt Stone here to see you." She paused and looked almost disappointed. "I'll send him right back."

She hung up and then stood, smoothing her skirt over her hips and motioned for him to follow her. "The sheriff said to take you right back. Is there anything I can get you? Coffee, tea? Something else?"

They stopped in front of a large polished oak door. "Nothing for me, thank you."

"Let me know if you change your mind. I'm sorry we didn't get to know each other better, Mr. Stone."

His entire life Wyatt had never known what to say to women when they flirted with him and he wasn't interested. He didn't want to hurt their feelings but he didn't want to give them the wrong idea either.

"Thank you again for your assistance."

He twisted the doorknob and turned his attention to the task at hand. He needed information and hopefully Sheriff Bickham would have it. Wyatt needed just one break in this case.

"Sheriff Bickham?" Wyatt stuck his head in the door, still unsure as to his welcome. "I'm Wyatt Stone. I'm a consultant working with the Birchwood sheriff's office regarding the murder of Mandy Roberts Hoskins. I was hoping I could speak with you."

A graying man with a large, bushy mustache waved him in.

"Come in. Sullivan gave me a call that you were coming but I didn't know when. Come in and have a seat." The man reached for the phone. "Can I get Cindy to get you some coffee or a soda?"

Definitely not.

"Actually, she already made that offer but I'm fine. I'd really just like to get down to it if you don't mind."

"I don't mind that at all. Have a seat. When your sheriff called me I took the liberty of pulling the case file and having Cindy make a copy for you. I hope it will help."

If only everyone that Wyatt came into contact with could be this cooperative.

"That sounds great." Wyatt settled into a chair on the other side of the desk from Bickham. "What can you tell me about the case, Sheriff? Were you close to finding her stalker?"

The sheriff frowned and lifted a folder from his desk, sliding it toward Wyatt. It wasn't as thick as Wyatt had hoped it would be.

"I had my suspicions, Mr. Stone. Deep suspicions. Unfortunately, I could never prove them. Then Mandy left town and we all sort of breathed a sigh of relief." He shook his head and pressed his lips together. "Dammit, I thought she was safe finally. I certainly didn't even imagine—"

The older man pulled a handkerchief from his pocket and wiped at his face. "She was a sweet woman and she didn't deserve this sort of an end. I want the asshole that did this and I'll do anything I can to help you."

Wyatt laid his hand on the folder, already itching to read its contents. "I appreciate that, Sheriff, and please, call me Wyatt. I'd like to hear your version of events if I may, before I look through the file. Reports are one thing but I tend to respect a cop's gut feeling."

The man's face was wreathed in smiles. "I've got plenty of that for you."

Wyatt took out his cell from his shirt pocket and placed it on the desk. "Do you mind if I record this? It's just for me and my bad memory."

Wyatt could barely read his own handwriting.

"Not at all, son. Where do you want me to start?"

"Just start at the beginning, Sheriff. When did you first learn about Mandy's stalker?"

Chapter Twenty-Five

WYATT HAD BEEN right. Several men showed up at the worksite, including the contractor Bill. They all wore sheepish grins and stared at their steel-toed shoes in embarrassment but Toni wasn't one to rub their faces in the past or dwell there either. She was simply happy to see them back and ready to work. The schedule would need to be modified and some items might have to be put off for after the opening but she had her crew back – albeit a smaller one.

The guest house was still off limits so Toni spent her time working on the pathway scare attraction. Without Wyatt, she couldn't reach any of the overhead pieces but there was plenty of other work to be done. The zombie creeping up slowly behind someone was going to be a huge hit.

So intent on installing the motion sensor, she didn't hear footsteps on the soft trail until a scream pierced the quiet along with a series of smaller screeches. Toni scrambled to her feet and had to slap her hand over her mouth to keep from laughing.

Barbara Ross was standing ten feet away, shrieking at the top of her lungs and flapping her arms at the witch Wyatt had helped install just days ago. Toni's mother must have set off the motion sensor and the witch had flown across her path along with a multitude of screeching black bats.

As tempting as it was to let her mother fight off some imaginary baddies, Toni was too good of a daughter to let it continue. Running over to the switch hidden in some brush, Toni hit the reset button and the witch and bats glided back into their ready positions, leaving Barb standing there with her mouth handing open and her normally carefully coiffed hair askew.

Cue the scolding in 3...2...1...

"For heaven's sake, Antonia, what the hell is that? It almost killed me. Is that what you intend to do to innocent people, your guests? You'll be sued for every cent you have on the first day you open. I can't believe a daughter of mine has so little common sense to do something like this. My God, that house is a death trap. What a money pit. Have you no sense at all?"

Barb finally had to take a breath, her chest still rapidly rising and falling. In fear? Disgust? Something else? Toni had no doubt she was going to hear a lecture of all the things she should be doing with her money, better things. Things that mommy and daddy approved of. Like giving most or all of it to Carla. Poor thing. She was probably down to half a dozen Chanel handbags and ten pairs of Prada shoes, all last year's style.

"Hello, Mother. It's nice to see you too."

Barb's gaze was darting back and forth, her head craned back looking at the tree canopy up above. "Those weren't real bats, were they?"

That was as close to a compliment as Toni's mother had given her in recent years. "Not at all. The flying witch was fake too, but thank you for thinking they might not be. That means I've done my job well."

"Job," Barbara scoffed. "Playing at monsters and skeletons. That's not a real job."

Five minutes with her mother was about all Toni could usually take and today was no exception. If she let Barbara continue, Toni knew how this conversation would go. There would be much whining about Toni's unmarried status, her childless status, and her occupational status. Then the comparisons to Carla would begin and damned if Toni was going to put up with it. She'd started the day out in a good mood and she wasn't going to allow it to go into the dumpster.

She wasn't going to pull any punches either. She'd learned early that the best defense was an exceptional offense.

"Have you come to congratulate me on my business success?"

When pigs sprout wings and fly.

Barbara had gathered her wits and was now giving her daughter a stern look that had worked when she was ten but had little effect now.

"I've come to talk to you because you won't answer your phone. There are things that need to be discussed and I won't allow you to ignore your family obligations."

Since Toni had always been a second-class citizen in her family, she wasn't too keen on any first-class obligations.

"Fine, let's go into the house and sit down. I could use a cold drink and a chair."

Her mother's gaze raked Toni head to toe, taking in the olive colored t-shirt, khaki cargo shorts, and steel-toed boots. "Is that all you had to wear today? My God, you dress like a hobo."

Pulling the cotton fabric of her shirt away from her sticky skin, Toni laughed and picked up the tools, leading the way back to the house. "My ball gown is at the dry cleaners. Are you coming?"

Apparently so. Barbara didn't say any more until they were in the small parlor that Toni and Wyatt had been using as an office. With the cross breeze and two fans, the room was actually pleasant to sit in. Toni grabbed a couple of sodas from the cooler and offered one to her mother.

"No, thank you," Barbara replied, wrinkling her nose at the metal folding chair before sitting down on it. "I'm rather put out that you forced me to come here today. If you had answered your phone it wouldn't have been necessary."

Popping open the can, Toni relaxed for the first time that morning, settling into the chair with a relieved sigh. Her back was killing her from bending down working on the sensor and she needed a long soak in a hot tub.

And after this conversation? A drink, very strong.

"No one forced you here, Mother. You weren't marched at gunpoint or tied up and thrown in a trunk. As for answering my phone, I've been quite busy here. What did you want to talk about?"

Toni didn't even mention finding Mandy's body and seeing Carla at the wake. Her sister must not have told their mother about that.

"Carla is in real financial trouble, Antonia, and it's your family duty to help her. She's in dire straits."

Toni would never allow any of her family to be thrown out of their homes and live in the streets, but neither was she willing to bust her ass to finance their lavish lifestyle. It was her money and she didn't live high on the hog, so to speak. She preferred a simple kind of life where people and experiences were more important than possessions.

"What happened?"

"I beg your pardon?"

"What happened?" Toni repeated. "How did Carla come to be in this situation considering Trevor owns a successful business? Has it gone under? Would I be *loaning* the money to help the company?"

Barbara fussed with her handbag and cleared her throat. "Let's not bring Trevor into this. The last thing we want to do is impugn his ability to take care of his wife. That can damage a man's ego."

Yes, let's all worry about Trevor's ego.

"You didn't answer the question. Has the business gone under? How did Carla find herself in this situation?"

Barbara lifted her chin and stared down her nose. "Carla has many expenses, too many to go into detail here. Suffice it to say that she needs your help."

"What about you and Dad?"

"Your father and I have already–" Her mother abruptly stopped and seemed to rethink her words. "What I mean is we've done what we can, of course, but we have our retirement to think about in just a few years."

A clearer picture was beginning to emerge and it looked like Carla had run through her husband's money, her parents' money, and now had her sights set on Toni's. She slapped the can down on the table and leaned forward, looking her mother right in the eye.

"Here's how this will work, Mother. There will be no nego-tiations. No deviation from this plan should it be put into motion. If there is a danger of Katie's school not being paid, I will pick up the tuition but I will pay it directly to the school. If they are behind in their mortgage payments, I will bring them current, but I will only pay the bank. If they need food, I will happily go to the store and load them up with a month's worth of groceries. If Katie needs clothes or toys, I'll take her shopping. If they need medical bills paid, I'm there. If they can't pay to fix one of their vehicles, I'm all over it. If Trevor has business expenses he can't pay, I'll help out. Do you see where I'm going with this? But if you are asking me to write Carla a check for some vague notion of expenses when I know very well she has about a hundred thousand dollars' worth of shoes in her closet, then you are delusional. I work too hard for what I have to let my flighty, selfish older sister blow it on designer clothes she doesn't need or maybe a boob job because the girls aren't as perky as they used to be. That's the terms, take it or leave it."

Barbara Ross was literally shaking with anger but Toni didn't back down. Not too long ago she might have allowed herself to be cowed into doing whatever her mother wanted but those days were gone. All her parents did was enable Carla to flit through life without any sense of responsibility and heaven knew what it would do to her little girl, Katie.

"I have never been so ashamed of you, Antonia Ross. Your sister needs you and you're sitting there trying to dictate the terms."

"Damn right I am," Toni retorted. "And I don't feel a bit

sorry about it. If her family truly needs help I'll be there, but the fact that you want to keep this from Trevor sets off alarm bells, frankly. Until you, Dad, or Carla is willing to come clean about this I'm not playing this game. I'm not about to write a check, no questions asked, knowing I'm never going to see a dime of it ever again."

Barbara jumped to her feet and began to pace the small space. "She'll pay you back."

Right.

"Has she paid you back, Mom? How does she plan to do it? She doesn't have a job so where is she going to get the money?"

Toni's mother stopped and whirled around, shaking her finger. "She can get a job if she wants one."

"Doing what? When was the last time she worked? I think it was that job at the cosmetics counter when she and Wyatt were dating."

Red. Barb's face had turned a violent shade of red. Crimson. Scarlet. Toni needed to calm her the hell down. She'd gone too far but then she'd been pushed. No excuse, though. It was her mother, for Christ's sake.

"Mom, just have a seat and relax. We can talk through this, I'm sure."

Barbara Ross was too far gone. She shook her head, her teeth gritted together. "You were always like this. You must hate me and your father. I begged you to be more like Carla but no, you had to be strange. Weird, with your drawing and your ugly clothes. Your resentment toward the rest of this family has gone too far this time. It's one thing to lash out at your parents but to do this to your sister is sick. Envy is ugly, Antonia."

Her mother actually believed that Toni was envious of her sister.

Toni stood on shaking legs, her heart pounding in her chest. She'd never shown her mother the door but she was about to. This action just might cement her excommunication from her family but it needed to be done. They were toxic and she couldn't allow them to poison the good life she'd managed to build.

Wiping her damp palms on her shorts, Toni took a deep, fortifying breath. "Mother, I think it's time you left. If you cannot speak civilly with me then I don't think we have anything to say. I've told you the parameters in which I'll help Carla. If they aren't acceptable then I don't think I can be of any assistance."

Barbara picked up her handbag and held it to her chest, her lips trembling with rage. For a split second, Toni thought she might be on the receiving end of a good, hard slap.

"Your father is going to hear about this."

"I'm sure he will. Can I show you the way out?"

Barbara wasn't done yet, apparently. She stepped closer to Toni, almost nose to nose. "I want you to think about today and what saying no means. I'm sure you'll come to see what the right course of action is."

Toni smiled but not with happiness. It was some sort of shocked reaction to her mother's words. Had she heard them correctly?

"Are you threatening me, Mother?"

"All I'm saying is that you either want to be part of this family or you don't. You can't expect to be a Ross and yet not fulfill your obligations."

Being a Ross wasn't looking too attractive at the moment. Maybe one of those mafia crime families was looking to adopt a daughter.

"Nothing comes free, huh? Except for Carla. Everything is gratis for her." Toni shook her head, tears pricking the backs of her eyes. "What did I do to you, Mother? I know I wasn't planned but that wasn't my fault. Why do you hate me so much?"

Barbara didn't answer, turning and heading for the door without a backward glance. Instead of showing her out, Toni stood rooted to the spot, her emotions churning, threatening to spill over. She would not cry on the worksite with all these workmen around. She would hold herself together and put on a professional front.

After all, tears in the past hadn't helped or changed a thing. The favorite was still Carla and Toni was simply around for a kidney or a lung should her sister need them in the future. Toni had long since stopped groveling for love and attention but she'd never been threatened with being thrown out of the family.

Something more was going on than Carla needing a new wardrobe or a fancy watch. Just what had her sister gotten herself into now?

Chapter Twenty-Six

❧

As MUCH AS Wyatt didn't want to see Carla he wanted to see her husband Trevor even less. At one point, he and Trevor had been buddies, best pals in high school before Wyatt went off to the Army and Trevor took over his old man's construction business.

When Wyatt was home from deployment, he and Trevor would hang out and have some guy-fun trying to hold onto a friendship that probably wouldn't have survived adulthood. As the years passed, it had been harder and harder to find time for each other and they'd begun to drift apart as people do when real life intervenes.

Wyatt had made the mistake of asking Trevor to check on Carla every now and then to make sure she was okay and see if she needed anything like a window fixed or lightbulb too high for her to change. Trevor had taken the request to heart and soon he was taking care of many of Carla's needs, including the sexual ones. Fast forward almost a year later when Wyatt came home from his last ever deployment to find Carla pregnant with Trevor's baby and asking for a divorce.

He'd given it to her without argument.

Trevor had shown up at the farm and tried to explain but honestly, Wyatt didn't want to hear it. It broke every bro-code rule and his friend fucking knew it, so what was there to discuss? Wyatt's marriage was broken beyond repair but then he'd known that before he came home. He and Carla had been fighting like cats and dogs since right after the honeymoon. She'd quit the facade of happily in love fairly quickly after the wedding. Once she had someone "won", she moved on to the next challenge.

He'd be lying if he hadn't wondered how Trevor was getting on with Carla but then he remembered he was supposed to hate his old friend's guts.

So it was with great reluctance that Wyatt stood in the foyer of Trevor's office asking if he was available. When Sheriff Bickham had told him that Trevor was the main suspect in Mandy's stalking it had shocked the hell out of him. Trevor was many things but he wasn't the type to stalk. Frankly, he'd never needed to.

Wyatt's friend must be doing well. Several employees buzzed hurriedly through the halls, low murmurs of conversation and a definite sense of urgency. The office wasn't the most luxurious Wyatt had ever seen but it spoke of a company making money. The carpets looked brand new, the walls freshly painted, and the furnishings, right down to the chairs and paintings, appeared to be well cared for.

"Mr. Wells will see you now." The young receptionist behind the desk pointed down the long hallway. "Last door on your left. He's expecting you."

A hallway had never seemed longer but eventually Wyatt was standing in front of Trevor's door, his hand suspended in midair, ready to knock.

All the junk he'd dealt with in the last five years, all the crap he'd taken from Carla and yes, even Trevor, slammed into him like a cement truck to the solar plexus. But a funny thing happened after the collision. He didn't feel like crawling away and hiding at the farm. No, he'd put up with too much shit from both of them and they needed their asses kicked from here to the moon. He'd given them a free pass for acting like assholes when he should have held them accountable for their selfish decisions.

He'd learned that little tidbit from Toni. She'd stood up to her parents and that had to be a hell of a lot harder than dealing with an ex-wife. If she could do it, then he could too.

Instead of knocking, he reached for the doorknob, twisting it open and stepping into the room. Trevor sat at a large, light oak desk with a wall of windows at his back. The man he used to call his friend stood and walked around the desk, a smile on his face and his hand held out ready to shake.

Fuck that.

Wyatt punched Trevor right in his pretty face. It had been a long time coming.

Now he felt better.

Landing on a chair, Trevor rubbed his chin and grimaced but didn't hop up to get his own lick in as Wyatt had expected. He instead chuckled and grinned before standing up, still nursing that jaw.

"I guess I deserved that."

"It's several years past due but I don't think there's a statute of limitations on being a terrible friend and an asshole."

Trevor walked past Wyatt and reached into a small refrigerator in the corner, pulling out two bottles of beer and holding one up. "Peace offering?"

Wyatt accepted it, twisting open the cap and tossing it in the trash can. "This doesn't make us even."

"No, it doesn't but it actually makes me feel a bit better. I always wondered why you didn't put a hurt on me before. I expected you to."

Wyatt took a long draw from the bottle. "I couldn't decide who I was more pissed off at, you or Carla. But looking at it now, I think you did me a favor and screwed yourself. You've probably suffered more than I ever did. Shit, at least I was in the Middle East getting shot at. You've had to spend pretty much every day with her."

Shrugging, Trevor waved Wyatt into a chair and then settled into his own. "Karma. I should have known something that was born in a lie could never be quite right. But Katie's wonderful. She's going to kindergarten in the fall."

"You should put some ice on that."

"I will later. You still pack a wallop. I don't remember the last time someone knocked me off my feet like that. Hell, it was probably you." Trevor tapped a pen on the desk and laughed. "It had to be Dallas. We went to that bar after the football game and we squared off with those three guys that didn't like the songs we played on the jukebox. You swung and the big one slipped on the wet floor, leaving me to take his punch because I was standing right behind him trying to wrestle him to the ground."

Wyatt had good memories of that weekend, what he remembered of it. "I haven't been to Dallas since. I'm not sure they'd let us back in the city."

"Good times, my friend. Good times." Trevor sat back in his chair, giving Wyatt a narrow-eyed look. "Is that why you came? To give me that long overdue beat down?"

"Not exactly." Wyatt watched his friend closely for any reaction. "Actually I've been asked to consult with police regarding Mandy Roberts Hoskins' murder."

Trevor blanched and sucked in a sharp breath. "Then I know why you're here."

"I was hoping we could talk."

Shifting in his chair, Wyatt's friend seemed to be searching for what to say. "First of all, I loved Mandy and probably always will. She was a wonderful woman."

Did that mean he didn't love Carla?

"She had a stalker and the cops think it was you."

Trevor scoffed and shook his head. "You mean Cole thinks I was her stalker. He hates my guts and for good reason, I guess, but I didn't stalk her. We were in a consensual relationship. We were in love."

Clearly, Mandy's life had become much more complicated after he'd left town. Back then her biggest issues were exams and her latest boyfriend.

"You were seeing Mandy? While she was married?"

Red stained Trevor's cheeks and he dropped his gaze looking anywhere but at his old friend.

"Yes, we were seeing each other. Mandy worked here at the office in the accounting department. We started spending time with each other during a particularly rough patch during the recession and things happened from there. She was planning to leave her husband."

"She said that?"

This time Trevor looked him in the eye. "Yes. Like I said, we were in love and making plans for our life together. Then she suddenly disappeared. No note. No message. Just seemed to vanish into thin air. I never heard from her again."

Taking another drink from the beer bottle, Wyatt considered his next question carefully.

"What did you think happened to her?"

Rubbing the back of his neck, Trevor seemed at a loss. "I was never sure. I know she was scared of this stalker. She told me she was but even if she hadn't, you could see it. The notes and letters were creepy as hell and it freaked her out that someone out there seemed to know her personal business so intimately. When she disappeared, there was a big part of me that thought she left to get away from him and that eventually she would be back."

"But she didn't come back."

"True, and by that time I was involved with...well, you know."

Yes, he knew.

"So why did the police think you were the stalker?"

"They've got nothing on me."

That was true. Sheriff Bickham only had a gut feeling and had admitted as much.

"That's not what I asked. How did you get dragged into this?"

"Cole knew something was up between Mandy and me. Things were so bad between them she didn't bother much to hide it. She said their marriage had been over for a long time and she shouldn't have married him so quickly but he'd swept her off her feet when he was new in town. Anyway, the letters knew things only people close to her would know supposedly, so the suspicion was on me but I'm still not clear what my motive was supposed to be. Why would I stalk my own girlfriend?"

He did ask.

"To make her so scared she'd run to you for protection," Wyatt suggested. "To keep her dependent on you if she was starting to think about leaving."

Trevor straightened in his chair, shoulders stiff. "She wasn't thinking about leaving me. I told you, we were in love. I wanted to marry her."

"I'm just saying that there are motives they could assign you. Did you have any opinion about who her stalker might be?"

"I was as frustrated as she was. They went through her old boyfriends, male neighbors. They even interviewed the guy that made her latte at the coffee shop. It was like she was followed by a ghost."

More spirit activity. Ironic considering where Mandy's body had been found.

Wyatt wasn't done questioning Trevor. He didn't truly believe that his old friend had stalked anyone but he also wasn't sure he bought the whole *we were in love* thing that he was trying to sell.

"I'm confused about the timing of your relationship with Mandy. It began in 2009? She disappeared in June of 2010 and Carla told me she was pregnant with your baby in January of 2011. Doesn't sound like you pined for her all that long."

He'd said it to get a reaction and Trevor didn't disappoint. The man came out of his seat, the chair flying backwards and crashing into the window frame with a loud bang.

"You are way out of line," he growled, his face twisted with anger.

"That's possible," Wyatt conceded. "But try to see how other people might look at the situation. To them you appear to be a serial home wrecker—first Mandy's marriage and then mine. Also, you and Carla didn't waste any time once Mandy disappeared. Some might even think you were seeing both women at the same time. If you were, it would make them more suspicious of you, that's for sure."

His chest rising and falling rapidly, Trevor rubbed the back of his neck. "I was not seeing both at the same time. Like you asked me to, I was looking in on Carla but I was dating Mandy. Carla knew I had a girlfriend and that I was serious. When Mandy disappeared, Carla was there for me." He leaned forward, planting his hands on the desk. "Look, I'm not proud of what I did. Frankly, I'm ashamed of my actions. I lost a good friend in you, Wyatt, and those are hard to come by. If I knew then what I know now…"

Wyatt believed that Trevor was sorry for what he'd done but actions had consequences. "Let me ask you something because I've always wondered. Just how did you think this was all going to end when I came home from deployment? What was the happily ever after you pictured there?"

Turning his back on Wyatt, Trevor stared out the window. "The truth? I was planning to end it with Carla. I was still in love with Mandy after all and thought she'd come back. But then Carla told me she was pregnant and everything changed. I felt like I had to do right by her. I knew I was ruining my friendship with you but I'd already betrayed you because I'd been weak. I was so torn up about Mandy that somehow I lost my moral compass. If it makes you feel any better, I've been paying for what I did every single day."

"It doesn't." Time for honestly all around. "In a way, I think I was more hurt by your betrayal than by Carla's. The only reason I think we were still together is because I was deployed for the majority of our marriage. If we'd had to live together every day I think we would have split up pretty quickly. She and I made each other miserable so I wasn't surprised she was having an affair. I was simply surprised that it was you."

Trevor turned, his eyes shiny and his lips trembling. "I was surprised it was me too. And I'll say it again, man—I'm so fucking sorry. You sure as hell didn't deserve what she and I put you through." He took a deep breath, his gaze dropping to the floor. "We're getting a divorce."

"I'm sorry, especially for Katie."

To his surprise, Wyatt was sorry. It didn't make him feel any better that Trevor and Carla were splitting up. He didn't want retribution or revenge or anything else. He simply wanted to move on from all the bullshit that had been holding him back for too long. Preferably with Toni but ultimately it was up to her.

"Thanks." Trevor sank back down into the chair. "Listen, before you go...you asked if I had a suspect in Mandy's stalking. At the time I didn't, but now I think I might. With hindsight, some things have become clearer."

"Let's hear it," Wyatt urged. "Any lead may make a difference in this case."

The other man sighed and raked his fingers through his short blond hair. "Carla. She knew I was seeing Mandy and sometimes it seemed like she resented that I wasn't available to be with her whenever she called. I would never have believed it before but now I've seen just how vindictive she can be." Trevor held up his hands in surrender. "I'm not saying I think she killed Mandy or anything. Hell, she wouldn't want to ruin her manicure. But I do think she was capable of trying to scare Mandy away. If that makes any sense."

It did. Of course that meant one thing.

Wyatt had to do the one thing he'd sworn he'd never do.

He had to talk to Carla.

Chapter Twenty-Seven

T HE FETTUCCINE WAS perfectly cooked and the sauce creamy. Wyatt was an excellent chef and had whipped the delicious meal practically out of thin air but he'd also been quiet the entire time, responding to her questions with simple yes and no answers and sometimes even a grunt. Whatever was bugging him, he didn't seem inclined to share it.

Too bad she wasn't a more understanding person.

Antonia picked up her wine glass and took a sip, watching him carefully over the rim. "I had quite the day. Did I tell you my mother came by the estate?"

Maybe if she talked about what happened to her, he'd talk about himself. He'd promised to fill her in, but so far he hadn't even confirmed he'd met with the sheriff.

Wyatt's wandering attention was suddenly laser focused on Toni. "Your mother? What did she say?"

Not wanting to admit how the incident upset her, Toni shrugged carelessly. "She said a lot of things, none of them very nice. Nothing new there."

"What did she want?"

"My money," Toni snorted. "Apparently Carla is broke.

Funny thing though, Mom doesn't want Trevor to know anything about this little transaction, which I found very disturbing."

Wyatt gave her a strange look. "She wants to keep it a secret from Trevor? What else did she say?"

"The usual. Blah, blah, blah Carla. Blah, blah, blah Carla. After awhile I just tune it out. But this time was a little different. She gave a sort of veiled threat that if I didn't give Carla the money, I would be out of the family. As if I'm really a part of it now."

"They must be desperate. I wonder why?"

"I assume Carla ran up the credit cards and she's afraid for Trevor to find out."

Wyatt reached for the wine bottle and refilled Toni's glass without asking. "I doubt that. I talked to Trevor today actually and he said that they're getting a divorce."

A divorce. Divorce. He talked to Trevor?

Toni reeled from the news and grabbed for her wine glass just as Wyatt must have known she would. "Did he say if it was his or her idea? Because if it wasn't her idea the shit is really going to hit the fan. She doesn't like it when her toys get a mind of their own."

"Tell me something I don't know," Wyatt replied dryly. "Trevor didn't say outright but I kind of got the feeling it was his idea. I could be wrong, of course. It makes this whole money situation that much more interesting, doesn't it?"

Yes, it did. Did Carla need the money for a high-powered lawyer? If it came to a custody battle Toni would be on Trevor's side. She wouldn't help Carla hang onto a child she had little interest in.

Wait…

"You saw Trevor today? What the hell for?"

Rubbing his temple, Wyatt sighed and threw down his napkin. "Because Trevor was a suspect in Mandy's stalking case. Apparently they'd been having an affair behind her husband Cole's back."

"Wow, Trevor likes them married, huh?"

The words popped out before she could stop them. This was one of the big reasons she was going to hell.

"I said basically the same thing to him. He denied that it was a fetish or trend. They met when she worked for him and supposedly he loved her and wanted to marry her. This was before he was seeing Carla. Supposedly. I've been lied to so many times by him I'm not sure what the truth is anymore."

Toni was having a hard time wrapping her mind around this new development. "So…Trevor was involved with Mandy before he was involved with Carla. She had a stalker but he claims it wasn't him."

"That's what he says. He thought she had disappeared because of the stalker but felt she would come back eventually."

"And when he was lonely and sad, that's when Carla moved on him, I bet? That's how she works. She preys on the weak of the herd."

Something Toni was determined not to allow herself to be.

"He might have gone after her," Wyatt reminder Toni. "We'll never really know the truth, although it doesn't absolve either one of them of guilt."

"Do you think he was stalking Mandy? Do you think…"

She couldn't even say the last part. It was too awful to contemplate. Wyatt took his time answering and she had to wonder if he'd been pondering those same questions all day.

"The man that was my friend could never have done those things."

"And this man?" Toni prompted. "What about him?"

Wyatt shook his head. "I still don't think he did it. He looked genuinely torn up about Mandy's death. I don't necessarily trust my bullshit detector when it comes to Trevor but my gut tells me he didn't do this."

Wyatt might not trust himself but Toni did. "So where does that leave us? What happens now?"

"I brought home the case file to look over. Again. I went through it before I saw Trevor but I need to do it once more."

"Sounds good. I'll help."

A muscle worked in his jaw and Toni had a feeling there was more to all of this than Trevor.

"There's something you're not telling me. Is it that bad?"

His lips were turned down in a grimace. "It's not good. When I asked Trevor if he could think of anyone who might stalk Mandy he said that he did have a name. One name."

"One name?" she prompted. "Who?"

"Carla."

Of course. Wyatt, the poor man, was never going to be free of Toni's sister.

She was like the proverbial bad penny. Just when you thought you'd seen the last of her, she'd turn up unexpectedly.

Toni wouldn't let him face this alone.

✦　✦　✦

TONI HAD THAT look on her face. Lips pursed. Forehead furrowed with concern. Eyes soft and full of emotion.

She was worried about him, and heaven knew it had been a damn long time since anyone had cared that much. It was nice to have someone in his life but he didn't want her turning herself inside out because of this. He'd had time to think about it and it was a good thing he was going to see Carla.

"Don't," he warned, shaking his head. "Don't make this molehill into a mountain. I'll be fine, honey. Carla doesn't have any power over me anymore."

"I'll go with you. I need to talk to her anyway. We can go together."

That sounded like the worst idea ever.

"No. I can do this alone. I'm going to ask her a few questions about the case. That's it. Nothing personal."

Toni sputtered into her wine, dabbing at her lips with a napkin. "And just how do you propose to keep the personal out of it? Carla won't play by the rules, Wyatt. You know that. She'll twist it all around and make you out to be the bad guy. I've seen it in action."

So had he.

"I know you might have a hard time believing this but Carla did not get her way all the time when she and I were married. I was on to her tricks fairly quickly and squashed her plans for minions and world domination whenever they rose up. I think that's why she ended up leaving me for Trevor. Whenever I was home from deployment, she found she couldn't do whatever the hell she wanted. She was anxious to see the back of me."

"I didn't mean to imply–"

"I'm sure you didn't but there has to be a part of you that wonders why I stayed with her. I bet it makes you respect me just a little less. Be honest."

Slumping in her chair, Toni nodded glumly. "Maybe. But I know how she pulls in people by being all wonderful and then how she treats you when she thinks she has you. But you stayed with her a long time. Years. It just seems like you should have figured it out earlier."

For the first time in a long time, Wyatt wanted someone's respect. That was the only reason he was picking at this particular scab. He reached out for her hand and tugged her to her feet, pulling her onto his lap and wrapping his arms around her securely. "I did figure it out early, honey. But you have to understand there were two reasons I stayed married to her. One, I was deployed for the majority of our marriage and frankly didn't have the time or the energy to deal with the state of our relationship. At first it seemed nice to have someone to come home to, although later even that turned on me. With everything going on, everything I'd seen over there, a crappy marriage was such a little thing."

Toni grazed his stubbly cheek with her soft fingers.

"And two?"

"I know it's an old-fashioned concept but I was brought up that marriage was forever. That I had to somehow make it work. Leaving wasn't an option but when she left me it was a relief."

For a long time he'd felt a landslide of guilt about that.

"That makes sense. I guess I simply wondered if there was

something about her that made you stay."

"There was. Our wedding vows."

Nodding, she seemed to understand. "I'm in sort of the same position. Trying to have any kind of relationship with my family that I can but knowing that it's really a losing battle. They're not going to change and neither am I. It's long past time to cut the ties. If they can't treat me the way I deserve to be treated then I can't allow their toxicity in my life."

As much as he hated that Toni was going through this he had to agree with the sentiment. The Ross family didn't deserve to have her in it. Even in the early days when he'd been dating Carla, he'd seen how they'd treated Toni but not understanding it. There had been a part of him that had wondered what she'd done to earn that attitude.

Now he knew. Not a damn thing except refuse to be anyone but herself.

"If you set the boundaries, they might come around."

Toni rolled her eyes and laughed. "Do you really believe that or are you just saying it because you think it will make me feel better?"

"It could happen."

"I could sprout wings and fly but it's unlikely."

His chest tightened painfully at the sadness written on her face. He wished he could take away all the angst and replace it with joy.

But he knew from experience this was something she couldn't skip. Mourning the loss of her family was an essential part of moving on. He'd done the same after his divorce. He'd just done it too long.

All however, was not lost. He could be there for her in one way.

"I won't let you speak with Carla or your family about the money all by yourself. I'll be there with you, holding your hand and standing by your side. I won't let them browbeat you or be nasty to you."

Her hand cupped his jaw, her skin warm against his own. "You can't protect me."

"I can try," he retorted. "Let me be there for you, Toni. You're not alone anymore."

Just like that, they were a team. It had snuck up on him but there it was. They were a united front and it felt better than he'd ever thought possible.

Her smile was like sunshine breaking through the clouds and his heart sped up in response. This little female affected him as no one ever had. "Neither are you."

The kiss that followed was a promise, a pledge that they had one another's back, but it quickly turned into so much more that they were hot and breathless when they broke away. Toni's breasts rose and fell rapidly, her cheeks flushed and her lips swollen. She looked amazingly beautiful and Wyatt was over-come with the urge to sweep her up in his arms and carry her down the hall to the bedroom.

"Can dessert wait?"

The urgency in his tone was raw and needy, but he didn't hide it. Not with her. He could see the same emotion echoing back at him in her gaze.

"I'm hungry, but not for food."

Right answer.

Chapter Twenty-Eight

MAKING LOVE WITH Wyatt was different than anything Toni had ever experienced. Used to men that thought about their own pleasure more than hers, it was slightly unnerving to be the subject of such single-minded focus. Intent on bringing her to the heights of passion, he made slipping out of her clothes its own event, letting his rough hands slide over her skin as he tugged each garment off her body and tossed it away. Every touch to her sensitive flesh sent a jolt of electricity through her veins and her limbs grew heavy and languid as he stripped off her last sock before bending his head to press a kiss to her instep.

Thank goodness she'd showered at her hotel before coming over here for dinner or she would have been mortified. Luckily, she'd even managed to smear on some scented body lotion in anticipation of a romantic evening.

Wyatt trailed the tips of his fingers lightly up the soles of her foot and she giggled at the tickling sensation and tried to wriggle away. "No fair."

It was different. This playful, teasing side of him. He'd been the adult in his marriage to her sister, so perhaps he didn't get the opportunity to just have a little fun very often. She needed to do something about that.

"All's fair," he chuckled, running his tongue up her arch and around her ankle bones sending her entire being into a tailspin. A moan escaped through her lips and she arched off the bed, her lids fluttering shut. It felt that damn good. "I think you like this."

"Whatever you do, don't stop."

He didn't. That talented mouth kissed a wet path up her legs and then back down again to tickle her other foot until she was writhing on the bed. Every touch of his lips ramped up the temperature inside of her until her abdomen was filled with molten heat. His tongue played with her belly button and she captured his head in her hands, her fingers digging into the scalp and running through his hair.

"Now," she urged breathlessly, the need almost overwhelming. "Don't make me wait."

"I've barely begun—"

She pressed her lips to his, cutting off his words as her tongue slipped inside his mouth, playing a game of tag with his own. "Next time you can draw this out all you like but I don't think I can wait another minute. Do you want me to beg?"

His answer was to rummage in the drawer of the bedside table for protection. He ripped it open with his teeth and with her help quickly rolled it on, although help might be a generous word. Toni's fingers were busy caressing every ridge and vein, the skin hot to the touch, and if anything she probably slowed him down.

Positioning himself between her thighs, he bent his head and captured a pouting nipple between his lips, causing her to arch off the mattress and moan her approval. "Wyatt. Now."

With one sure thrust he was deep inside of her, exactly where she needed him to be. Each sure stroke rubbed sweet spots inside of her that no man had ever found and she allowed her lids to drift shut as a liquid heat began to spread from her abdomen to every nook and cranny of her body. Her toes curled in ecstasy as they rocked together in perfect synchronicity, Wyatt's face tucked in the crook of her neck, his breath warm against her skin.

Her fingers curled into the muscles of his shoulders, holding on for all she was worth, needing something solid to keep her grounded or at any moment she might fly apart into a million shimmering pieces.

Wyatt grunted deep from his chest, his jaws snapped together tightly as he held back. She was ready to go over but she needed something more and her movements grew more frantic as she tried to push herself to that peak. Seeing her distress, Wyatt reached between them, rubbing circles around the swollen button, giving her the friction she desperately needed.

Fireworks burst behind her eyelids as blood roared in her ears, blocking out the world and all its trials and tribulations. At this moment, there was only her and Wyatt in this private universe they'd created. They couldn't stay there forever but she could revel in it for a short time, savoring every ounce of pleasure as if it were her last.

When they collapsed in a heap of arms and legs, Toni stroked Wyatt's damp back, feeling the muscles move and bunch under her touch. He was nipping at her shoulder and she giggled when he ran his tongue over the flesh, tickling and soothing at the same time. As good as the sex was – and it was out of this world – this was good too. The closeness, the cuddling, the feeling that they had nothing to do, no responsibilities to worry about.

Eventually, Wyatt rolled onto his back taking her with him, her head pillowed on his shoulder. She enjoyed the quiet for awhile but her stomach had other ideas. With a loud gurgle it demanded dessert and she groaned, hiding her face in the sheet.

Now is not the moment, stomach.

"This was supposed to be romantic," she whined when he levered to a sitting position and tugged the sheet away from her flaming face. "So much for being sexy and mysterious."

He gave her a lopsided grin. "Was that what you were going for, honey? Personally, I like a woman who can just be herself. It lets me know that I can just be who I am as well."

Sniffing delicately, she retreated to the pile of pillows against the headboard. "Does who you are like dessert and if so, would they be willing to go down to the kitchen and bring some up here?"

Barking with laughter, Wyatt slid from the bed and pulled on a pair of black boxers. "Who I am is also hungry and would be happy to. Wait here."

She had a sneaky suspicion she'd wait on him anytime and anywhere.

Chapter Twenty-Nine

WYATT AND TONI stood on the steps of Trevor and Carla's home in Harper Falls, neither one eager to push the doorbell. It had been over five years since he had seen his ex-wife and it wouldn't have bothered him to go for fifty or more, but it wasn't to be. Even if he didn't need to speak to her, he wouldn't allow Toni to step into the lion's den all by herself. She was a strong woman but she had a soft heart. Carla wasn't above playing dirty to get what she wanted.

Toni nudged his arm. "Are you going to ring the doorbell?"

"I thought you were going to do it."

Rolling her eyes, she reached across him and pressed the button. "Very funny. Let's try and act like we're not in hell even though we clearly are."

"I think we should reward ourselves in some way if we get out of here in one piece. How about pie or ice cream?"

Toni snorted and dug her elbow into his ribs. "If I get out of here alive I want pie *and* ice cream. None of this either-or crap. Oh, and a pony too."

Wyatt smirked as he watched a figure coming towards them through the window by the door. "He can keep my unicorn company and we can go for rides in the moonlight."

Laughter bubbled up and she had to grab his arm and yank hard on it to keep from bursting into laughter just as the door swung open. Carla stood there, her gaze darting back and forth, from Toni to Wyatt and back again. They'd surprised her by showing up together and that was just the beginning.

"Carla, I think we need to talk."

He and Toni had agreed he'd take the lead in the discussion, although he was to step back if the conversation veered toward money and whether his ex's sudden need for cash had anything to do with the case he was working on. He hoped it didn't go that way but his ex was unpredictable.

Carla scowled at both of them and looked over her shoulder for a moment before turning back to them. "I never thought to see you again, Wyatt. You look good."

He could feel Toni stiffen beside him so he reached behind her and placed his arm around her waist, trying to settle her down. She had nothing to worry about. When Carla had opened the door he'd felt nothing. Not anger. Not hurt. No pleasant nostalgia. No shame. And certainly no attraction. It was if that part of his life was so far in the rear view mirror it was barely a distant memory. An instructive one, of course, but it no longer wielded any power.

"Can we come in or do you want to talk out here where your neighbors can see?"

Carla's lips turned up at the corners in a calculating smile. He could practically see the wheels whirring in her head as she tried to figure out what they were doing on her doorstep.

"I might let my baby sister in, Wyatt, but give me one good

reason I should let you past the threshold?"

He'd been prepared for that question.

"Mandy Hoskins."

Fury passed over Carla's face so quickly a stranger would have missed it but it was clear as day to Wyatt. She was a master at hiding her true emotions but she was getting sloppy. She swallowed hard and stepped back, allowing them to pass.

His hand still on Toni's lower back, he guided them into the opulent home and followed Carla into a living room off the foyer. The room was light and airy with high ceilings and gleaming wood floors. He sunk into the sofa cushion and pulled his phone from his pocket, setting it on the coffee table in case he needed to record something. Carla sat opposite the two of them on an uncomfortable looking dark oak Queen Anne chair.

Carla folded her hands in her lap, looking calm and composed. "I'm not sure how I can help you." Her eye narrowed at her younger sister. "Both of you. What's your interest in this, Toni?"

Crossing one leg over the other, Toni sat back and studied her older sister. "I'm curious as to whether your recent financial difficulties have anything in common with your ties to Mandy Hoskins."

To Carla's credit she didn't even flinch, although Wyatt noticed a definite iciness in her blue eyes as she gazed at her sister. There was certainly no love lost between these women. It was worse than it had been years ago.

"I don't have any ties to Mandy Hoskins," Carla replied smoothly, her fingers steepling together on her lap. "She worked for Trevor and then she left."

"You were at her wake," Toni observed.

"Lots of people were there. You were there too and you never met her. I was simply paying my respects to a former employee, that's all." Carla leaned forward, her gaze raking Toni head to toe before moving on to Wyatt. "Why are you here together? I didn't even think you two liked each other."

"Focus, Carla," he said sharply. She was taking the conversation away from the subject at hand which he was sure was intentional. "I'm here to talk about Mandy, not my relationship with Toni."

Her brows shot up to her hairline and she laughed as if hearing the most ridiculous joke.

"Relationship? You two have a relationship? She's hardly your type, darling. Really, I think you could do better."

No, he couldn't. Toni was the best he'd ever found and he'd be a fool to let her go.

"Did you have someone in mind, big sister? I hear you're back on the market these days."

Damn, she was feisty. He shouldn't be proud of her but she was staying in control even when pushed.

This time Carla did betray some agitation, her hand fluttering to her throat in a protective motion. "I'm sure I don't know what you mean. My marriage is fine."

Wyatt could have argued that point, but honestly, he didn't care enough to do it. Her marriage was her issue and he didn't want to get himself – or Toni – involved.

Time to redirect. Again.

"Trevor was seeing Mandy before you got married, correct?"

"He was but I don't think it was serious or anything."

The opposite of what Trevor had said. Interesting. Wyatt wasn't inclined to believe one of them over the other. They'd both lied numerous times.

"So he wasn't upset when she disappeared?"

Fidgeting with the hem of her blouse, Carla seemed to consider the question. "I don't think upset is the correct term. He was disturbed that she'd left without a word. After all, she was working for him and that left him in a difficult position at the office."

"And you two began seeing each other soon after?"

"Should we be talking about this? I don't want to bring up bad memories that will only hurt us both, Wyatt."

Funny, this didn't bother him at all. He'd moved past it and seen the entire time for what it was. He deserved better and he'd found it.

"I'm okay with it," he assured his ex-wife. "So you started dating after Mandy disappeared?"

Her fingers tightened on the arm of her chair, not happy with his response. "Something like that. It was years ago, after all, and I didn't keep a diary. Does it matter?"

It might matter that her husband was pointing the finger at her for a felony.

"It does. I went to speak with Trevor yesterday about Mandy." The knuckles on her hands turned white where she was gripping the chair. "He has quite a different story to tell. He says he wanted to marry Mandy and he said that he wouldn't put it past you to be her stalker."

Carla's lips trembled and she shot out of the chair, her arms crossed over her chest. "I don't have to listen to this. Trevor is crazy to have said something like that."

"Why would he say it then?"

"We had a fight a few days ago. Maybe he's still angry."

Toni's eyes went wide and she stared at her sister with horror. "Holy shit, you had to make him pretty pissed off for your own husband and father of your child to try and throw you under the bus for a crime you didn't commit."

To Carla's credit she tried to defend her husband. "He didn't mean it. We had an argument and he wants to hurt me. It's no big deal."

"It's a big deal to me," Toni declared, rising to pace the room. "What kind of person does something like that?"

Toni was allowing herself to get dragged into the middle of her sister's marriage and Wyatt needed to put an immediate stop to it. She was too trusting and caring, no matter how much she tried to show her tough, businesswoman side. Nothing good could come from this.

Carla also stood, tears welling in her eyes. "Trevor can be difficult and moody. That's why I need your help, Toni. You're my last hope."

Stopping in her tracks, Toni turned to her sister. "What do you mean?"

"I know Mom has talked to you about lending me some money. If Trevor didn't have all these financial pressures on his back, I know that he wouldn't be so hard on me and Katie. He just needs a little bit of breathing room."

And I'm a monkey's uncle.

Intently watching Toni, Wyatt held his breath. Was she buying this tearful act?

"It's not you but Trevor that needs the money?"

Carla nodded, relief showing in her expression. "Exactly. Business has been slow and the stress on him has been terrible."

Toni tapped her chin and then smiled. "I'll write his company a check."

Carla's head jerked up in surprise and she moved to stand in front of her little sister. "No! I mean, he has his pride. You can just write me the check and I'll sneak it into the bank account. No one has to know."

Toni looked at Wyatt then back at Carla. "We'll know. Mom and Dad will know. Somehow the accountant at the firm will know and I doubt it will stay a secret. No, it's best if everything is out in the open. I'll have my accountant call Trevor tomorrow and they can draw up loan papers. I'm sure he'll want to make this as official as possible."

"Just write me a check," Carla said through gritted teeth. "It's not a big deal."

Toni smiled and Wyatt breathed a sigh of relief. She hadn't fallen for her sister's act. Thank God.

"I don't think so. I told Mom how things would be and I haven't changed my mind. The fact is I wouldn't write you a check with a gun to my head. If this money is truly for Trevor, then I'll deal with him."

It happened so fast, Wyatt couldn't stop it. Carla raised her hand and slapped Toni hard across the face, the smacking sound echoing off the twelve foot ceilings. Wyatt shot to his feet and inserted himself between the women, his arms gently cradling Toni. He should have seen it coming.

"Bitch," Carla spat, her skin a mottled red of fury. "You

think you're better than everyone else, dressing in black and drawing skulls and witches. It's no wonder our parents like me best."

Toni was cradling her crimson cheek and her eyes were bright with tears, but her chin was lifted in defiance. Toni was pissed the hell off. Another reason for them both to get the hell out of here. If it ever came to a catfight between the two women, Wyatt's money was on Toni. She might be little but she was scrappy and determined. She wouldn't care if she got dirty and messy.

"Back off," he barked at his ex-wife. "What the hell is wrong with you? She's your own flesh and blood, for Christ's sake. Do you ever think about anyone but yourself?"

Carla was shaking a finger at Toni. "She started it."

No wonder I liked being deployed thousands of miles away.

"Well, I'm ending it. We're leaving."

"That saves me from having to throw you out." Her lips were pressed so tightly they disappeared into her face. "I know why you came here. You think I killed Mandy, but I didn't. I didn't like the pale-faced wimp but I didn't stalk or kill her. Frankly, she was no competition to me. I already had Trevor."

Wyatt looked down at the woman who had shared his home and name for the longest time. He had no idea what he'd ever seen in her and he felt sorry for the naive young man he'd been. Her flattery and attention had caused him to close his eyes to what she really was and he'd kept them closed in an effort to salvage whatever he could from their relationship.

What had he learned? Never underestimate the stupidity of a young man in lust nor the ability of the human mind to fool itself and rationalize all sorts of shit that wasn't true.

At some point, Toni had rounded him and was now standing next to her sister, a vivid handprint still branding her cheek. "If you're what I have to be to get Mom and Dad's love I think I'll pass. I give up, Carla. You win. They're all yours and honestly nothing really changes because they've always been yours. From this moment forward I am removing all toxic people from my life. You never have to see me again."

Feeling a mixture of pride and sadness for Toni, he wrapped his arm around her shoulders and led her toward the door. The whole visit had been one giant clusterfuck.

He'd found a peace with his past but now Toni was an outcast in her family.

Quietly they climbed into the truck and pulled away. Wyatt didn't say anything because he didn't know what to say at a moment like this. Silence seemed like the best option. He'd wait for Toni to speak. They were at the Harper Falls city limits when she finally did.

"I don't think Carla did anything to Mandy. She's a lot of crappy things but she's not a stalker or a killer."

"Those are generous words about a woman that hit you less than thirty minutes ago. I'm not sure I would be that charitable, honey. You're a better person than I am."

Toni slumped in her seat and gave a heavy, tired sigh. "Would you believe it's not the first time?"

"Yes, and you're still a better person."

"I'm just a tired person. Tired of begging for the scraps of affection my parents toss my way occasionally. I'm tired of twisting myself into a pretzel to be something I'm clearly not to win their approval. They wanted a blonde, blue-eyed beauty queen and they ended up with me. It's their right to be disappointed but it's also my right to decide when I can't take any more. I'm there. Finally. It doesn't feel all that bad, actually. It's kind of a relief."

Wyatt reached over and placed his hand on top of hers. "I know I'm not much but you have me, honey, and you don't have to be anything but yourself."

"You can just be who you are too."

He only hoped he would be enough.

Chapter Thirty

TONI FELT LIKE a huge weight had been lifted from her shoulders. She realized that once she had given up on the idea of "winning" her parents' love, she was now free to be and do whatever she pleased. The little girl inside of her would probably always be sad but the women she was now had made peace. She'd be happier without her family. At least for now. People could change and if one of them reached out to her and sincerely wanted to make a connection she wouldn't slap their hand away.

Speaking of slap…

Wyatt had insisted on her putting some ice on her cheek even though she thought it might be overkill. It hadn't hurt any worse than those red gym balls that used to smack her in the nose when they'd played dodge ball on the playground and she hadn't been scarred for life then. Of course, she was happy to never play that game again. People were vicious and took winning much too seriously.

"I've got a bunch of chicken we can throw on the grill with some corn on the cob," Wyatt said, his head stuck in the refrigerator but it gave her a good view of his splendid backside. "If that doesn't sound good we can go into town."

"Chicken and corn on the cob sounds great. Besides, we need to go through that file one more time. What was it you said? Time to go back to the beginning?"

Wyatt put the chicken and a bottle of barbecue sauce on the counter and began assembling spices from the cabinets. "It's a standard technique when a case has no good leads. Back to basics. Go over motives and timelines. Anything that might aid us going in the right direction."

Toni had been anxious to help but even more so now that her own family was seemingly involved. She didn't think that Trevor and Carla had anything to do with Mandy's murder and for Katie's sake, she wanted the world to know that no matter how difficult things might be between her and her sibling.

"Can I help?"

Wyatt laughed and began sprinkling the chicken with salt and pepper. "With dinner or with the case? How about you shuck the corn? That should be safe enough."

"Funny. It's a good thing you're a great cook or I'd take major offense but instead I'm going to let you do all the work and feed me." Wrinkling her nose, she stood to assist but the peal of the doorbell interrupted her. "Are you expecting company?"

Wyatt frowned and shook his head, running his hands under some soap and water. "No, not at all."

He strode to the door and looked through the peephole – the one she was too short to see through – and grinned. Yanking the door open, he laughed and welcomed a handsome blond man into the living room, slapping him on the back.

"Dammit, Logan, I had no idea you were coming here. I

would have picked you up at the airport or something. Get in here and tell me what's going on."

The man named Logan lugged a duffel bag into the center of the room and tossed it on the floor. "Jason sent me. I'm here to help with your case. And I didn't fly in, so you couldn't pick me up at the airport. I drove. I was about twelve hours away and I've been on the road since before dawn. I don't suppose you have any beer in this house?"

"That I do. Come on in and take a load off. You've been in the truck all day?"

Logan trailed after them into the kitchen. "I have and if you don't mind I'll stand for awhile. Sitting on my ass for hours is not my idea of fun. I need to stretch my legs."

Wyatt retrieved a beer from the refrigerator and handed it to Logan before putting his arm around Toni's shoulders. "Toni, I want you to meet my friend and boss, Logan Wright. Logan, this is Antonia Ross, the owner of the haunted hotel and also my friend."

Logan did everything but waggle his eyebrows. Clearly, he could see there was more going on between her and Wyatt than simply friendship but to his credit he finally just grinned and took a swig from the bottle. "It's very nice to meet you, Toni. Is that chicken you're fixing for dinner?"

Toni had to laugh at his hopeful expression. "It is but I'm not the one cooking it, Wyatt is. And yes, there is plenty to go around."

"That is good news. Now why don't we let Wyatt do all the work while I tell you stories about him?"

Wyatt shook his head and smiled as he washed his hands

again, ready to cook. "Go right ahead. West is the one with the embarrassing ones. Besides, Toni and I have known each other for years. She might have a few to tell you."

Logan was easygoing and fun to be around. During dinner, he didn't just tell stories about Wyatt, he told stories about all the guys at the consulting firm and even a few from his own wild childhood, stopping only to take a call from his wife. From the soft expression he wore while they spoke, it was clear he was deeply in love with the woman named Ava. He also talked to his toddler twins, which was hilarious as he sang "Itsy Bitsy Spider" into the phone. Big macho former cop definitely had a gooey heart for his family and Toni couldn't help but like the guy.

They all three helped clear the table and did the dishes, although it was pretty tight in Wyatt's small kitchen. By the time she sat down in the living room and spread out the file on the coffee table, it was almost nine o'clock at night.

Sitting on the floor, they each took a section – Logan the photos, Wyatt the police reports, and Toni the statements. There was no sound in the room except the shuffling of papers and a sigh every now and then. Eventually they traded until they had each seen the entire file. Wyatt stood and retrieved three sodas from the kitchen and placed them on the table. No one had said a word yet and Toni couldn't take it anymore.

"So...what do you think? I'm not a cop or anything so I'm not sure if this file looks normal or not."

Logan leaned back against the couch, stretching out his long, denim-clad legs. "Let me ask you a question first. Now that you've read the file, what do you think about the case? Is your intuition saying anything?"

Toni thought about the question and everything she'd studied in the last hour. "It was low on details. It felt like they barely did any investigation at all. They couldn't prove anything and they had no forensics or clues. It seems like they were relieved to decide that her stalker was Trevor but that they couldn't prove it."

"You're smart," Logan observed. "You could have been a cop. Or maybe a mystery writer like Ava."

"Don't give her any ideas," Wyatt growled. "I have enough difficulty keeping her out of trouble. She likes to think she's invincible."

"I do not," Toni retorted. "I simply like to take care of myself, that's all. I don't think I'm a superhero or anything."

"Well, your instincts are good." Logan pointed to the copies of letters from the stalker. "Better than the cop that did this investigation. Did you notice anything when you read through these? Something jumped out at me and I bet it did for Wyatt too."

Wyatt nodded gravely. "I was thinking it was just me but since you see it too… There were way too many personal details for the stalker to be a stranger. It had to be someone that knew her well, maybe even lived with or close to her."

"That's what made them creepy." Toni shuddered as she remembered how the stalker would talk about Mandy's clothes, meals, books, and television shows. "It was like he had a camera on her personal life twenty-four hours a day."

Logan pounced on her comment. "But he didn't because they checked for hidden cameras and bugs. None were found. That's the clue. Right there. They missed it."

Frowning, Toni shook her head, confused. "It could still be Trevor though. He spent every day with her and she could have told him that personal stuff."

"If she told him why would it creep her out? No, these were details only someone very close to her would have known."

"Someone who lived with her," Toni murmured, the picture becoming clear. "But that means…"

Wyatt slapped down the soda can on the table. "Her husband. Cole Hoskins. He had access and more than a little motive—after all, his wife was having an affair. Jesus, if you look through this file it's like they didn't even look at him seriously. They barely talked to him. He was given a pass from day one."

Logan's eyes narrowed and he lifted the stack of papers from the file and then dropped them down again with disgust. "The most dangerous person for a woman is the man in her life. Statistically speaking, that is. So it's mind-blowing that they didn't bother to investigate him at all. He should have been their first and strongest suspect."

"Why would a husband pretend to stalk his own wife?" Toni asked. "It doesn't make any sense to me."

Wyatt gathered the papers together and slipped them back into the folder. "Maybe he was angry about her having an affair. Maybe they had a very unhappy marriage and they got on each other's nerves and this was his way of getting back at her. Maybe he was using it to set up her murder and create a scapegoat. I've seen people do some evil shit to the person they supposedly love. I'm not surprised by it anymore."

Considering her own family, Toni shouldn't be shocked either. "So what happens next?"

Logan pulled his phone from his jeans pocket. "We call Jared and ask him to dig up what he can on Cole Hoskins. We might see something in his past or finances."

"We also go see Sheriff Bickham tomorrow and ask him why the investigation never focused on Hoskins," Wyatt replied. "Plus we contact Sheriff Sullivan here in town and ask him to get a warrant for Hoskins' home and bring him in for questioning. I'm assuming he'd lawyer up but we can try."

"Why do you assume that?"

"I assume everyone will," Wyatt replied with a laugh. "I'm cynical that way, honey. It wouldn't be smart to talk to an experienced lawman without an attorney whether you were guilty or innocent."

Logan had walked into the kitchen to talk to his friend and co-worker, leaving Wyatt and Toni alone. "So what do we do now?"

Wyatt stood and pulled her to her feet before pressing a tender kiss to her lips that left her breathless and wanting more. "You don't do a thing. You go back to the estate tomorrow and continue with the renovation crew. Logan and I will go talk to the sheriffs and get the warrant moving. If Cole Hoskins is the stalker, and maybe even the killer of his own wife, justice has waited for over five years. It can wait one or two more days. He has no idea we've decided to focus the investigation his way. He thinks he's in the clear."

It could wait but Toni was the impatient type. If Hoskins had terrorized and murdered Mandy, she hoped Wyatt and Logan could prove it. Then Mandy could finally rest in peace.

Chapter Thirty-One

THE NEXT DAY Wyatt and Logan spent the morning with Sheriff Sullivan pulling their case together so he could request a warrant to search Hoskins' home and business. After much discussion, they'd decided not to tip him off by questioning him until they executed the search warrant. That way he wouldn't have the opportunity to get rid of anything incriminating, supposing that he still had evidence all this time later. That was why cold cases were so hard to solve. Witnesses disappeared or died. Evidence was lost. Memories faded.

Once they had that organized they headed to Harper Falls to see Sheriff Bickham but he was out on a call. They ended up spending most of the afternoon shooting pool and darts at the local watering hole waiting for him to come back. It was after five o'clock when Logan's phone rang. It was Jared and from the grim sound of his voice they were on the right track with Hoskins.

Not wanting anyone to overhear, they exited the bar and sat in the truck, putting Jared on speaker.

"Okay, shoot," Logan said. "Wyatt's taking notes if we need to write something down."

Jared Monroe was Logan and Jason's partner but he tried to stay close to home, which was Seattle. His impressive computer skills had saved their bacon on more than one occasion and Wyatt hoped this case wouldn't be the exception. They had very little on Hoskins and getting a warrant wasn't a slam dunk by any means.

"As soon as we're done here, I'll email you all the information," Jared replied, his voice sounding muffled on the cell. He was probably at home with his wife and young daughter and didn't want to wake her from her nap. "So I checked into this Hoskins' background. Turns out Mandy wasn't his first wife. She was his second, actually. The first Mrs. Hoskins died in a tragic drowning incident in Minnesota where they lived. She and Hoskins were out on his boat and she fell overboard. According to his testimony, he jumped in the water to try and save her but she'd disappeared. They had to drag the lake to find her body. She had a contusion on the back of her head, which Hoskins said was from falling on the boat. Her death was ruled accidental."

"Accidental, my ass," Logan growled. "So that's two women with bashed-in skulls that made the mistake of marrying this asshole. That's enough for me."

Jared snorted. "It doesn't have to be. Hoskins' behavior has been strange to say the least. His dad was in the military and they traveled all over the world, never staying in one place too long. When Hoskins became an adult, he continued to do that, taking jobs all over the country. As a computer programmer, he could get a job pretty much anywhere. He moved at least once a year, taking contract after contract."

Wyatt groaned, his fingers tightening painfully on the pencil. He'd met this guy and it hadn't tripped any of his radars. He'd been too preoccupied with Mandy's death and Carla's appearance. Sure, he'd questioned Bickham in the beginning but he'd accepted the "he didn't do it" explanation without pushing back at all.

Fuck.

"I was in the same room with the asshole. I talked to him."

"Don't do this to yourself," Logan ground out. "Ted Bundy was considered charming and intelligent by friends and police alike. I'm guessing that Cole Hoskins is cut from the same cloth. We're going to have to check every place he's ever lived for missing women. If he's killed twice there's a good chance those aren't isolated incidents."

"He seemed genuinely tore up. Like he really loved her."

"Sociopaths are terrific actors because they really believe what they're saying," Jared replied. "That's why they can pass polygraphs too, so don't let him suggest taking one to clear his name."

"This is all speculation," Logan pointed out, his tone reluctant. "We could be jumping on the wrong bandwagon. Maybe his wife did die tragically and Mandy was chased from his life by a stalker that wasn't him."

"Could be," Wyatt conceded. "But if we're not wrong then any woman in Hoskins' life could be in danger. We need to find out if he has a girlfriend."

Jared clear his throat loudly. "Do you think I half-assed this, gentlemen? I checked and he does have a girlfriend. Her name is Virginia Hodell and she's thirty years old. She works as a kindergarten teacher in the Harper Falls school district."

"He likes them young," Logan muttered. "When did he start dating her? Was he seeing her when he was married?"

They heard Jared shuffling some papers. "Supposedly he started dating her about eight months after Mandy's death but his credit card transactions tell a different story. Dinners at fancy restaurants. Hotel charges from out of town. Lingerie purchases. All from about six months before Mandy disappeared. Unless he wears that shit himself and if so, I don't want to know about that."

Wyatt didn't care of Cole Hoskins wore pink panties every day of the year. He only cared if he killed his wife. Or both of them, for that matter. They talked a little more with Jared and then ended the call, both Logan and Wyatt quiet as they worked through all they had learned.

"What are you thinking?" Wyatt finally asked Logan. "You're the only man I know who has solved a serial killer case. Does this look like one? Do you think we might have that here?"

"I'm not sure," Logan said slowly, his expression a mask of concentration. He was probably thinking about the vigilante case that he'd closed and how close to home it hit for him. "This could be. My gut tells me that at the very least this Hoskins guy stalked his own wife, but whether he killed her is another matter—although it's not necessarily a huge jump from stalking to murder. It happens every day."

Wyatt's phone buzzed and he checked the incoming text. "It's the sheriff. He's back in the office and ready to talk to us. I'll send Toni a text and let her know we'll be late picking her up. She's always saying she has lots of paperwork so hopefully that can keep her busy. I think the crew will be working late as well to try and make up some of the schedule so she won't be alone."

"Let's go then. I'm anxious to find out what Bickham thinks of Hoskins and whether he knew about the previous wife."

Wyatt's guess was a big, fat no.

TONI STRETCHED HER arms over her head and yawned widely, fatigue beginning to get the better of her. After Wyatt and Logan had dropped her off this morning at the estate, she'd spent the better part of the day working on the pathway or dealing with the crew sent out to install the below ground pool. The hole was dug and pipes installed, plus the concrete was schedule for day after tomorrow. With any luck, it would be ready by the opening.

A cool breeze wafted through the small makeshift office and she twisted the lid off a bottle of water and took a long swallow. The day had been hot but the temperature had dropped quite a bit and the house was comfortable with just a few windows open. The heatwave was finally over and more reasonable weather should prevail, which was a relief not only for her but all the workers on the site.

Grimacing at her laptop, she cracked her neck as she tried to buckle down and get back to the reports and emails she should be reviewing. A business didn't run itself and although she had an excellent staff, some things needed her attention and wouldn't wait. She'd sent some new designs to her fabrication department head and he'd sent back a few tweaks that might make construction easier. He needed her to review them and say yes or no. Her first reaction was to say yes but she needed to be sure.

She didn't get far, however, as her phone rang and interrupted her concentration. It was from a number she didn't recognize and for a moment she thought about sending it to voicemail, but then remembered that Wyatt was with Logan and this call could be from him.

"Hello."

"Hi, is this Antonia Ross? I'm Jason Anderson. I work with Wyatt."

Ah yes. Antonia relaxed back in the uncomfortable metal chair, her butt almost numb. She remembered this man's name. He was Wyatt's boss; one of them, anyway.

"Yes, hello, Mr. Anderson. What can I do for you?"

"I have some information for you, and please call me Jason."

Wyatt was lucky. Jason seemed like a nice man.

"Thank you, Jason, I will. What information do you have for me?"

There was a small silence before Jason answered. "Wyatt said that your sister was asking for a loan and he wanted me to check out their finances since you weren't getting any answers from your family. I hope he told you I was going to do that."

Wyatt had but with everything going on…

"He did," she assured Jason. "I've had a lot going on here and it slipped my mind."

"Wyatt said you're opening a haunted hotel," Jason chuckled. "I have to tell you my wife Brinley would love something like that. Please let us know when you open. I'll bring her for a weekend."

She'd make sure he and his wife had the best suite in the joint. "We'd love to have you as our guests. Your wife likes ghosts and scary things?"

"She does. Halloween is an event around this house."

To Toni, Halloween wasn't a holiday. It was a complete way of life.

"That's wonderful. I can't wait to meet both of you in person."

"Looking forward to it. Now to get to your sister's finances." Jason cleared his throat and Toni thought he seemed rather reluctant to continue. "Your sister's husband owns a construction business, correct? From what I can see, the business is sound. No huge debts that I can find. His credit is solid and his reputation in the business community is outstanding. I don't see any red flags there."

"That's a relief. So they don't really need the money?"

It made it much easier to say no if that was the case.

"Well," Jason drew out the word. "I wouldn't say that. I dug into their personal accounts and they seem fine. They're house rich and cash poor but that's not all that unusual these days. His work is seasonal and that might account for cash flow issues."

Toni sighed. From Jason's cautious tone, she knew there was more he hadn't told her yet.

"I know I'm going to regret this but just say it. You found something awful, didn't you?"

"I did." Toni groaned and ran her fingers through her already mussed hair. This was going to be bad. "Your sister has gotten herself into serious personal debt."

"Personal debt," Toni repeated, her mind not comprehending the words. "Wait…what kind of personal debt?"

She'd asked although she was pretty sure what the answer was going to be.

"Your sister goes to New York and Los Angeles for shopping sprees. She stays in luxury hotels for days and orders room service and expensive spa services along with the mountains of designer clothes, handbags, and shoes she buys. She was able to keep up with the payments for awhile but I'm guessing the monthly minimums became too much to handle."

Leave it to Carla to get herself into trouble like this. She probably thought that she deserved to have all these things because she was so special and beautiful.

Dammit. Fuck.

"How much?" Toni croaked out the question, already doing math in her head. She couldn't allow her sister to be thrown out of her home. Not because she was concerned for Carla but Katie was another matter. For her, Toni would do most anything.

"Seventy-five thousand."

That was a hell of a lot of shoes. A lifetime's worth. How empty did Carla have to feel inside to think that expensive things would fill that void?

"When does she need it?"

She heard some shifting and shuffling in the background before Jason replied. "Listen, Toni. I don't want to stick my nose where it doesn't belong but your sister's husband makes enough money to pay this debt. They have enough stocks and bonds that they could sell. When I said they were cash poor, I didn't mean they didn't have any assets. They have plenty of assets that could be easily liquidated to take care of this. My guess is that your sister doesn't want her husband to know."

That explained Barbara's whole spiel about how they had to protect poor Trevor so he could feel like a man.

"Are you sure? They can pay it and not be broke?"

"I'm positive. It's not my place to give you advice but I can say with utmost confidence that they can pay this debt and move on with their life, unless of course there's something even worse out there that I wasn't able to find."

"Do you think you found everything?"

"Yes."

That was good enough for her. It was clear that Carla and Barbara, and possible Dad too, was playing Toni for the money. Save Carla's marriage at the youngest daughter's expense.

It hurt even though Toni had made her peace with her family situation.

"I appreciate all your help, Jason. More than you know."

"I think I can imagine. I'll let you go then. Goodnight and I hope we meet soon."

"Me too. Thank you again."

Placing her phone down on the desk, Toni stood and walked over to the windows staring into the pitch black night, only the sounds of the crickets to keep her company. The old Toni would have simply let this go and been silent but the new Toni wasn't going to keep her mouth shut.

She walked back to the desk and picked up her phone, pressing the speed dial for her parents.

Time to stand up for herself.

Chapter Thirty-Two

BICKHAM FROWNED AND shook his head. "You boys are barking up the wrong tree with Hoskins. I've never seen a man so broken up when Mandy disappeared nor a man more determined to have justice when she was being stalked. He was a devoted husband."

"But you never spoke with him as a suspect?" Wyatt pressed. "It never crossed your mind?"

The sheriff's face was red and he shifted uncomfortably in his chair. "What you don't seem to understand is that Cole Hoskins is a respected member of the community here in Harper Falls. He volunteers at a soup kitchen and runs the annual town rummage sale for the benefit of the children's charity. He's been on the town council for the last four years and works on civic affairs. He co-sponsors a Little League team. There is no way that he stalked or killed his own wife."

Hoskins had worked hard in the last five years to be seen as an upstanding citizen. Almost too hard, perhaps, if his actions were looked at through this new lens.

Logan leaned forward, his expression neutral. "Then you knew Hoskins was married before Mandy? And you knew she died of drowning despite being a strong swimmer?"

The man's mouth gaped open like a fish out of water. "I–I–I didn't know that but it doesn't change a thing. Cole Hoskins is a pillar of the community. If he was married before it was his business. He was probably too broken up to speak about it."

"Possibly," Logan conceded. "His first wife was inebriated the night she drowned so it may have all been a tragic accident. But when a man loses two wives before the age of thirty-five it makes me pause and think about things. He might have the worst luck in the world in relationships or he's helping these women into the great hereafter."

Tiny beads of sweat had broken out onto the sheriff's fore-head. "I'll admit it does look suspicious. In light of that knowledge, I might have looked at him more closely when Mandy disappeared." Bickham wasn't going to go down without a fight. "But he hired a private investigator to look for the stalker. What man would do that if he was stalking his own wife? What is the point of all of it?"

Wyatt rested his ankle on his opposite knee. "About that. My firm checked with the private investigator and he basically found nothing actionable. In fact, the leads that Hoskins had him check out all seemed to go nowhere. As for why a man would hire someone to investigate himself? I'm guessing a man who wanted to control the case. Wanted to know everything that was happening and push it in the direction he wanted it to go."

"And the reason he was stalking his own wife?" Logan que-ried. "I think Cole Hoskins was planning to kill Mandy and he wanted someone to blame it on. A shadow to keep the cops busy while he plotted and planned. He invented a stalker and all eyes were on this pretend person. In the meantime, Hoskins killed Mandy and garnered all the attention and sympathy."

It was simply theory at the moment but Wyatt's gut was talking loud and clear, right along with Logan's own intuition. Hoskins had never been truly investigated and they would be derelict in their duty not to question him.

"I just can't believe it." Bickham shook his head. "He's a good man. He's a friend to everyone."

Logan gave Wyatt a cynical glance that said all the things they wouldn't say out loud. Like perhaps the sheriff should have recused himself from the case if he was friends with the husband. Or that they should have spoken to the private investigator, which it appeared they never did. They'd trusted Hoskins' word instead.

"I hope I'm wrong," Wyatt said, feeling distinctly sorry for the lawman although it was tempered with a dose of anger. Bickham had let his personal feelings cloud his judgment. "We're trying to get a warrant to search his home and workplace. If we can get it, then we'll question him after we serve it."

"You don't want to talk to him now?" the sheriff asked with a frown. "I can call him and get him over here."

Wyatt held up his hand. "Don't. We don't want to tip him off that we're looking at him yet. I don't want him to have a chance to get rid of anything incriminating he might still have before we can get the warrant."

"Whatever you say." Bickham straightened in his chair. "How can I help you?"

"Keep this quiet," Logan answered bluntly. "Don't even mention it to your deputies. News has a way of traveling around a small town and we need the element of surprise on our side. Can you do that for us?"

"I can," Bickham promised. "You can trust me."

Wyatt and Logan stood, the meeting at an end. He hadn't enjoyed making the sheriff look bad but the man had made a few mistakes that couldn't be ignored. Luckily, he was still cooperating.

"Thanks for seeing us after such a long day." Wyatt shook Bickham's hand. "I'm sure you want to get home and eat dinner with your family."

"I'm headed there in a few minutes. Just have some paperwork to finish."

Logan thanked Bickham as well and they headed out to the vehicle.

"What do you think?" Logan asked Wyatt. "Because I think that was a strange conversation."

"I can't argue that. It's hard not to wonder if Bickham suspected Hoskins but they were friends—or they were friends—and Bickham never suspected a thing. Either way, he doesn't come out of this looking all that good. I also question his ability to keep this quiet."

It didn't really matter either way. They had to deal with where they were now. Crossing his fingers, Wyatt hoped for good news about the warrant. Hoskins might be the key to the case.

He fired up the engine and put the truck in reverse. "Let's stop and see how that warrant is shaping up and then we can go pick up Toni and get some dinner. We can fill her in on the case over a steak and potato."

✦　✦　✦

SHERIFF BICKHAM'S SHAKING hand hovered over his phone. The two consultants had just left his office and he was still reeling from their accusations. They honestly believed Cole Hoskins might have stalked and killed his beloved wife.

Bickham didn't believe it. He'd seen Cole and Mandy together and how happy they were.

Well, except for the fact that she was having an affair. Cole had said he forgave her, that he was a difficult man to live with, and Bickham had believed him. After all, everyone in town admired Cole and trusted him.

With a grunt of self-disgust, Bickham grabbed the receiver and brought it to his ear, dialing the familiar number. It rang a few times but his friend picked up.

"Cole? It's Gary. Listen to me carefully, will you? Those law enforcement consultants that are working on Mandy's case? They just left my office. I need to warn you that they're looking at you, buddy. I know, I know. I told them you were devastated when Mandy disappeared but they have no leads so they're flailing and looking anywhere they can. They're going to try and get a warrant for your home and work, then try and question you. You may want to get a lawyer."

The conversation went on for a few minutes and then the call ended. The sheriff sighed in relief, feeling better than he had since Stone and Wright entered his office. He'd done the right thing. His friend shouldn't have to be victimized again after all he'd been through. He couldn't let a couple of outsiders come into town and open up old wounds. It was his job to protect the residents of Harper Falls and that's just what he intended to do.

Staring at the phone, Bickham realized he hadn't asked Cole about his first wife. The one that he'd never mentioned before. He made a mental note to do that the next day. It had been too long since they'd hung out and had a couple of beers.

Chapter Thirty-Three

I T WAS LATE and Toni was exhausted. Wyatt had texted her about an hour ago that both he and Logan were talking to the sheriff about the warrant and Cole Hoskins. She'd assured him she was fine to stay at the site a little longer but after a more than twelve hour day she wanted a long hot bath and a pizza. Extra cheese and sausage. Luckily, he and Logan should be showing up any minute as it was almost ten o'clock and he was a punctual man. Maybe because of his time in the military.

Standing, she wandered over to the open windows where a cool breeze wafted over her skin, the smell of cut grass and fresh earth tickling her nose. The air refreshed her senses and helped wake her up after sitting at the desk for way too long. Paperwork was not her idea of fun.

Leaning against the window frame, she listened to the crickets in the distance and the rustle of leaves against the house. After a day of heavy machinery it was so peaceful.

She frowned as a different noise was carried to her on the wind. It sounded like voices but that was impossible. All the workmen were gone for the day hours ago. She was alone.

Straining her ears, she listened intently and again heard what sounded like a man and a woman speaking – one voice deeper than the other. Those voices shouldn't be here. For a moment, her gut clenched at the thought of visiting spirits in her backyard.

I must be delirious with overwork.

Toni snorted and shook her head at her foolishness. She didn't believe in ghosts, goblins or witches. But she did believe in people and their inherent curiosity. The realtor had warned her and apparently she'd been lucky up until now. It was probably a couple of kids on a ghost hunt. She ought to jump out and scare them before giving them a lecture about trespassing. Hopefully the male hadn't brought the girl here for some kind of groping make-out session. That was something she didn't want to walk in on or interrupt.

Quietly she exited the house through the back door and made her way down the deck steps following the soft voices. They seemed to be coming from the swimming pool area and she headed in that direction, their words still too far away to be clear. It was only when they were in sight that she could make out the words.

Still contemplating what she would say to the little trespassers, she ducked behind the old greenhouse that was being used to house the crew's tools although they never bothered to lock the doors, which she'd questioned. Bill had told her the area was safe because the residents were afraid the house was haunted.

Standing next to the freshly dug pool were two figures – one male and one female. She couldn't see their faces in the dark, the only illumination from the moon overhead but they didn't sound like kids. The female voice had a mature quality to it that indicated an adult.

Were they the only two? Had a group of ghost hunters come to check out the premises? They didn't need to sneak around. If they'd asked, she would have said yes which was exactly what she was going to tell them.

She began to move from her hiding place but something – some instinct, some voice in the back of her head – made her hesitate… hang back and listen some more. Edging back farther behind the greenhouse, she waited until one of them spoke again.

"Are you sure it's here?" the female asked. Toni could see her shadow bent at the waist and combing through a line of bushes at the far edge of the pool. "I don't see anything."

Both the male and the female had flashlights so Toni kept well back in case the beam of light traveled in her direction. They were looking for something, which was strange unless they'd been sneaking in here regularly after everyone left. Maybe they'd lost their car keys.

"I'm sure," the male piped up in the darkness. "We have to find it."

The female spun around, her flashlight illuminating the male's face for a moment before landing on the lawn. Toni sucked in a breath as she realized she'd seen that face before. It was the man with the flat tire in front of the estate a few weeks ago. What was he doing here? And more importantly how many times had he been here before?

"There's nothing here," the woman said, frustration in her tone. It was then that the flashlight shown on the woman's face briefly and Toni wasn't surprised to see it was the female companion that had been sitting in the car that day talking on her cell phone. Clearly there presence at the estate hadn't been as innocent as she and Bill had assumed.

"Try over there," the man suggested. "Around that flower bed."

The woman dutifully moved to the left while the man sidled over to his right, bending over to pick something up.

A shovel.

Maybe he was going to dig for treasure. Or perhaps he had buried something back here.

But the man – she couldn't remember the name he'd given her that day – didn't start digging a hole. Instead, he crept up very slowly behind the woman, not making a sound on the soft, freshly turned over earth.

The woman was on her hands and knees, intently combing through a bed of azaleas looking for whatever was lost when the man stood behind her and began to raise the shovel over his head.

Adrenaline took over and Toni didn't even realize the scream that sounded came from her until afterward. Jumping out from her hiding spot, she ran up to the man, trying to shove him aside or knock the shovel from his hands.

"Stop! Stop!"

She was too late. The shovel came down on the poor girl's head and she slumped to the ground, her body limp but Toni heard a small moan. Thank God, she was still alive. But for how long?

Toni took several steps back, her heart racing and her ears ringing, realizing she'd done something completely stupid. But she'd had little choice. She couldn't just stand there watching the man kill that poor woman. However, she couldn't wrestle him for that shovel either.

I am so dumb. Now what?

The man's silhouette was stiff and unyielding and even in the almost dark it was clear he was angry. His body language seethed with fury.

Shit. Fuck. Shit.

She had no plan whatsoever. Some pissed off guy who wanted to bust open his girlfriend's skull had now turned that anger Toni's way and basically she had no strategy for getting out of this.

Her pulse galloping and her gaze darting all around, she figured the house would be the safest place but apparently he'd had the same thought. At some point while she was trying to figure out what to do, he'd moved in between her and the house, cutting off that escape route.

That only left one option. The pathway that led to the barn.

Like something out of a horror movie, he hefted the shovel over his shoulder and began striding toward her. Not running, at least not yet. But luckily for Toni, she'd seen practically every horror movie ever made and more importantly she'd paid attention. She wouldn't be making any of those too stupid to live mistakes. Any more, that is.

Because the pathway through the small forest was her territory.

He might have superior strength and speed, not to mention a shovel, but she had something more important.

She knew where every damn motion sensor was on that path.

She could only hope they would cooperate and work. This might be the most important scare of her life.

Blood surged through her veins and that little annoying voice in her head started barking out orders that all basically said the same thing.

Run.

Pivoting on the heel of her steel-toed boot, Toni did just that. She wasn't any sort of athlete and running made her boobs bounce no matter what kind of bra she strapped them down with but she pushed herself to the limit, wanting as much distance between the two of them as she could get.

She pumped her legs hard, listening to his own swiftly gaining footfalls on the grass behind her. Despite the coolness of the evening, Toni was covered with cold sweat and her heart was thumping against her ribcage, frantically trying to get out. She shot a quick look over her shoulder but it was too dark to see much of anything. She could only hear her own rapid breathing and the blood that roared in her ears, almost drowning out any external sound.

Darting off the path and behind a tree, she waited as quietly as she could but at the same time giving herself an internal pep talk. She knew Wyatt and Logan were on the way but right now it was just her and the man. She had to be smart.

The people in horror movies always made the same mistakes. The opened a door when everyone in the audience was screaming for them not to. They allowed themselves to be chased up a staircase and then trapped on an upper floor. Or they would run into a shed or garage and be cornered until the bad guy swung his knife or machete in their direction.

That wasn't going to happen to her. She had him out here where she could run in all directions and there was no place to be trapped.

A random thought ran through her mind that she was glad she and Wyatt hadn't had sex this morning. She hadn't wanted to make any noise in case Logan could hear them. But now she was simply glad they had abstained. Everyone knew the first to go in a movie was the couple that had sex.

Jeez, I've lost my mind. Focus.

The pounding of running feet pulled her attention back to the pathway. He was getting closer...any minute...just one more second...

Toni held her breath as the dark figure was only a few feet away but as she'd feared he was on the far left side of the pathway. She hadn't been able to get this sensor working all the way across so she'd have to help it. Reaching out with just the tip of her boot, she waited until the right moment and then broke the invisible beam with her foot.

1...2...3...

It would take five seconds for the witch to fly across the path and the bats would swarm a few seconds later. That gave her the distraction she needed to get away and hide until help came.

Toni hadn't realized she was holding her breath until the ugly green witch with the long flying robes came out of the trees and flew right into the face of the man. Not waiting around to see how he reacted, she hurled herself forward and onto her feet, running into the trees that had grown close together over the years and praying that the bats would do their job.

She heard some yelling and cursing and allowed herself a

small smile of triumph, but she couldn't rest on her laurels too long. Her chest ached and a stitch in her side had her almost doubled over in pain, but she didn't even pause until she came to a spot where three large tree trunks converged and were surrounded by thick weeds. It looked like a good place to hide, although perhaps too obvious?

It was going to have to do because she could hear his footsteps coming up behind her even as he yelled again, cursing the zombies that he must have activated. She dove down behind the trees and under the weeds, hoping her head wasn't sticking out as she heard him scream a third time.

The Grim Reaper.

That fake scythe probably scared the crap out of him from the sound of his yelp but she had to give him credit…he wasn't giving up. But she had one more little surprise in store for him.

The Bloody Skeleton.

Toni had to muffle her chuckle when he screamed again, this time over and over, high-pitched and terrified. The footsteps had stopped and there was only the man, whining and talking to himself.

Had he given up?

Her hope surged but it was extremely short-lived. His yelling ceased and the running started again, coming closer until she could see his shadowy figure through the weeds. He was standing about ten feet from her, his head swiveling back and forth, clearly looking for her and still holding that damn shovel. She willed every muscle in her body to freeze, not wanting even a hair on her head to blow in the breeze in case it made a noise. She had to press her lips together to keep from screaming as he just stood there, his shoulders rising and falling with his heavy breathing.

The little fucker was waiting for her to make a mistake...a move...a sound...

Chapter Thirty-Four

WYATT PULLED UP in front of the estate and killed the engine. The house was quiet and deserted, which he had to admit made it seem more sinister than it truly was in the daytime. In all the time he'd been there he'd never personally witnessed anything spooky going on but seeing it late at night like this made him understand why the town stayed away.

"Grim, isn't it?"

Logan chuckled as he too studied the edifice. "I know your girlfriend likes all this haunted ghost stuff so I'm guessing it looks that way on purpose."

"Actually it's looked like that for decades now but she's not doing much to change it. It suits her purpose perfectly."

Wyatt swung out of the vehicle and pocketed the keys, anxious to find Toni and head home. His stomach was growling and he knew she had to be starving as well. He had so much to tell her. Funny how he wanted to share everything with her when before he'd been content to be by himself all the time.

The sound of yelling pierced the quiet and Wyatt only hesitated for a moment, listening closely to what direction the sound was coming from before shooting off to the back of the house.

"Check inside," he called over his shoulder to Logan as he crossed over the back deck and headed for the pool area and the pathway, trying not to trip in the darkness. There weren't any lights this far from the house and one tree root could send him sprawling and put him in a cast for weeks.

The cursing and yelling didn't sound like Toni. It sounded male and extremely angry.

Wyatt's breath came in pants as he flew to the entrance of the pathway, which was about a mile long and led directly to the barn. If it wasn't Toni back there then it was a trespasser who probably found out about the motion sensors the hard way. It might be a kid trying to find a ghost or someone with more nefarious intentions but either way Wyatt would find out what was going on. He only hoped Toni was in the house doing paperwork. Safe and sound.

Since he knew where the motion sensors were Wyatt stuck to the right of the path, not wanting a flying witch or zombie to slow him down. He was beginning to think he'd imagined the whole thing as he didn't hear any more voices, loud or soft, and he halted for a minute to catch his breath. Sucking in gulps of air, he walked as quietly as possible through the thick trees until he saw a figure about a hundred feet away. A tall man holding a shovel.

Wyatt had heard ghost stories about this house for years but he hadn't heard any about buried treasure, so why that man was holding a shovel was a mystery. That he shouldn't even be there was a fact, though, and it looked like the intruder needed to be assisted off the premises. Easy or hard – it was his choice.

"Listen, buddy. This is private property. You need to–"

The man swung around, the beam from the flashlight illuminating his face. Shock rooted Wyatt to the spot and just that quickly this situation went from a simple trespasser to something completely different. Something dangerous.

It was Cole Hoskins.

Son of a bitch. The one man they were looking at for Mandy's stalking and murder just happens to show up here after Wyatt himself had told Bickham about their suspicions? It was too much of coincidence.

The sheriff had tipped off his buddy.

"Put the shovel down, Hoskins. The cops are on their way and there's nowhere to run. We know you killed Mandy and your first wife."

That was a bold-faced lie but he needed to rattle the other man a little bit. Too bad it didn't work. Hoskins didn't throw up his hands in surrender like Wyatt hoped he would, instead lifting the shovel and balancing it on his shoulder.

The two of them stood there for what seemed like a lifetime but was probably only a minute, maybe two. The tension between them stretched painfully and all of Wyatt's senses peaked as he waited for something to happen. He could hear the chirp of crickets and the rustling of the leaves. He could smell the strong odor of sweat mixed with grass and dirt. Mostly he could feel his own heart pounding, each beat pushing a rush of blood into his extremities. Waiting was the hardest part but he'd always been a patient man. The first one who moved…lost.

It was almost a relief when Hoskins made his move. With a roar that echoed into the night, he ran toward Wyatt, shovel at the ready to crack his skull or bust his ribs. Whatever the man needed to do to incapacitate his opponent so he could get away. Where he was going to go Wyatt wasn't sure.

"Wyatt, watch out!"

Toni's voice distracted him for a second and a glancing blow came down on his shoulder, sending a shaft of pain down his arm and spine. Recovering quickly, he ducked the next blow, bending double and running full speed at Hoskins' gut, knocking him to the ground. The shovel fell out of the man's hands and Wyatt now had the advantage, positioned on top as he landed punches in the abdomen and jaw.

Hoskins didn't give in easily. Throwing a punch to Wyatt's ribs and then another to his already sore shoulder knocked the breath from his body and sent a wave of pain ricocheting to his fingertips. It was almost impossible to suck air into his burning lungs and Wyatt knew he needed to end this fight quickly. He was injured and he wouldn't last long. Losing wasn't an option either as Toni wasn't tucked up safe somewhere. She was here and vulnerable with a possible double murderer a few feet away. Hoskins was desperate and a hostage might seem like a good idea.

Gathering every bit of strength he had, Wyatt reared his right arm back and gave Hoskins a vicious upper cut to the solar plexus, the hit shoving the air from his chest and causing his muscles to go limp. Wyatt lifted up off the man and Hoskins rolled to his side, curled into a ball, and coughed several times as if he was going to retch all over himself.

The thud of footsteps behind Wyatt had him spinning around but it was Logan who was wearing his trademark grin. "Looks like I missed all the fun."

His shoulder and torso beginning to throb, Wyatt struggled to his feet, his gaze seeking out Toni. She was standing several feet away looking definitely worse for wear with grass in her hair, sweat and dirt smudged on her face, and tears gathering in her eyes. He held out his arms, wincing when he moved his left arm. Shit, his shoulder was dislocated. This was going to hurt like a bitch to get it put back in place.

Toni ran into his open arms, her tiny little body colliding with his much larger one but he still had to grit his teeth at the shooting pain that threatened to send him to his knees. No way was he going to look wimpy in front of his woman. Dammit, he'd just saved her. Or something like that. What in the hell had Hoskins been doing here in the first place?

"Easy, honey. Will you tell me what's going on here? What was Hoskins doing here?"

She was holding onto him so tightly he could barely breathe, but his last question seemed to get her attention. Her head tilted up sharply, her brows pulled down and together.

"Hoskins? That was the guy who had a flat tire out front a few weeks ago." Her eyes widened and she struggled out of his arms, looking ready to flee. "The girl is by the pool. She's going to need an ambulance, Wyatt. He hit her with the shovel and then he chased me."

Logan had slapped some cuffs on Hoskins in the meantime and Wyatt sure as shit was going to ask his friend why he carried a pair when he wasn't even a cop anymore. Force of habit? Whatever, it came in handy today.

"I'm way ahead of you," Logan assured them, pulling Hoskins to his knees, the man still coughing and struggling for breath. "I called 911 and we should be hearing sirens any minute now. You want to watch him while I go check the girl?"

"Do it. I've got him."

As if on cue the sound of sirens could be heard in the distance, faint but discernible. Every bone and muscle in Wyatt's body ached but before he even took an aspirin he needed to get the story of what had happened here tonight.

"Are you okay?" he asked Toni, running his gaze from her head to toe and back up again. "Did he hurt you?"

Toni shook her head, the color coming back to her skin. "No, he hit that girl. I yelled at him to stop but it was too late. Then he chased me but I knew the locations of the sensors on the pathway. I don't think he likes witches and ghosts."

Ignoring the pain in his shoulder, he pulled her close again, running his hand on the good arm through her tangled hair. "You did good, honey. I'm proud of you."

And I love you. Forever.

As soon as they were alone, he'd tell her. And hope to hell she felt the same way.

Chapter Thirty-Five

THE SUN WAS coming up and Toni was in Wyatt's kitchen trying to rustle up some breakfast after one long damn night. No one other than Wyatt had managed a wink of sleep and the only reason he had was because the painkillers made him drowsy. She didn't know exactly how they put a shoulder back into place but the mere thought made her shudder. When she'd finally been allowed in the little room where they'd treated him, he'd been rather pale but otherwise fine. The doctor had put his arm in a sling, handed her a prescription, and told her not to let him overdo for a few days.

"Need any help?" Logan stuck his head around the corner. He'd been in the living room with Wyatt.

"Did he doze off again?" Toni asked, plating the scrambled eggs and bacon. She wasn't the best cook in the world but she could handle this.

"No, he's hungry and worried that you're burning the bacon. He said it should bend over a fork."

The toast popped up and she grumbled while placing it on a plate. "You can tell him I know how to–"

"Tell me what?" Wyatt asked, lumbering into the kitchen,

his dark hair askew and fatigue drawing circles under his eyes. She felt a pang of thankfulness that he was all right, that they were all okay. The whole thing could have gone the other way.

"That I know how to cook bacon," Toni huffed. "I may have issues in the kitchen but I'm not that bad."

"I'm sure you can. I just don't like it burnt."

Logan helped her carry all the plates to the table. "I like my bacon crisp, personally. Different strokes and all. Ava makes a mean scrambled eggs. One of the reasons I married her."

Wyatt's phone rang and he sighed, beginning to rise to get it but she waved him off, quickly retrieving it from the end table in the living room. He wouldn't let her spoil him much but she was certainly going to try at least for today.

He listened for quite awhile before thanking the other person and hanging up. "That was Sheriff Sullivan. He says that Hoskins woke him up early this morning and wanted to make a statement. He admitted to killing Mandy but he claims it was an accident. That they argued and she hit her head. He panicked and buried her body in a wall at the estate thinking that she would never be found since no one would buy the place, thinking it's haunted and all. He knew about the estate from some guy he worked with."

"But I bought it."

Wyatt nodded, digging into his eggs. "You did and by the time he found out the construction crew was already there. The day you saw him and he had the flat tire was the day he and his girlfriend came by to see if they could move the body. They quickly saw it was too late and they could do nothing but sit back and wait, hoping that somehow Mandy wouldn't be found."

"He implicated his girlfriend? That's quite a guy," Toni observed. "First he drags her into a murder plot and then tries to kill her too. This is why women like their cats."

Logan choked on his orange juice laughing. "It doesn't say anything good about the male animal, does it?"

Toni eyed Wyatt across the table. "There are a few good ones left."

"So did Bickham warn him?" Logan asked. "That had to be what set him off."

Nodding, Wyatt popped a piece of bacon into his mouth. "He did and now that's a big mess. Bickham's probably going to be prosecuted for obstruction of justice. At minimum, he's going to lose his job and ruin his life. All for a friend who at the very least killed one person and tried to kill another. And we haven't even discussed Hoskins' first wife. They'll probably re-open that case. But yes, when Bickham called him he decided he needed to wipe the slate clean and run. His girlfriend was a loose end that needed tying up so he told her he had left a personally identifying object in the backyard all those years ago and now that they were on to him he needed to retrieve it. That's what they were doing when you caught them last night."

Toni couldn't believe the audacity of Cole Hoskins. He actually believed that he could get away with murder after murder. "So he brought her back to the estate? That doesn't make any sense."

"Actually it does," Logan said. "Going back for evidence was a good cover story to get her somewhere dark and deserted. I also assume he was planning to hide the body there, which is kind of genius. The police had already finished their search and investigation of the estate. They weren't coming back so technically it was a safe hiding place."

Wyatt wiped his mouth with a napkin. "He was planning to bury her body in the pool. Once the concrete was poured in a few days she would never be found."

"Another soul to haunt the estate," Toni sighed. "I'm glad he didn't get away with it. How is she doing? Is she cooperating with the sheriff?"

"She's going to be okay but whether she's talking, I don't know," Wyatt admitted. "If I were her, I'd get my lawyer to make a deal before Hoskins does."

Logan's phone rang and he pulled it from his pocket, a grin spreading across his face. It had to be his wife Ava. "Excuse me, I'm going to take this outside."

Toni watched with a smile as he hurried out to the back porch. "I think he's anxious to get back to his family."

"I think he is. You should meet Ava sometime. She's the only woman in the world that can keep Logan in line."

Since Wyatt had given her an opening, she'd take it.

"I'd like that. I'd like to meet all your friends. Do you think I'll be around to do that?"

Their gazes met and a frisson of electricity ran up her spine. He was smiling the kind of smile she'd been hoping for all her life. He didn't need to say the words; she could see it in his face but she wouldn't stop him if he wanted to.

"I think you will be." Wyatt placed his fork down and reached across the table for her hand, their fingers tangling together. "I love you, Antonia."

The tone was soft but so sincere that for a moment she had trouble catching her breath. Her heart felt too big for her chest and her throat had closed up as well but somehow she managed to croak out her words.

"I love you too."

Because she did. More than she could articulate. She hoped he could see it in her eyes but with any luck she'd have a long time to prove it to him.

"Your parents and Carla aren't going to like this."

No, they wouldn't but she wasn't going to let them interfere in her life anymore. She'd always thought that Wyatt deserved better and fate had played a funny trick on her. It was now her responsibility to make sure that's what he got. She'd do her best to be that.

"They don't get a say. You make me happy. They don't, and let's face it. Nothing I do makes them happy so I might as well do what I want."

His expression was sober and a little fearful. "I just don't want you to regret this someday. I don't want you to feel like you gave up your family for me."

"I didn't and I won't. But if they want to be in my life, they have to respect my boundaries." She fiddled with the handle of her coffee cup. "I guess I need to be thinking about moving here to town. I only expected to stay during construction."

"We have time to work that out. I don't expect you to turn your life upside down for me."

She pushed out her lower lip and pretended to pout. "You don't want me here."

Standing, he pulled her into his arms. Well, arm. The other

was in the sling, but the one did just fine holding her tight against his warm body. She could feel the heat of his skin through the thin barrier of their clothes and she rested her head on his chest, his heart thumping under her cheek.

"I want you here so much I don't want you to leave the house, honey. You took a guy who wanted to be left alone and turned him into someone who wants you around every minute of every day. I'm actually living again and I have you to thank for that."

Her eyes burned as she attempted to blink back the tears that threatened to fall. "Then let's make sure that all those minutes are everything they can be. Have you ever climbed a mountain, Wyatt?"

Laughter rumbled in his chest and he tugged on her hair so she was looking up at his smiling face. "No, but I have a feeling that's something we're going to do. Have you ever been white-water rafting?"

"No, but bring it on." She patted his chest, smoothing the fabric of his shirt. "But maybe we can just stay home sometimes too?"

"As long as I'm with you, I don't care what we do."

"Can we watch horror movies?" she asked hopefully, her lips curling into a grin. "I can't believe you haven't seen all the classics."

He leaned down and kissed her lips, tender and sweet and over too soon.

"I'm too busy watching you."

She wouldn't argue with that.

Chapter Thirty-Six

TONI ADJUSTED THE neckline of her fairy costume and then checked her wings in the dresser mirror. Halloween was a special night for her every year but it was even more special this year. The hotel was open and hosting a huge party.

And of course Wyatt. He made everything better.

There were still parts of the estate that weren't ready. With the police investigation, they'd had to suspend construction for quite awhile, but they'd opened a few days ago at maximum capacity. The guests didn't seem to mind that the pool wasn't finished or that the hayride wasn't ready. The scary pathway was operational and she'd already received several compliments from the guests. They didn't know those witches and zombies had probably saved her life.

"Do I have to wear this?"

Twirling around so the sparkly, scalloped edge of her pink and green skirt flowed around her thighs, she smiled indulgently at the man she adored. Wyatt had become something of a horror buff in the past few months as they'd gorged on scary classics but dressing up in a costume was something else entirely. Still, he looked dashing dressed as Indiana Jones, all macho and rough.

He'd vetoed several of the outfits she'd suggested and had seemed content, if not thrilled, with this one.

"If you're not in costume, people will stare at you."

He probably wouldn't care but she thought it only fair to warn him.

"I look ridiculous."

"You look sexy. And hot. Women will be hanging off of you all night. I'll have to beat them back with my wand."

She looked at the silver wand and frowned. "Maybe I need something bigger."

Wyatt looked in the mirror and straightened his fedora. Damn, he looked good.

"You could just put them under a spell." He turned and enveloped her in his arms. "Like you did with me."

Wrinkling her nose, she touched his forehead with the tip of her wand. "For someone under my spell, you're not very obedient."

His warm chuckle sent a flush of desire through her abdomen. He didn't realize sometimes the effect he had on her just by being himself.

"I'll work on that," he assured her. "In the meantime, are you ready for your guests? This is the big night. Honey, I'm so proud of you."

Toni took a big deep breath and smiled. "Thank you. It's going to be amazing. I can feel it. Tonight will be a night to remember."

"Just in case, I wanted to make sure of that. That's why I waited until now to tell you my big news. I told Jason, Jared, and Logan that my new home base was going to be Denver. I sold the farm."

Her mouth was hanging open but she couldn't seem to muster the brain function to close it. They'd talked about this a million times but she'd assured him he didn't have to do it. She would commute back and forth.

"I can't believe– I mean– I don't know what to say. Are you sure?"

He tilted her chin up and rubbed her lips with his callused thumb. "The farm was my parents' dream. I kept it because it was a great place to hide away from the world. I'm not hiding anymore. Besides, you've made so many compromises for me."

When Toni's family found out that she was with Wyatt they'd literally thrown a screaming fit. They'd actually accused her of "stealing" Wyatt from Carla despite them being divorced for over five years and ordered her to cease seeing him immediately.

It had only taken a moment for her to decide she wouldn't. He was the one person in her life who had been supportive – okay, not at the beginning but he was now – and she wasn't going to end that to be emotionally battered by her parents and sister. Carla had spent the last several months playing the victim about not only Wyatt but also her split from Trevor. She'd been forced to come clean about her debts and understandably Trevor had been livid, filing for divorce. He'd paid her debts but hadn't been willing to forgive.

Thank goodness, Katie was spending most of her time with her father. Funny how Toni and Trevor were friendlier than ever and she was able to spend more time with her niece than before. Even Wyatt was warming to his former buddy and they'd had dinner together once.

Up on her tiptoes, she pressed a quick kiss to his lips. "This was a big compromise though. One that I didn't expect."

"I'm excited about it and looking forward to being able to spend more time with you. You're not having second thoughts about me, are you?" he teased, tugging gently at her wings.

"You're stuck with me."

"I don't feel stuck."

"That's my magic spell at work."

He nuzzled his nose along hers before giving her a kiss that took her breath away and made her wish she didn't have over a hundred guests downstairs. Maybe no one would notice if they were a little late.

"No, honey. It's love."

Thank you for reading
Danger Incorporated – Danger in the Night
Sign up to be notified of Olivia's new releases:
oliviajaymesoptin.instapage.com

About The Author

Olivia Jaymes is a wife, mother, lover of sexy romance, and caffeine addict. She lives with her husband and son in central Florida and spends her days with handsome alpha males and spunky heroines.

She is currently working on a series of full-length novels called The Cowboy Justice Association. It's a contemporary romance series about lawmen in southern Montana who work to keep the peace but can't seem to find it in their own lives in addition to the erotic romance novella series – Military Moguls and the romantic suspense series – Danger Incorporated.

Look for Olivia's new romantic suspense trilogy Midnight Blue Beach in Fall of 2016!

Visit Olivia Jaymes at
www.OliviaJaymes.com